# CONTENTS

If you asked me how I got to "where I got" I'm not sure I could answer you.

I do know that in spite of ourselves sometimes we luck out and other times we just have to deal with life. None of it's personal, but the storms and the rainbows are going to happen and you can either make up your mind to steal on through or you cannot.

I would come to know the souls of some who could, and some who couldn't, and along the way I would learn about them and myself.

They would reveal things I doubt they ever would have when they were alive and with it would challenge me and make me reflect on my own existence, where I was and where I wanted to go.

I'd learn things about the living too. I'd see greed, desperation, and depravity that I'd always just hoped didn't exist. Lust and loss-adventure and pain - closure and renewal. What money could buy, and what it could not no matter how much a person with the resources was willing to spend.

Some questions I would find answers too but many I would not, and that's cool.

I would come to understand fully that it really doesn't matter how many bad things happen to a person, in the end you make a conscious decision that nothing and nobody is going to break you and to quote the man in the movie you either "Get busy living, or get busy dying..."
I chose to live.

# THE STREET SINGER

I couldn't feel the rain but I really couldn't feel anything most days. My shift was completed so I'd made my usual stop off to the corner liquor store for my customary fifth of medicine and some ice-cream. As I looked down into the blue freezer, I pondered tonight's fix, my appetite thinking Ben and Jerry's or Klondike bars, my mind on the conversation I'd had earlier with the dead dude I just transported to Ann Arbor. By now I was getting used to it, or I guess as used to having the spirits of the dead share their life stories with you as a human being *could* get.

It had started several months ago, I don't really recall the time, either week or time of year, but I sure as hell remember the first time I had a voice start talking in the cab of my transport vehicle, a voice that was supposed to be permanently silent, riding in the refrigerated rear of my vehicle, but the living have no control over the dead and so it was.

The name on the sheet and on the toe tag I had automatically verified said Tabor.

I quickly went over the things I needed to know as the morgue attendant zipped up the body bag; weight 162 lbs., time on ice 6.25 hours, the donation particulars, and the cut off time for transfer.

I didn't usually read any further as I really didn't want to know anything else, some of the freaks in this business wanting to know all the gory details but I protected myself by not becoming one of them. I typically never even looked at any part of the corpse that I didn't absolutely need to. Part of it respect, part of it simple self-preservation as I had seen plenty of fucked up shit already in my life and I didn't feel like adding to the cinema of horrors already playing on a regular basis in my head.

I signed the exit time sheet had the attendant witness my signature and down the quiet white corridor I went with 162 pounds of dead weight making the wheels of my gurney creak slightly in the cold midnight air.

Into the back of the truck without a problem, gurney locked down, doors closed tightly and a quick call to dispatch as I adjusted my power seat and turned on the heater in the front cab.

"Truck 219 to dispatch"

"Go ahead 219"

"En route to Ann Arbor Donor station with one donor body, Tabor, identity confirmed"

"Roger that 219, what your travel time and ETA?"

"Travel time 2 hours twenty minutes, ETA 0230 hours"

"Roger that, we'll tell them you're on the way"

I double clicked the mike in response which automatically confirmed their last transmission and I put the van in gear as I headed for the highway.

I hit I-96 and set the cruise control at 82 mph as I took a sip off my coffee. I could have gone faster if needed, the police always giving us professional courtesy when we were on a run, but tonight I didn't have a cutoff and I was waiting for a live podcast interview with Jimmy Buffett on the trucks satellite radio so this was going to be a casual ride, that is until Tabor said hello.

At first I thought I was hearing things, perhaps road noise or a rattle from the truck as I turned the radio down, but there it was again.

I had a hard time processing it at first, it sounded almost like static coming from the radio and I fiddled with the volume again, still not sure just exactly what I was hearing and then glancing towards the passenger seat I noticed what I can best describe as a partial, clouded and vague apparition, more of an energy shape than anything else, riding *shotgun* beside me. I'm not sure if that makes sense to you, it still doesn't always make sense to me, but a chauffeur and apparent confidant to the voices of the dead I had just become.

It was pitch black out as I slowed the vehicle and pulled off onto the shoulder, I was trying to sort this out and I was going to need a few minutes at best to do it. WTF? was obviously the first thing going through my brain. Being around the dead was something I was fairly okay with, but part of that was because they didn't talk. I did my job and they did theirs, no talking. So why did tonight need to start being different, but Tabor was the one to answer my question.

"You do realize not everyone can hear us, right?"

I actually looked around as if I didn't know the voice speaking was coming directly from right next to me. It shouldn't have, it never had before, but tonight sure as shit it was coming from the glowing orb now growing in both size and clarity into the somewhat recognizable form of a human, and I was still freaked out.

"You hear me, I know you hear me."

Finally, I answered and said yes I hear you, now who are you and why are you in my truck?

I can't tell you what that felt like, slight relief in the form of validation, validation of something my ears admitted to me but my brain challenged from every possible angle. Looking back I think it felt like having at minimum slight control, because at least I was engaged in conversation and not just some manipulated bystander.

"I'm in your truck because you're taking my body somewhere and my spirit is stuck here not knowing where or when to go. The way they explain it is partially because you are a living life form that has the ability to sense my vibration, even though I'm dead, but again not everyone has the ability to hear the dead, in fact most do not."

*Lucky me* I thought.

"Luck is not something the universe believes in" he replied.

Hold up a second, now you're telling me you can read my mind.

"Unfortunately, yes and I apologize, you know in my living self I was actually a really private dude" he replied.

"I didn't even try to overhear other people stuff, mainly wanted to avoid drama if you know what I mean, but where I'm at now the rules are different, so again apologies my man."

It's cool, I mean it's not, but it isn't your fault I guess was all I could say.

What the fuck! I'm talking with a dead man! I yelled out loud and I guess Tabor recognized from his new reality that this situation might take a bit for me to process so he didn't reply and allowed me to try and get my mind wrapped around what was going on.

I was parked on the side of the highway for a good 20 minutes before he spoke again and this time I was a little more prepared as he asked me how and why I drove dead people around for a living.

*Great* I thought, now I'm being interviewed by a dead dude but this time he didn't confirm that he was reading my thoughts which at that moment I really appreciated.

I took a sip off my coffee as I put the truck in gear and rolled back up onto the highway, looking to the now clear form of a middle-aged black dude riding next to me I said this might take a while.

"It's cool brother," he said, "I got nowhere to be..."

After I'd finished giving him the short version of my life I wanted to know more about him. Normally this was territory I avoided like the plague but for some odd reason I had begun to form a slight bond, and with it a curiosity about who he was before he passed. He began to tell me how he was actually born and raised in New Orleans, having lived there in his younger days. He began telling me about the harsh life for a black man in the south, but also the wonderful sights, sounds and smells of his life in The Big Easy.

"I was born in the ninth ward, the one that took the ass whooping by Katrina a few years back. Growing up we had nothing to speak of, my momma had four children, which by normal standards wasn't even that many but it was still a lot of mouths to feed. Two brothers, one sister, our daddy got killed early on in a knife fight over another woman so momma never spoke much on it. Maybe because it hurt her, maybe out of anger or embarrassment, or maybe 'cause he left her with four mouths to feed in a place that was hard as hell to survive in anyway. I really don't know, like I said she never really spoke on it. My childhood was sparse of any extras but it was still a good childhood. My momma like many poor folk could make something out of nothing and the woman could cook. Monday was wash day so red beans and rice was supper year-round every beginning of the week. She'd roll out biscuits, sometimes homemade pickles, and always a bottle of pepper vinegar and a big glass pitcher of sweet tea to wash it all down. Dinner was the only meal we all saw each other and my brothers, both older than me, would talk about work, a little of sports, and sometimes about the girl they were dating currently but always with respect in their words and tone with my mother present, other times not so much. My sister who was two years younger than me was always quiet and didn't say much, ever. Mom just usually sat quiet herself and listened, doling out bits of advice from her hard-earned years of wisdom, but I think mainly she just wanted to sit, relax, and enjoy whatever brief time she had with her children, not having to work for that one small hour of her day.

My mom, like many women in our community, always had two jobs and did side work for extra. She sewed up pants, skirts and such, she also helped butcher at the hog yard on the outskirts of town when they were busy which we always looked forward to as she could bring home as much of the cheaper cuts as she wanted. They were just going to throw them away anyhow and she would pack wicker bushel baskets with fresh hog maws, feet, heads, and anything else she could cook down. She was a small woman, but strong and she must have made quite a sight riding the bus back home with the baskets slightly dripping blood in specks onto the dirty floor. Blacks still sat in the back at that time, and by themselves, so no one troubled her much. Riding the bus was a luxury and she would actually walk to the slaughter house but no way she could carry all those baskets back home by herself so she paid her 15 cents for the ride. She wanted my sister to help her but only one time was all it took and the young lady passed out from the sight of all that blood, so momma never brought her back. I helped her a couple times but she said I was too slow and the boss man had given her a talking to about it so she never brought me back neither.

She knew how to can goods, vegetables and such, so after she got home and washed herself of the blood caked onto it seemed every part of her body she would get to washing and cooking the meat. One time my aunt had stopped by and thought someone had gotten stabbed again from all the blood my momma had washed off her in the side yard with a garden hose. We all had a good laugh over that, even my mom who was always too serious to laugh. My aunt didn't think it funny at all and stayed sour the whole night over it. My mom went about her work, talking with my aunt and sister as they begrudgingly helped her salt and season the various pieces, packing them into the reused glass jars and boiling them down until the tops popped which meant they were done proper and would keep for months or years if needed. We had a neighbor with an old metal shed that he had made into a smoker and he and momma struck a deal that he would smoke whatever she brought him and they split the finished product 50/50 which was real nice for us and we'd have side pork and ham hocks for the months to follow.

I was just turned 16 when two things happened to me, I started liking girls, and I started liking their clothes too.

At first, I would just feel the soft cloth when I knew no one was around, but then one day I put on a pair of my momma's drawers and I liked it. I was very confused, I didn't want to be with boys, but I began more and more to appreciate things only women were supposed to like. I knew to keep it hid, nobody in my neighborhood would have accepted it and I knew sure as hell I'd have gotten the tar beaten out of me if it ever got out. Slowly I got more comfortable with it, putting on my sister's spare dress and stockings when no one was home, but I always knew to keep it hid. Anyway, I also had a singing voice and one day my neighbor who had heard me before asked if I could come down to the French Quarter and fill in for one of the fella's in their duct tape street band who'd got sick and couldn't sing."

I had to interrupt as I asked Tabor out of curiosity what a duct tape band was and he chuckled and explained how most street bands were of this kind, being they were all so poor that the instruments they had were in many cases literally held together by duct tape, wire, or whatever they could hustle up to keep the train rollin'. Tabor continued on.

"I asked the fellow how much I get paid first off and he replied that this depended on the crowd but being it was early spring and there was plenty of tourists he said if I sung good I would make 50 bucks for the day.

I remember feeling real quiet for a few minutes, $50 was more money than I'd ever seen.

*Fifty bucks?* I repeated to him.

Fifty bucks, *if* you sing good...

Oh, I said with confidence, for $50 I'll sing like Jesus Christ himself was sitting front row.

He told me to get my things and I told him I was already set so off we went, him carrying his trombone and an old plastic bucket which I wondered why he brought it but decided not to ask. Me carrying only my voice and the thought of coming home with some cold hard cash at the end of the day. We picked a prime spot on the corner of Chartres and Toulouse and with the rest of the band showing up we started putting out some music right quick. Some folks walked on by, some stopped briefly, and some a while longer, but almost half tossing coins or small bills into that old bucket. Sitting out front with the small microphone and old amplifier connected to it by barely a worn out old brown wire I belted out what I figured was popular for folks and you know something, that old bucket started filling up right beside me. By only four o'clock we were splitting up over $300 and there was only four of us. I was so excited I would have sung until midnight but the other members had families or habits to tend to so we called it quits.

Two of them said they liked my singing, which I figured out real quick was their way of saying bring this young buck back, apparently they hadn't hit money that good in quite a while and needless to say they wanted it to continue.

I'd have been ready the next day but for some reason they wanted to spread it out a little so we agreed to meet up again Thursday, same time same place. On the way home we stopped and each got a cold coke and walking along we laughed to ourselves, talking about music, women, and fishing. When my momma got home I showed her what I made and at first she got real angry, thinking I'd made it like so many other boys in the ward do either stealing, slinging dope or running with the wrong people. I explained to her what I'd done and how Id earned my money, suggesting she ask the neighbor if she didn't believe me, but with respect in my tone.

She smiled slightly as she said, "You made that kind of money singing?" and I replied "yes Ma'am."

For the first time in my life I could ever remember anyone looking at me that proud she smiled again and said, "well son you just keep on singing then" and she walked out of the room.

I took some of my money the next day and bought myself a used dress shirt, pants and shoes at the local thrift store and I got a proper haircut at the corner barber much earlier than my usual of every three months. When I showed up at our playing spot on Thursday, I looked sporty and I knew it. A couple of them razzed me a bit but I knew what I was doing and started right off with some fancy romantic songs, making it a point to serenade the women in the crowd indirectly. I say *indirectly* cause most of them had boyfriends or husbands and even though they was probably from up north it was still the south and a black man had to be cautious of getting too cool with a white woman.

I played it sly, I sang it soft and sweet, and that old bucket started filling up quicker and fuller every day. The band was ecstatic, one fella I think slightly jealous but he didn't mind his cut of the cash so he kept it to himself. I found a flower shop on the way to the French quarter and one day as we were making our way to the gig I stopped in and bought up a dozen of their day-old pink and white roses for $2. I asked the old man to trim them for me and for an extra dollar he wrapped each one individual in green paper with a little stem of baby's breath like my mom had showed me one time. My neighbor and the rest of the boys thought I was nuts but them tourist women ate it up. I started figuring which ones was single or the closest to it and I serenaded them personal like, just before the end handing them one of my flowers and some of them almost start crying as either them or their beau dropped a 10 or 20 in that old plastic bucket of ours.

It was prime tourist season and that night when we finished, we counted out $838 plus change and the band was off their heels, slapping me on the back, calling me one slick young dude, smooth operator, and one even said I was a motherfuckin' genius. I wasn't used to hearing real strong language, being brought up by a Christian momma, but the compliments sure felt good and I ain't going to lie, I ate it up.

As we walked home that night Gerald my neighbor said he wanted to stop in and have a drink to celebrate. His misses wasn't going to be home and he wanted to tie one on but there was only one problem. I was just turned 17 and my momma would be waiting for me when I walked in sure enough. If she smelt liquor on me it wouldn't matter how much money I had or how I explained, it would have been the end of my singing with the band and I knew that just as sure as I believed in the sun coming up. Gerald told me the place we was going to my age wouldn't matter, but I said Okay, but what about momma? He smiled a toothy grin looking sideways at me and with one

arm around my shoulder said "Don't you worry 'bout that neither, it's all gonna be cool little brother."

We had to cut back three blocks off the main street but sure
enough off from a dirty old alley with nothing particularly
good about it sat this run-down clapboard shack with no windows and only one door. As we approached, I could hear music
faintly drafting out of the cracks in the faded grey wooden
boards of the walls, the walls themselves lookin' like they
could blow over in a stiff wind but Gerald laughed again and
reassured me we were in the right spot as we let ourselves in.

The inside didn't look much better than the outside but they
had a juke box and some half broke neon signs here and there
that lit up the darkness a little bit. The bartender knew my
neighbor and poured him a beer but I still wasn't sure as I
ordered an orange soda and looked around nervously at the
seven or eight hard looking men and women seated at their
own tables. Gerald whispered something to the man serving
us and he glanced over at me pretty serious but looked back at
Gerald as he walked to the end of the bar and came back with
a single cigarette and a pack of matches, sitting them both in
front of Gerald, looking serious at me again like I didn't belong
there and walking away again.

I never seen my neighbor smoke cigarettes before, I didn't care
as it wasn't any of my business, I just never seen it but as he
looked over at me again grinning he lit it up, blew on the end
of it for a second and passed it to me.

No thank you, I don't smoke. I said politely.

"I know but this ain't tobacco, and you going to like it, that
I guarantee. Plus, your momma can't smell it like booze and
even if she does you can just say one of the fella's was smoking
next to you."

"Trust me, ain't nobody 'cept me and you gonna know anything, and you need it anyway. You a good singer but if you want to be great you need to loosen up and this is just what the doctor ordered my man."

He was still holding the smoking hand rolled cigarette out in front of me and even though I was scared to death I was more scared of him and the band wanting to put me back on my front porch and never singing again, so I took it.

I wasn't sure what to do and again he laughed and told me to just suck a little air through it, not holding it too tight, and not taking too much in at once. I held it right but I must have took too much as my lungs filled up quickly and I coughed hard as I blew out the smoke, coughing again for what seemed like forever with everyone in the bar laughing a little at the sight of my virgin attempt at smoking weed. The bartender handed me my orange soda, telling me it would help, and now looking upon me more like an uncle or a friend than the man I remembered just a few moments earlier. He took a hit, Gerald took a hit, and they passed it again to me, quietly warning me again not to take so much. We passed it around once more with one of the women behind me asking us to share. She was kind of worn looking but had big breasts and she smelled exotic as I handed it to her. The warm wave started to hit me as I watched her toke on it like a pro, her wonderful red lips making me start to have wicked thoughts and I swear everyone in that bar must have known it, or maybe it was just my first time being high, I don't know but I was sure happy right then.

"You cute... baby boy," she said looking hungrily in my direction.

I wasn't so nervous anymore but something on the back of my neck said *danger* and yet right then I didn't care. The weed rolled over my mind and she took my hand like a school teacher leading a child, which was pretty much what it was, as she led me to a smaller room in the back with a big red couch.

I ain't gonna say what she did, let's just say it felt good and I let her have her own way. In the months to come we stopped by that juke joint a few more times, me having my little fun every time, but then I began wanting to taste other fruit and would occasionally stop at a different place on the way back to my momma's house. I had money, I had looks, and I could sing, so getting some lovin' was never hard at all after that."

Tabor went on for a while describing his increasing fame and financial status in the community, and then told me about the day it all ended.

He explained about coming home late one night to find their home in fire with only one of his brothers making it out alive.

Even as a spirit I could hear the lingering anguish in his voice as he described he and his other brother trying to first come up with the money to bury the family and then figuring out how to find and afford another place to live. His older brother was sweet on his girlfriend of three years and planning to get married anyway but Tabor now found himself homeless. He rented a room for a while but he also started drinking and smoking more weed to kill his pain, eventually getting a taste for the low level street cocaine that so many other musicians favored and pretty soon he was spending all of his cash on any-thing but what was good for him. He was soon to learn rent ain't free and he also learned what it felt like to sleep on the ground when the boarding house would no longer let him in.

He told me that even at the bottom he still didn't really care, the pain of loss still the main thing on his mind as soon as the sun came up every day.

"Then one day I got a break," he said. A man from Chicago heard me and the band and asked me if I'd have a mind to come work for him at his club up north. He offered me twice what I was making right then and my own apartment above the club, the one thing was he had a strict *no dope* policy. I shook my head and promised him I didn't have that problem and he stepped right up to me, looking me straight on and said, "Young man let's not start out our relationship with a lie, and you damn sure better not think you can play me for a fool or you won't last at my place."

"I bowed my head a little, embarrassed for my deception, and just said "yes sir."

"Well alright then, meet me at the train station tomorrow at 10 AM sharp and we will see how you like Chi-Town," reaching out his manicured and muscular right hand to seal the deal. Two days later I got my first look at Chicago and other than my own New Orleans it felt like home. I sang with his house band for the next 20 years, still smoking a little weed but leaving the hard stuff behind me. I was able to buy me some nice clothes, eat in some mighty fine places, and spend a lot of private time with some beautiful women both white *and* black. Yes sir Chicago treated me right but I was getting older and so was my voice, and my looks.

After a while I couldn't bring 'em in like I used to and one day the man and me had to sit down with what I knew had been coming now for a while. He was kind about it but he was a business man and I respected both. He gave me an envelope with $1,000 to help me with a new start and offered me a month to figure it all out and look for my next job but I didn't know how to do anything but sing and we both knew I was too old to live off that now.

I thought about going back to the big easy but it had been so long I knew there was nothing for me there now anyway but I also knew that the car factories was always hiring and they'd train you too. I wasn't much on charity or waiting around so the next day I hopped a bus to The Motor City!

I got me a job pressing parts right off. It wasn't my dream but I'd been living my dream for a long time now so it wasn't that hard to accept. I met up with a few fella's in the plant who were also musicians and pretty quick we formed a band and started getting part time gigs on the weekends which threw me some side money and allowed me to continue to meet some lovely ladies. Everything was going strong until I met a woman, fine and rich, in a club one night. She spoiled me right off and even though she was married we had our fun. Her husband was gone a lot and I actually came to love her, and I thought she loved me but I would find out the hard way that getting in the way of her money train would be the end of me.

She dressed fine as hell and one night when we went back to her place and were pretty lit up on whiskey and weed I confided in her my old taste for women's clothing. I remember her laughing at first, not believing me serious, but then she offered to let me rummage through her closet and when I came out in nylons, high heels and a red dress I thought she'd fall out of her damn seat. I was embarrassed but I was who I was and she was cool with it or at least that's how she let on. I didn't push it and we stayed having our fun for a few more months but after a while I got the idea to ask her to leave her husband which brought a laugh again, followed by cold silence. I was serious but came to find out what I really was, an occasional play toy that could sing and fuck good, and nothing more. Our relationship became less frequent and more tumultuous. I began to resent her, and she figured it out. One night she played on like it was all cool, even letting me put on her most expensive outfit, and then very cold like, with a look of more *scorn* than anything she told me to get out and not come back.

I was stunned but I turned to go change out of her stuff and she smirked and said, "No, you can keep it. Just leave and consider it a parting gift."

I hadn't been hurt by anyone in so long and even though I'd seen the writing on the wall long ago I was still stunned. She didn't love me, that was clear, but I loved her and the room turned ice cold as a single tear came rolling down my cheek and then she leaned back in the white upholstered chair she'd been sitting in, silver cigarette holder in her hand, and smiled as she nodded her head towards the door. I was so stunned I didn't even grab my own clothes from the bedroom and as I walked unsteadily down the front steps I saw her husband and another large man were waiting for me, baseball bats in their hands. I only felt the first time they hit me and I went down to the icy pavement, warm blood flowing from my forehead as they both hit me and called me faggot, homo, and every other vile thing they could come up with.

I don't know if I died right then but I remember being so very aware of her dark hate towards me and that hurt me as much as anything I could recall since my family had passed so long ago. I remember laying in the morgue, knowing rationally that it was cold but not truly feeling it. The emotion of betrayal was what I felt the most. I guess in our human form we have exchanges of energy in our lives, love and hate, but when you're dead they become much more pronounced and that woman was the closest thing to love that I'd had in a long, long time. Losing it the way it went down burned my soul like some evil god had engraved my spirit with a vengeful torch. You have little concept of time when you die so I don't know how long I felt it, or how long I been in the ice box, but now, being with you, I don't hurt anymore. I know it ain't like me and you are friends, I just don't feel negative energy coming from you and it helps to ease the dark way I had to die. Thank you for that."

I had just been listening as we drove and had no reasonable reply other than to say, "You are welcome Tabor."

We were 20 minutes out from the drop off and our conversation tapered off other than a few more questions from Tabor about my life and him asking me if I was alright. I could only say that honestly, no, I was not alright but I was trying to find my way there. As I pulled up to the big roll up door of the harvesting facility I called it in on the radio, telephoned the people inside the building from my cell, and put it in park.

"What they going to do with my body?," he asked.

The way I understand it they harvest the organs, bones, or tissue that you agreed to and then they send you to whatever funeral home is handling the funeral.

"What if I'm not having a funeral?"

Then they just bury or cremate you, whichever is specified in your will or with your next of kin.

"What if I don't have a will, or next of kin?"

Then I guess they bury you in a paupers grave, the state will take care of it.

"You mean nobody's gonna know where I lay?"

No, I'm afraid not.

"No one's ever gonna hear me sing again." More of a *statement* than a question I thought to which I shook my head slightly and softly replied, "No, I'm afraid not."

We kept waiting for the attendant to open the door so we could pull in, sometimes it took them 15 or 20 minutes and he asked "Can I sing you a song? I don't feel like I can go to heaven if I can't sing one more time. It was the only thing I was ever really any good at."

I told him that I would be absolutely honored to hear him sing and from the air of my cab the sweetest voice I think I'd ever heard broke into a slow a capella version of *Amazing Grace*. I could see his image begin to fade away but in that moment neither one of us any longer had any pain.

# QUESTIONS

I got back to our building around 5 AM and with my shift over I handed off my truck and radio to the oncoming driver at 0600 sharp and headed to the nearest convenience store to get what I needed. I was off the next three days and with the way I knew that my brain was going to be constantly process the events of the last night I'd have preferred to be working, but it wasn't my call. Mainly I thought about how anybody ended up with nobody to miss them when they died. I was pretty close to the same situation but not all the way, at least not yet. My ex-wife might show up, then again she might not or if she did I wondered if it would only be to spit on my grave.

I couldn't have blamed her either way, to her damaged soul I had taken away the one thing in this world she had loved more than herself or me. No way I could blame her for hating me. I had a few friends, a few distant cousins that had either walked away or been pushed away after my daughter died. There is one person I still kept in my heart but I'll talk about her maybe later. I was never that close to many people anyway and when Chloe died I fell even deeper into my own depths.

I remembered back to the day we buried her. It was strangely pleasant, the sun was out, birds chirping, 73 degrees as I recall and it never made sense to me that such an amazing young lady so full of love and promise now lay in a grey coffin, and yet the world didn't seem to notice or even care. I noticed, I cared. It was all that I could see for the years that followed because in my mind I was at minimum part of the problem that had put her there. In reality, I hadn't but it was close enough for me to be an easy target and in spite of being cleared in the investigation it didn't take long for my wife and a bunch of others to put a bull's-eye on my back. I didn't have the drinking problem then that I had now and sometimes I wished I did. It would have been easier to accept all the blame and maybe *off* myself at the conclusion, but instead here I was still alive and breathing, my only contribution to the world now shuttling the dead so they could give their last gift to somebody else. It was supposedly somewhat noble work but to me it was simply a place to hide from the world with decent pay.

I had a small apartment walking distance from two solid watering holes with rent that wouldn't kill me. I could afford a few channels on cable and as I was typically up most nights I kept my hand close to the remote control and a glass of booze, clicking through the bizarre television shows I always thought were positioned at this particular hour for the odd people of the world like me. I thought back to the accident many times. I wasn't drunk that day but I had been drinking. The driver who broadsided us had been two sheets to the wind but also from a wealthy family that could afford him the best legal defense available. We filed a civil suit after but during the preliminary investigation they somehow uncovered a minor in possession charge that I'd gotten as a juvenile. It was supposed to have been expunged and non-admissible, but their hotshot attorney got the judge in our case to allow it in to demonstrate a 'pattern of alcohol problems' on my behalf. Once that happened the attorney who had assured us of a slam dunk victory would no longer provide legal representation and the case was later dismissed. The man who had killed my girl, Mr. John Kruger III, celebrated his success by flying down to his family's vacation estate on St. Simons island off the coast of Georgia and got so drunk the second night he crashed into a parked car. Thankfully no one was in it but he got locked up for DWI and spent the night in jail. The next day his lawyer got him out, challenged the blood test, got that thrown out, with a little assistance from the local judge and was sipping martinis with young mister Kruger later that night. So much for justice, right?

I'd always loved history, geography, and animals and to anyone who doesn't already know it this is pretty much what they fill the television channels with from midnight to sun up which suited me just fine. I thought back to when I was growing up and actors could actually act, not like the plastic, inflated, mind robbing dribble of the current day. What the fuck was a *Kardashian* I thought to myself, and how on earth could they have their own shows? I admit the girls showed well, being women of full and curvaceous figures, but once they opened their mouths it was all I could do to not throw my television out the window. Thank God for National Geographic and the history channel is all I could think. I had my shift beginning again mid-week and for now I'd rest, clean my apartment, and try to think of where I might go with my life someday. The first two weren't a problem, the last however was about as easy as catching as a rabbit on a football field. Where would my life go some day, really?

If I'm honest, other than breathing, I'd died long ago so rebirth was a fool's illusion or maybe some desperate personnel anchor for a future I saw in other people, just not me. Sure, I had some very small dreams. I thought maybe I'd meet someone again someday, but it also scared the hell out of me and I fast forwarded in my brain to the eventual conversation where she asks about my past, me never being a good liar and disclosing that my ten year old daughter had died in a car accident that, even now, I believed I could have or should have been able to prevent. I knew that it didn't matter how good a woman I might meet, no woman was going to tie themselves to someone like me with my minimal income, balding head, morbid profession, and ever present baggage. I thought that maybe I could eventually save some money and move out west, I'd always wanted to see Colorado, Montana, and Washington state but what would I do for work and even though these past years I had pretty much been alone I feared forcing a situation that in my mind could make me even more so.

Jesus, why am I such a damn pessimist! I felt like I had said it out loud but knowing I had not. Life had broken me when Chloe died and now I barely had the energy to walk down the stairs, let alone set aside the extra luxury of having emotions. I took another sip of my drink, saw the sun beginning to peak through the blinds and turning off the small lamp beside me, crawled into bed.

# THE DAYCARE LADY

Wednesday came soon enough and within one hour of clocking in I had my first run of the night. The e-mail said it was a 44 year-old female with pick-up at Grand Rapids Metro. They gave no cut off and I set my ETA at 19:45 as it was only 25 minutes away. I backed up to the rear loading dock knowing that the morgue was most easily accessed from here, without having to wheel a dead body through the entire hospital as was often the case. I called security and they said the officer would meet me at the entrance which was unmarked for both professional reasons and security. You might not think it but there are some odd, gory bastards that will actually try and sneak in to see bodies or sometimes worse. I remembered how just last year over by Chicago some cult of idiots had actually stolen a corpse for their own messed up rituals. What can I say, people are nuts and that's why I preferred working with the dead most days. Calling in to dispatch I started walking up the ramp with my gurney and saw a bunch of the hospital staff looking down at me through the large glass windows. I was pretty sure they didn't know what I was there for so I just waved and kept walking. Nobody waved back but I had a job to do and as I got to the door of the morgue a short, military looking wanna-be cop came shuffling up with a very serious and stern look.

"Where's your security ID," he asked rudely.

I typically preferred things to run smooth but I'd dealt with this guy before and most of the other members of our team had as well. They all said he was a prick and I came to agree with them fairly quickly.

"Where's yours," I asked back with a slight grin.

He wasn't amused and told me he didn't have or need any fucking ID even with a Spectrum Health plastic badge clipped to his front pocket.

"Well" I said, "That cheap polyester uniform and napoleon complex ain't going to get you anywhere with me." Lying I continued, "Tell you what sport, if you want to deal with the corporate boys from this hospital and my company, and the team of lawyers involved when the recipient of this donors heart dies because you wanted to demonstrate your nonexistent authority by being an asshole and delaying my transport , I'll be happy to stand down until you get an a attitude adjustment. I get paid the same either way but if I was you I wouldn't count on long term employment here if you screw this up because you couldn't get into the academy and you want to take it out on everyone else."

By now his face was beet red but he knew I was 100% right as he angrily punched the code into the keypad on the wall. "Thank you," as I pushed my gurney ahead of me through the open door.

They had three in the ice box and we easily found my donor, confirming the toe tag with my paperwork:

Leslie

DOB- 3/13/1976

Weight 172 lbs

Donation organs, retinas, bones, tissue, without limitation.

Now this might freak you out right there, assuming they'd be sending back a skin covered bag of nothing after they took what the needed but it doesn't work that way. The harvest would include anything that matched a needing recipient but they had artificial bones (basically bio degradable PVC) to fix her back up again for the funeral and the makeup people at the funeral home would have her looking just fine for the viewing.

They could work miracles with the body when the families absolutely *insisted* on having an open casket. Just last year I transported a victim of a gang drive by hit out of Detroit, the client having been shot in the side of the face with an AK 47. The destruction is obvious without going into great detail but the mom of the banger demanded an open viewing. I remember asking the mortician how in the hell they could pull that one off without the body looking like a bad Picasso painting. Chicken wire, papier mâché, a little fake hair and some recent pics to build it from. It won't be perfect but we can get it close enough for no one to throw up when they see it was all he said.

Still pissed off the surly and now grinning security guard spoke again; "Well I guess this bitch got what she had coming." Not knowing what he was talking about but seeing the blood splatter on the inside of the body bag by the head area I decided to just ignore him, but he kept on. "Yea," he said with an arrogant smirk, "this is that lady who killed that kid in her day care. Hope she rots in hell, of course swallowing a bullet the way she did that is guaranteed."

I'd had enough of this dickhead from the second words out of his mouth and I knew morgues don't have cameras, so it was just him and me. Setting my clipboard on the gurney I spun around and grabbed him by the collar with both hands, slamming him right into the wall just two quick steps forward.

"Listen to me, you insensitive, despicable punk. I don't know this lady and neither do you. What she did or didn't do in this world is between her and whatever god she worships. It ain't my business and it sure as fuck isn't yours so you're gonna keep your mouth shut from here on out, you're gonna help me load her up, you're gonna sign the paperwork, and you're not going to say another word to me. If you can't or won't do that I'm gonna wipe this morgue with your skinny ass and I'll deal with the outcome. Either way you aren't going to disrespect this woman again, or you will pay the price. We clear?"

Letting go of his clothing I stepped back, waiting for him to take a swing or run his mouth, he did neither. Man, I thought, I haven't gotten that mad in longer than I can remember but truth be told it felt good.

I must have got my point across because he didn't say a word and did exactly as I had instructed.

"Truck 219 to dispatch"

"Go ahead 219"

"En route to Ann Arbor with one donor- Leslie, identification confirmed"

"Roger that 219, what's your travel time and ETA?"

"Two hours and forty minutes, arrival time 23:30" (figuring for traffic en route)

"Roger that, we'll tell them you're on the way. Drive safe."

"Roger that, thank you," and off I went.

It was quiet for the first hour and I began to think the last run *ghost conversation wise* was a fluke but with one small whisper of a woman's voice the reality of it came reeling back.

"I'm not a bad person you know, anyway I wasn't before."

I paused, not knowing how to reply, really not knowing anything about what she had just said and all I could come up with was a slightly canned response of in my experience we can all be saints or sinners, it just depends on the day.

"I'm no saint," she said, "trust me on that. I had a dope habit

31

that no one knew about and it made me take a child's life."

I thought back to my ride with Tabor and actually thinking back, getting past the initial shock, it was incredibly interesting and while it may seem a stretch, somewhat pleasant. In my mind I thought that this is not going to be that.

"You don't like me do you? It's okay I don't like me much either," she spoke.

I had forgot about the dead being able to read our thoughts and all I could come with in what was a clearly uncomfortable situation for us both was "I really don't know you, so I don't like or *not* like you. I'm just driving your body to the transplant center and I honestly don't have an opinion one way or the other." Silence again, thank God. After another ten minutes of highway time I turned the radio up, falsely assuming she was done speaking to me. I had it on the Ray Charles station on Pandora, the melody of *I Got a Woman* filling the cab when she decided to interrupt.

"Do you think I'm a bad person, a bad mother? Please, I'd like to know."

I truly didn't know anything past what that dip shit in the morgue had told me and I'd been around long enough not to take the word of a fool like that, still some curiosity and doubt remained as I answered. I don't know, I was told you killed a kid and you confirmed it. Was it an accident or did you do it on purpose would be my first step in forming an opinion of you on my own?"

"It was an accident, but a preventable one and yes, it was my fault."

This was leading into some serious grey area but we had another hour and a half to ride so I asked her to fill me in.

"I owned a daycare center," she said, "or at least I did."

"We did a good job, everyone on our team loved kids and our popularity grew fairly quick. I had three part-timers, one full, and me. We ran three shifts and even though I hadn't wanted to offer third shift at first my main girl committed to it and the money was hard to turn down. Basically, on third the kids just slept so to a certain degree we could to. It was typically the quietest, easiest shift that we had and then my full timer got into a spat with her boyfriend who didn't want her gone every night and she quit, no notice, the bitch just quit so I had to pick it up.

At first it was pretty doable, like I said the kids mainly slept, but I couldn't really sleep as I worried about them rolling over in their cribs and suffocating or waking up and getting into something that could get them hurt. Like I said you sleep, but you don't really sleep. Anyway, it started to affect me during the day. I was drinking coffee and Red Bull like a mad woman just to keep up and then one day a friend of mind turned me on to Adderall and it was like being 20 again in the middle of summer. I didn't feel like I even needed sleep and I could just go and go. I lost 20 pounds the first month so my husband wasn't complaining either. I knew I was dancing with danger and I tried to find someone to pick up nights again but then I made the second biggest mistake of my life.

With my weight loss I was looking better than I had in years and there was this one dad who was really good looking and started being extra nice to me. I figured he was just being friendly but he kept on, and he started stopping by even when his kids weren't there. One night he came by later than usual, with a bottle of wine, saying he and his wife were arguing and would I mind just hanging out for a little bit. The kids were all sleeping by then and my husband and I were also fighting so I don't know why, but I said okay.

Before I knew it the wine and the Adderall started working

together and I got hornier than I can remember in years. I must have been moving my shoulders a little and he asked if I was alright? Just sore I told him. I'd been working a lot lately and I think it's catching up to me. Moving closer he asked if I would like a massage. My husband hadn't asked me that in years. I still knew I shouldn't have, and the drugs and alcohol can't be my excuse, but I let him get behind me and before I knew it he was rubbing my head and neck, and then my shoulders, and then my breasts. I didn't tell him to stop. We ended up on the couch and truth be told it wasn't the revelation of passion I'd always thought an affair would be. It was just sex, and it wasn't even that good. "Soon after we finished he got up and left. Wham bam-thank you ma'am I guess; a quick good night and an insincere good bye kiss was all I got. I felt horrible and fucking stupid. I was able to get four hours of restless sleep before day shift began and I just went through the motions, not wanting to think about what had happened. I was holding a toddler, Kevin while I talked to one of the moms and I was bouncing him a little in my arms like I did with all of the kids, when suddenly I lost the grip in my right hand and he fell backward, hitting his head on the counter next to me. It wasn't that far of a drop, maybe two feet, or that hard of a hit or so I assumed, but it knocked him unconscious and we all freaked out. One of the girls called 911 and all I could think was to lay him on the couch while we waited for the ambulance.

I got an ice bag and placed it under his head and then the police showed up, stabilizing him as best they could and eventually helping load him into the ambulance. As the vehicle took off with the lights and sirens going the officer turned to me and looking me hard asked "Ma'am, have you been drinking?" In my mind I thought yes, but it was only two glasses and it was hours ago. In the end it didn't matter, they arrested me for child endangerment, drawing my blood at the hospital which came up positive for both alcohol and Adderall. Kevin died two days later and I was charged with negligent homicide on top of the other charges. During the investigation it came out about my one-night affair and as soon as my husband heard he filed for divorce. I was out on bail and he also filed for sole custody which, current circumstances considered, was a slam dunk once we got in front of the judge. Nobody, and I mean even my closest friends, wanted to hear my side or how I got to where I got. All that seemed to matter was that I was now an adulterous, drug addict, child murderer. The state closed my daycare, and they had every right, but now on top of it all I had no income. What little I had saved went to my attorney's retainer and the judge had even ordered me out of our home, giving my husband sole custody and no visitation for me with my children. A part of me can't even blame him for that but it didn't help the pain I felt inside not being able to see my own children.

I found a job working in a bar 20 miles from where we lived and thankfully no one recognized either my face or my name so I could make a living while I waited for my trial. I told them I would plead guilty, because I was, but the prosecutor wanted to do a full investigation to make sure there weren't other instances of abuse or neglect. He even interviewed my husband and my kids who by now weren't my biggest fans. I think, I hope, that my kids still loved me but truth be told in the last two years I was working so many hours away from them I can't blame them if they had resentment towards me. I can't blame my husband either but I wished I could have told him that I was so incredibly sorry, it was a big mistake and it was my fault, but it was the only time in our 14 years of marriage that I had honestly even looked at another man. Once I got off the dope I could see so clearly and I didn't like what I saw. I was working to make money so we would have a better life but I lost sight of who I was supposed to be, a mother and a wife. I remember being able to take the family away for a four-day weekend the winter before this all happened. We ate out every meal, the kids being able to basically do whatever their hearts desired at the indoor amusements. Money wasn't an issue and I bought my husband this really nice University of Michigan track suit we saw in a local shop. It was 200 bucks but I knew he wanted it and I also knew he would never have said so. We were used to living on a shoe string budget and a purchase like that couldn't have even been a consideration before I had opened my business.

That's all just a memory now, but I'm glad I have it. I hope someday my children will remember me for who I was and not what I did in the end. I simply couldn't live with what I had done to them and my family and I started getting into cocaine working at the bar. One of the bartenders dealt it and it was free, at least that's how I saw it. I ended up sleeping with him too so I guess it wasn't really free but with what was going to happen and where my life was headed what did it really matter? My trial was coming up the following Wednesday so when I woke up Monday around noon I knew what I was going to do. I knew my husband would be at work and my kids at school, I also knew where he kept his pistol and I knew where the key was to the box he kept it locked in so after letting myself into the empty house I penned a brief note apologizing for what I had done and was about to do, putting on a pair of my favorite pajamas that I was surprised he hadn't taken to goodwill or thrown out, and I climbed into our bed one last time. I didn't want him or the kids to see my body so I had put a note on the front door saying 'call the police, don't come in to the house. I love you and I am so incredibly sorry.' As it turned out the Fed Ex guy was dropping off a package just as I pulled the trigger and he called the cops. I was never a very good shot and I remember shaking like a leaf when I pulled the trigger, wouldn't you know it I couldn't even take my own damn life the right way. They kept me alive but on life support which I hated having done to my ex but at that point I no longer had any control over any of it. He let my kids come see me one last time and I wish he hadn't. He gave them the order to pull the plug that night and it's weird but I could see him crying on my chest as my last breath left me. I wasn't dead yet but still I could see him and knowing that I was the one who had caused it all I cannot find peace, even though I was always lead to believe that after you die this was the one gift you could count on."

Leslie went on and said, "I heard what you said to the security guard in the morgue and I appreciate it."

"It's okay," I answered. "The dude was a dickhead and he deserved every bit of it."

"You know in this business some people become so calloused they tend to handle it without any sense of compassion for the person. We see some pretty messed up stuff but I always figure it isn't my place to judge anybody no matter what they did. Take you for instance, I have no idea what I would have done in your situation. I lost my daughter a few years ago and I'm still not right about it."

She asked if I'd ever considered handling the loss the way she had and I told her more times than I could even count.

"Why didn't you," she asked," and why did I?

I had to really chew on this for a minute and when I answered her I said, "first, I don't honestly know."

"Everyone handles things differently in their lives. Some of us are stronger or weaker in different areas, or maybe more sensitive and less sensitive is a better way to classify it. When my daughter passed I felt all of the blame was mine but in reality it was just a case of bad things happening to good people. I couldn't have prevented the car accident from occurring, I wasn't drinking or speeding. The weather wasn't even that bad. It was raining that night but nothing extraordinary. I'm not even sure if it was completely the other driver's fault. He was drunk but I can't rationally answer if that caused the crash although so many times I wished the court would have convicted him so I could have blamed somebody, anybody but myself. My wife was a different case.

Our marriage had been rocky at best in the last couple years and Chloe dying was more than she could take. I think we would have been divorced long ago if not for our daughter, neither one of us wanting to raise a child of a broken home. We had both come from divorced families and we had always agreed we wouldn't do that to our own kid no matter what. In hind sight maybe we should have but instead her last memories of her parents included more arguments and icy conversations around the dinner table than laughter and love. I think sometimes I feel more guilty about that than anything else."

"Does your ex-wife still talk to you?" she asked.

"Not in years, but like you I don't blame her."

"Did she remarry?"

"I don't know. I hope so, I want her to be happy."

"Do you ever hate her for leaving you, I mean it wasn't your fault your daughter died. I can't imagine what that must have felt like."

"Hate was never an emotion that I leaned towards. It hurt, and I wish we could have had more of a Hallmark card way to handle it but that's not reality. When people are hurt it's just too easy to find someone to blame so they can justify the anger they have over something they usually couldn't have controlled but happened just the same.

No, I don't hate my ex wife. I just wish what happened hadn't happened, but it did.

"I remember thinking in my head about our daughter's wedding day, walking her down the aisle and holding my wife's hand while she cried with tears of both joy and loss, our first grand baby being born, Christmases with bad sweaters and political disagreements at the dinner table. It's funny how we can so greatly miss the things that never happened in our life."

I dropped Leslie off, called our base to confirm my drop off and got back on the road with plenty of thoughts about my last ride. It made me reflect on my own situation, how it happened and how I got to where I was now in my head. The $1 million dollar question being what was I going to do with the remainder of my own life? The answer being that I didn't really have a plan. Yes, working with the deceased can make you reflect, and ponder, consider, and hopefully appreciate your own existence, but it isn't always that way. For many of us it just becomes a job after a while. Like any job it has its highs and lows but at some point it is again, just a job and like I had found with my other jobs in the past it was up to me to get something out of it, learn and expand my consciousness, or not.

Right at that moment the highway was clear, the late night air warm and sweet, and the tiny glimmer of living again had entered my head but it also scared the hell out of me.

I would first need to open myself to the concept of more complex interaction with another person, maybe a version of love if you will, and that meant I could get hurt again. I'd been hurt enough so my first inner reaction to my own proposal was to kick it right off the front porch of my being, like a Jehovah's witness banging on my front door too damn early on a Saturday morning. Still, the thought persisted.

I could and probably would get hurt. I knew it; man let's face it every relationship is a loss that just hasn't happened yet. People die, people change, people leave you and sometimes they just get flat out *weird* with no rhyme or reason to explain it. Still the memories of the good times I had known, both in my marriage and before, was enticing. I had belonged to several groups in college, my church, and had what I recalled in a blurred fondness as quite a few friends once upon a time. It was definitely harder to maintain relationships as I had gotten older. When you get married you tend to hang out with other married couples, when you had kids you hung with other people who had kids your age, and when you got divorced you either hung out at the local bar to complain and compare your ex or you locked yourself in a safe hole of singular existence and let the world pass by your front door to infinity. By now you know the choice I had made.

It was three in the morning by the time I got home and before I tried to sleep I checked my truck; fuel full, oil and wiper fluid good, all mechanicals and blinkers solid, refrigerator box clean, gurney clean and locked in place, body bags and back stock good, latex gloves and chainsaw ready to go (just kidding about the saw, I didn't want to lose your attention). I grabbed a quick shower, hung my uniform over the kitchen chair, made sure my Keurig coffee maker was full of water, placed my phone on the night stand by my bed, and off to sleep I went.

Two months later it came out that the fall Leslie had believed caused the death of young Kevin had not in fact been the cause of death. Kevin's parents had brought in their five year old daughter for a supposed accident not long after their young son's untimely death. The injuries to the little girl were more consistent with child abuse than the parents let on and when child services got involved the wife broke down and admitted the husband sometimes got rough when disciplining their children, but according to wifey he was a good man, and a good father. Sure he was I thought, he just let someone else take the rap.

The young boy's body had to be exhumed, and past medical records showed injuries that resembled those much like when a football player receives a closed head injury but goes back on the playing field. The abuse to the young boy was a ticking time bomb that had been set off by the accident that had happened with Leslie. She was not in fact the child murderer that everyone had so quickly labeled her. She was just a person who had made a few bad choices, but her children were still without their mom, her husband was still a widower, and she was still dead.

# MY WAKEUP CALL

Noon sharp I heard my cell phone vibrate with an incoming email. Rolling over I grabbed my reading glasses and rubbed the salt from my eyes as the message came into view.

Jesse James

DOB-07/04/1995

Weight- 201 lbs

**Time sensitive- out of state air transfer**

The last part grabbed my attention as I quickly sat up, got my mind tight and sent my response. Out of state transfer meant that, at a minimum, when I responded 16 people across the national network would be activated to handle the process from electronic document transfer to the necessary organizations, pickup and transport of the body, and finally the harvest and transplant of whatever organs were being dispersed. Time sensitive meaning there was a cut off, I assumed in consideration of air time and operating time. A private plane would be waiting in Ann Arbor once the harvest was completed, with a private emergency EMT black suburban (running full lights and siren) transporting the transplant team of doctor, nurse, and anesthesiologist to the waiting aircraft.

I gave my ETA to dispatch, threw some water in my face, and dressed in five minutes flat. This was a new pick up location for me and upon arrival I had to circle the block twice before I figured out where to pull in. The morgue was actually on the seventh floor of a medical school that handled all the action for the four surrounding counties so needless to say it was more of a meat plant than the typical dignified and somewhat serene environment I was used to working in. Security met me at the ground floor service elevator and after checking my documents up we went. It was a woman guard and although fairly friendly and not unattractive there was something *off* about her, or maybe it was just me.

We got upstairs and waited ten minutes for the head technician to even let us in. This was not starting off on a good note, little did I know just how strange the next day was going to get. When we finally did gain access, they had their paperwork screwed up and incomplete which meant more delays. They made it pretty clear that they didn't really care and I thought to myself I'll bet the people on the other end care, a lot. Like I said this place handled multiple jurisdictions so other than Detroit it was the busiest place I'd ever been in and as my friend Doc always liked to share with a grin, the rules weren't about to change for my white ass.

I had to kill time waiting for them to get their program together so I filled the air with some small talk about college football with the chick guard. She asked me if I was married and I said no. Kids? Again no. "Hey," she asked, "it looks to be a minute while we wait, would you like a tour of the place? It's brand new and state of the art. We have some pretty incredible technology here and seeing how it's the weekend I can give you a private VIP tour of the entire place."

She was kind of weirding me out a bit but I was bored and I was on the clock anyway so what the hell? "Sure, that would be great," I politely replied. Our first stop was the lower floor where they actually had hologram surgery simulators for the students to practice on. She explained that the doctors could actually program a procedure into the computer and the student would be graded on accuracy and completion, with alarms that went off if they did something that could injure the patient. It was kind of like that old board game Operation that I had remembered playing as a teenager. I still had unpleasant recollection over the times my hand wasn't steady enough and had touched the toy surgical instrument to the metal sides of the game board, sending off a loud screech and making me jump every time. Over the next 20 minutes we ventured deeper and deeper into the labyrinth of the large medical school, my tour guide always insisting I go first and following behind me in a slightly *stalking your prey* kind of way so although still pleasant, Ms. guard was starting to really give me the willies.

Wanting to get back up to the seventh floor where there were more people I quickly fake looked at my watch and said, "thanks for the tour, but we really need to get that paperwork cleared up and get the donor on the road." In the back of my mind the instinct of self-preservation was really starting to hum and I wanted to keep all of my own body parts intact so I made her walk in front of me the rest of the way back. Call me paranoid but I intended to leave here in one piece.

When we got back to the morgue everything had been cleared up so we headed to the cooler to get my guy. Wheeling my gurney around the corner I quickly realized that they maintained an open autopsy room with three fresh ones out in plain sight. Like I've suggested before I have seen my share of bodies but this place was a whole different animal with modesty of any kind a commodity these folks weren't afforded. One of the medical examiners was actually eating half a damn sandwich as he smiled and waved to me, hovering over a dude who had apparently swallowed a bullet. I was guessing the cause of death was fairly obvious but what do I know.

The cooler here was the biggest I'd ever seen with a smaller cooler actually attached to it, I guessed for overflow. They had 30 plus bodies laid out on the stainless steel shelves and as we were looking for the client a tech came in and opened the door on the smaller room inside, a stench rolling out that cleared up my misunderstanding of an overflow room. If you have ever smelled a decomposing corpse you know the smell. If you haven't, consider yourself lucky. The dude left the door open as he looked for whomever he was trying to find and my former tour guide was beginning to look a bit green as I guessed she wasn't as familiar with this part of the job as she let on. The tech found his next candidate and as he rolled them out on his gurney he slammed the door (thank God) and pointing a thumb back at the room he had just exited exclaimed with a slight degree of panache, "that's where we keep the rotters," as if the fucking smell didn't say it all by itself.

We were having a hard time finding Jesse so I asked the tech for help to speed things up and get me the hell out of this macabre place. He started flipping through the contained bodies with the bedside manner of a giant with a Rolodex but he quickly found my dude. Apparently, his first name wasn't actually Jesse, it was his middle name but somehow it got recorded the other way. Whatever I figured, let's just wrap this up. Slapping the dead guy's chest through the thick plastic wrapped around it he said, "here's your guy, his personal shit is on him."

I asked what he meant and with a slightly annoyed look abruptly unzipped the body bag, flinging the two sides of it wide open as he pointed to a large zip lock bag with cell phone, wallet, etc. duct taped to the chest of the body. The abruptness wouldn't have bothered me quite so much as I realized some people were more desensitized to this than others, what bothered me was the unexpected, and unprepared for on my part, visual of seeing a young man who I came to find out had gone through his car windshield the night before at 95 miles an hour after hitting a tree. Believe it or not Jesse didn't actually die at the scene and made it back to the hospital. Dude must have been tough I thought but some things even the toughest can't make it through and he was pronounced dead at 3:11 that morning. They had cleaned him up which was a gift for those looking at him but he was still too damaged, too young, and too dead, but he would help a few others live so it was time to get back to work. I got down to my truck and was ready to load when the female guard casually asked if I'd like to get together some time? I just wanted to get back on the road and hopefully never see this freak show of a morgue ever again but to avoid an argument I said sure, that would be fine.

She smiled, whipped out a small piece of paper and a pen, and proceeded to use the cold, dead, body-bagged person on my gurney as a desk, quickly writing down her name and number as she smiled at me and said, "it's my cell, call me any time." I was slightly numb as she handed me the paper and I just said thanks. Her number getting crumpled up and tossed out the window as soon as I was a block away.

Fucking people.

I called in to dispatch, explaining the delay, but thankfully we still had plenty of time on the cutoff. I cranked my ride up to 85 and put it on cruise as I always believed in giving myself plenty of time and no way I was risking letting this young man's death go to waste. About 20 minutes into the drive I could sense more than *hear* the sound of the rock and roll tune "Johnny Be Good" beginning to resonate in the air around me.

It may sound weird, and I realize it is a pretty upbeat song anyway, but I started to get this good groove inside me. Positive energy, whatever you may call it, and then Mr. Jesse James (not the notorious outlaw with the same handle) started to appear, riding *shotgun* right next to me.

"What's shakin' amigo?" were the first words I heard and I thought to myself that this dude must of been pretty hip in real life if even as a ghost he introduced himself this way.

"Just taking you for a little drive, or what left of you that is," I replied.

"Yeah man, I hit that tree like a rocket didn't I? Man, I always did like to drive fast and I thought I had my sled under control, that is until I didn't," as he looked over at me with a wink. This brother has sure got personality, I thought to which Jesse offered a very hearty "thank you!" I was still learning the tricks of interacting with my clients and had forgotten the whole read your mind angle.

"So your name is really Jesse James, like the famous outlaw?" "Same name, no relation," as he went on.

"Sure glad they thought to throw my Jerry Lee Lewis tape in my personals. Wouldn't have wanted to head into eternity without the killer by my side," he said with a grin.

I didn't know his car had a tape player, hell these days everything was cd or wireless and reading me again he said "Ain't the same. You will never, and I mean never, get the same sound out of a plastic disk or a radio signal. I remember my old man telling me about vinyl back in the day and I guess they are making a comeback but for me I always liked my cassettes. You can fit them in your shirt pocket right next to your smokes. Heck some good tunes, my Marlboros, and an ice cold Coca Cola in the glass bottle and I am good to go brother!"

"No offense," I said, " but you had a little more than Coca Cola in you my friend. Not judging you, it isn't my place, but you must have had one hell of a buzz when you got in your car last night?" The air went silent for a good five minutes and I thought for the very first time one of my ghost riders had decided to walk away from our conversation. Wrong again.

"I needed to get right," was all Jesse finally replied.

Right in your head, right with God? What kind of right I

thought.

"Right in my head," he spoke.

"You might not believe this but the reason I got all tanked up, revved up and rolling fast, was my dog dying."

"I can actually buy into that, but please go on" I replied.

Jesse began. "You see I come from dirt poor, hard, cold people. My whole life that's what I knew, but I never caved in to it. I always saw life as music. I was curious, sometimes furious, but always digging the journey for as long as I can remember. As a little boy I was frequently off on some imaginary adventure, most often alone. I had a few friends but I was usually too unpredictable for their tastes. Most of my buddies were terrified of the ass whipping they'd get if they got in trouble. Me, I just never cared. Trouble never bothered me and my grandma used to make me go grab a willow switch from the big tree in the back yard when she would whip me for screwing up. I recall that at first I grabbed a small one, thinking it would break quick, but grandma wasn't born yesterday as she often reminded me. She would look at the tiny wisp of a branch I'd brought to my own sentencing and shaking her wrinkled head would walk out back and pick her own.

Every time I had marks from it for a week but I wasn't about to stop having my kind of fun and finally one day when she'd sent me out I walked back into her house with two big, hard, two foot long sticks. I was only ten years old but I looked her straight on and said, old woman I brought one of equal size for both of us so it's a fair fight, but after today you ain't never gonna hit me again, not without taking a few yourself.

She looked at me, told me to get out of her house and I was never invited back. Not that it was a big loss. Growing up my buddies talked about their grandmas being these sweet old ladies that cooked good meals and baked fresh pies serving it all up with love and kindness. I guess for me it just wasn't meant to be. My grandma was a nasty old biddy and she couldn't cook to save her soul. The only nice thing she ever did for me was kicking me out of her house and my mom and dad weren't much better. I lasted with it another year and a half but by right around my 12th birthday I'd had enough and decided to give it a try on my own.

I had a friend who lived a couple miles away and with his mom raising him and his two brothers as a single woman she said she could use some help and had a soft spot for my situation so for a 100 bucks a month I could crash in her basement and get fed. She let me borrow their old beat up lawn mower so I could make money cutting the local neighbor's grass. The lawns in our area were small so for 10 bucks I mowed people's lawn and weed whacked too. Miss Gina told me I had to go back to school in the fall but it was summer and I was able to do three or four lawns every day. I could have worked on the weekends too but that's when me and her son Sidney liked to fish and shoot hoops so I worked my butt off during the week but on my days off we really enjoyed ourselves.

I was only a kid but even after paying for gas, paying rent, and eventually buying my own mower I began saving my cash and before I knew it I had almost 500 dollars saved up in the glass jar by my bed. Man, I was rich and I don't just mean money wise. For the first time in my young life I felt loved and I felt like I was actually part of a real family. There was trust and affection in that old rundown house that I never knew before and I gave my new mom extra money when I could to help out, which she really appreciated. I became curious about cooking, partly out of liking to eat but mainly wanting to know how to feed myself as I knew I wouldn't live here forever. Over the next couple years she taught me how to find my way and not just around a kitchen. She taught me how to live, not only survive. Our whole family went to the local Baptist church on Sundays, always dressing up for Jesus as she liked to call it, and even though I stuck out being the only white boy in the congregation, nobody treated me any different. After every service we would meet at a different person's home for Sunday supper and the food was primarily southern and amazing. Fried chicken like I'd never tasted, potatoes, dressing, sweet potato casserole and succotash, fresh biscuits and homemade jam, peach cobbler or banana pudding with those vanilla wafers. Man, it was fantastic!

That year at Christmas Miss Gina got all us boys brand new sweaters and snazzy shoes which she reminded us we'd better take care of and they were only for special occasions like church. I was back in school but still doing lawns until the snow fell and then I was able to shovel snow for most of the same folks I cut grass for in the summer. I wasn't quite as busy but I'd saved my money so I could afford the luxury of a little more down time and I got interested in reading, something Gina pushed me towards and in truth I'd have never pursued if it wasn't for her support.

I wasn't a really good reader at first, stumbling over the big words, and it wasn't because I wasn't smart like my old family had always made me feel. Miss Gina said I was smart as anyone else but educating yourself was a lifelong pursuit and I started going to the local library quite frequently. I started to mature physically and made both the high school basketball and football team, which were neither very big or hard to get accepted to being such a small town but it built my confidence up much like being told I was smart.

Everything was going great until Gina had a new fella come into her life. Trevor or Mr. James as he insisted we call him smelled like a hustle from the first time I laid eyes on him. I knew momma had been alone for a very long time, focusing on raising us boys rather than addressing her own needs as a woman, but this dude was shady and little by little he and I began to *not* get along. I think I challenged him with my confidence and he didn't think a white boy fit into their family so it wasn't long before Gina pulled me aside one night for a talk. She explained that her and Trevor were going to marry and I didn't protest. I'd been trying to tell her for over a year that something about him wasn't legit but I was still a kid, she was an adult, and love is love, even if it comes in a greasy bag.

I guessed it was better than the loneliness she must have felt as a woman for a long, long time and she didn't owe me a thing. No one I ever knew had looked out for me truly, the way miss Gina did. They were getting married in a couple months and she asked that I find a place before then. I won't lie I was still very hurt but I couldn't be mad at her and I found a friend that would rent me a room a couple towns over. Two weeks later I spent my first night alone and I couldn't even sleep. I was kind of numb if you want to know. I had manned up mentally, telling myself it was just part of growing up and the way life is, but it still hurt. I got introduced by my roommate to a group of local bikers and they took me under their wing, now replacing my two former families. I still ran into my old friend Sidney occasionally and we got along fine but he told me things were different at their place since his momma got a new daddy. I was sorry to hear it but I now had my own survival to concern me and I focused on that. I had graduated high school by now and was looking to improve my bank account with no particular skill in mind. The bikers had some ideas though.

I had my own car now, used but fast, and they offered me a gig running cigarettes across the state line. Part of their mentality being hardly anybody would look at a clean cut, young white dude. Even if I got pulled over, which I did, the cop just gave me a warning or told me to slow down, no tickets and no vehicle search, ever. I started making three runs each week and I wanted to make more but they told me that I couldn't. They didn't want to run the risk of a cop recognizing me or my ride, and it made sense, plus I was banking more from working three days a week than I had been working six or seven before. I had a car, I had money, and I now had friends that wild women liked to be around so it wasn't long before I also had a venereal disease. I was so embarrassed, and it hurt like hell, but when they found out they all cracked up, patting me on the back and saying welcome to the club little brother. It's weird but it felt like a family too me. A fucked up, criminal one, but still family. I realized fully that the main focus of the club was to first make cash and second have fun, but they offered something that I was missing and I fell right into it.

I was ambitious and capable so it wasn't long before more work was offered to me, but the dirt was getting deeper and before I knew it I was breaking more laws in a single days that I had my entire life before. That summer I started liking cigarettes, whiskey and women, and I found rockabilly music. I picked up a cheap guitar and although I could never play it very well it did get me laid a lot." He peaked over and gave me another wink.

I thought back on my own summers as a young dude and I got a vibe of the high energy I only now remembered feeling. Girls, music, and yes, even a little trouble I thought, and it made me smile.

"What's your story?" he asked.

I wasn't sure how far I felt like going, even though he was now part of the after universe I maintained slight reservation. I told him a little about my life, the cliff notes I guess you'd call it, not talking about Chloe but this doesn't work with the dead. Along with the whole read your mind thing I learned that their energy could read and see pretty much everything past and present.

"You got your share of pain and loss amigo, and Chloe said to say that she loves and misses you, and she knows it wasn't your fault."

Jesse's comment hit me something like a cross between a left hook and forgiveness by a priest. Right then the truck wasn't the only thing running on cruise control and I could feel my eyes beginning to water as I involuntarily shook my head, mainly to myself.

"Seriously bro, I can even see the accident before and after and it's like watching a movie where I already know the ending, but I agree with her completely it wasn't your fault."

I felt a slight ping of hostility inside. I mean who does this dude think he is, but he was trying to help and before today he was completely unknown to me so he would have had no vested interest one way or another to mess with my head or my life. I was able to slowly begin to believe him. The sun was beginning to drop in the west and soon I would be in the dark world I usually preferred but for some reason now I wanted it to stay up a little longer.

Jesse spoke up again.

"You know I lived fast and furious during my brief tenure, and I always said I wouldn't mind dying just as long as I lived while I was alive, but now I know that's a lie. The night I crashed I hurt so much I thought I wanted to end it, and I had no business going as fast as I was with all that liquor in me. It's my own fault, no sense blaming anyone or lying, but man I wish I could feel the warm sun on my skin again. I wish I could smell a spring morning, have a girl run her fingers through my hair and tell me she loves me even when I know it's only for the night.

You want to know how my dog died? That son of a bitch Trevor killed it. I hadn't seen him in a few years and one night I was in a bar and saw him in a booth going heavy with some woman that *wasn't* miss Gina. I wanted to confront him, never liking the dude anyway, but part of me thought why tell Gina when in my own mind she had picked this fool over me. I guess deep inside I was still hurt over it and hurt usually turns into anger or resentment. Resentment. It's funny, I remembered Gina teaching me the word one night when we were talking about my biological family and how I felt about the way they had usually treated me. Anyway, I didn't approach him but I still couldn't leave it lay and one day a few weeks after, I drove two towns over when I knew the grease ball would be at work. I would tell Gina, what she did or didn't do with it was her business. Either way I owed her the truth. She didn't believe me, I guessed simply because she didn't want to, and she told me to get the fuck out of her house. I understood in my young mind that she wasn't really mad at me, but she had to be mad at someone right then and I was the closest target. What shocked me the most was hearing her cuss. Being a church going woman I'd never heard a swear word cross her lips, let alone the word Fuck.

It didn't take long before, in spite of her own self-interest, she confronted her husband. Of course, he denied it and then demanded she tell him who said it so he could protect his good name. Good name? Right, but she eventually told him it was me. He went off saying I was just making it up because she had kicked me out. It actually might have seemed plausible (another word I learned from Gina) but the truth was the truth, any way he tried to paint it.

She was going to forgive him, not wanting to be alone again, but he got drunk a few nights later, came home and put a whooping on her. I guess we all show our true colors eventually and Miss Gina called the police and told him to get the fuck out of her house. The police came and made him leave and I remember thinking I hoped this cussing of Gina's didn't become a habit. It would have changed the internal vision I had of her and while I realize it's silly, I didn't have many true and pure role models in my life and I needed to protect in my mind my vision of this one. It probably wouldn't make much sense to anyone else but it did to me.

That weekend Trevor found out where I lived and he come knocking on my door. I answered the door in just a pair of blue jeans and he immediately went off, yelling at me and tried to grab and hit me. I pushed him back hard in the chest, knocking him down into the grass and I didn't want to fight him but he wasn't going to give me the choice. He got to his feet and charged me which only got him a hard right to the jaw, but he kept coming. My roommate heard the commotion and came to my aid. I would have never went two on one in a straight fight but this asshole deserved no favors from me and we put it on him hard. Typically when a dude is down I stopped but I had a rage in me from what he had done to both my happy home and the woman who had treated me like a mom, so like I said we put it on him.

No one called the cops, in my neighborhood nobody gave a damn about a fist fight, and eventually he wore down to just cursing and threatening me. I figured fine, come on back if you want another whipping. I'll be happy to oblige.

What I didn't realize is that he was really a coward and would try to hit me when I wasn't looking. It took him a while to get me back and when he did he hit me where I never expected, and never knew it would hurt as bad as it did.

I had a dog that I picked up as a stray a year back. I'd never had a pet of any kind so Gus and I bonded fast. He cleaned up good after I gave him a bath and I packed some weight on his weary bones, putting white bread and leftovers in his dish along with his regular food. Within a couple months he was a solid 80 pounds and went almost everywhere I did. He was always just happy to see me and I came to understand how people loved their dogs so much, then I got home one night and Gus was laying on the back porch, not getting up to greet me like he usually did and not looking right. Sometimes if it was nice out

I would leave him for a few hours in our fenced in yard and come to find out that one day when I wasn't home that rotten bastard Trevor came and fed Gus meat with rat poison in it.

I took him to the vet, they told me they couldn't do anything for him other than put him out of his misery, and that he had been poisoned. I brought his body home, burying it in the woods behind our house, and at the time, for some reason the thought of Trevor having done it never crossed my mind. I cried and cried and believe it or not I had never cried a single tear in my life. Even when I was just a boy and my grandma beat me and my family was so mean, I never cried. I got mad, plenty mad, but I never, ever cried.

Guess I had it built up in me from years of not and then I went down to the cellar and grabbed a fifth of some stolen liquor I moved occasionally for the bikers. It was 90 proof Old Grand Dad and I turned up half a bottle before I'd known it. My body was feeling warm, my pain getting distant. I grabbed two packs of smokes off my dresser, another fifth from the basement, and headed out into the night. I filled up my gas tank at the local convenience store, turned off my cell phone and headed out to the highway with Jerry Lee blaring out of my radio and tears running down my face once more as I could only think of my friend Gus the dog. The rain started coming down, I don't recall what time but I felt the pavement under me start to get slick and I remember looking down just before the crash; 95 miles per hour and climbing.

I had my window down, six crushed out butts in the ashtray, a near empty bottle between my legs and nothing but sorrow as the road suddenly swung to the right and my ride went into a spin. I spun 360 twice, straightened out for just a second and launched right off the black, dark road. Airborne for just over 20 feet until I hit that big old tree head on. The car stopped but I didn't and I went right through the damn windshield before you could say jack rabbit. I was coming to, laying in the wet grass, and I could taste the salt of my own blood but I couldn't see and I couldn't move. I wasn't drunk anymore at least I didn't feel it. I didn't think I was going to die but inside I knew I would. I heard the sirens and people shouting to each other up on the highway above the ditch I was laying in. It's weird but it was kind of peaceful and I swear Gus was laying right next to me trying to keep me warm. I was rubbing his yellow fur when the first medic got to me, but I was actually just running my hands through the weeds and grass around my body. I felt them inject something into my left arm and it went right to my chest, making everything seem very calm and I didn't hurt like I knew I should have right then.

I was laying under a very bright light once we got to the hospital, the nurses and doctors were working on me frantically and I couldn't believe all these people were trying to save the life of a nobody, roust about, like old Jesse James. Attention was foreign to me most of my life and in those last moments before I headed to the final dance those people trying to save my life touched me inside, and it gave me peace. Strangers giving a damn about me living or dying, still kind of can't wrap my brain around that one."

I guess we both just needed to let his last comments lay out there for a minute. I couldn't read his mind but for me it was a mix of melancholy and loss over a life gone so young. It was a little similar in that regard to when I lost my own daughter, too damn young and too damn fast. I never even got to say goodbye. When I had woken up in the ambulance she was already gone and for years I had ached over the void inside of not being able to hold her or tell her I loved her just one more time and that was a pain that I came to accept, but it never went away before today.

"She's okay you know, your daughter that is."

"In our world we have a connection to other spirits and energy and you can't explain it to someone from your world usually but Chloe is okay and she is glad you didn't have to suffer from what was going to happen that you never even knew about. She had cancer, she was going to start to get very sick the week after the accident and she couldn't have been saved. She didn't want you or your family to have to go through that and she is actually very happy that you didn't. The funny thing is that up here we are both our wisest older self, and our happiest younger self. We have no pain other than our concern for the people we loved and had to leave but our older self tells us that we can't do anything other than try and come to you in your dreams and sometimes in beautiful acts of nature that reflect the pure energy of what love is all about. Again, it is hard to explain if you aren't here, you just have to trust me, Chloe is okay."

I could feel my face getting wet from my own tears and as I began to hold on to the gift Jesse had just given. I was okay, more okay than in as long of a time as I could remember.

"Now we need to talk about you, and your daughter agrees with me."

I turned to look at him as I had no idea what he was talking about.

"Bullshit, brother you know exactly what I'm talking about," he quickly replied. "You been a dead man walking since the accident and you're young, heck you never even got a tattoo or told anyone you're really a rocker at heart." he challenged.

"I don't want or need a tattoo," was my obstinate response but he was right.

"Again, I'm calling bullshit when I hear it and you're seriously going to lie to a dead person who you know can read your thoughts! Ha!" He laughed at me with a mischievous rumble. "I'm not trying to get in your cool-aid amigo but we both know that sitting on that couch of yours, drinking booze, eating ice cream and thinking about all the reasons your life isn't worth moving forward is only going to put you in the dirt with the rest of the folks you've been riding around talking to."

It made me think, it also scared the shit out of me but like when I'd gotten angry with the morgue attendant a few weeks back the stimulus of the emotion felt good.

"Okay Dr. Phil, what would you do if you were me?" I answered him with obvious sarcasm.

Laughing again Jesse went on.

"First thing brother you need to get some action back in your program. When's the last time you got laid? When is the last time you just sat down with a woman who made you tingle a little, even when you hadn't gotten down with her yet? I know that after your situation, you're gun shy. I can't say I get it because I've never been married or lost a kid let alone had one of my own, but people go through hard times and brother it's time to get back on the highway, crank up the tunes and smell that sweet air again. My life is over for now but yours isn't. *What would I do*? Man, *what wouldn't I do* is the real question. I'd buy a motorcycle, get more tattoos, look at life every damn day like a Friday in summer, and I'd find me a woman to love, even if only for one night."

I got the message.

# ENTERING THE DARK SIDE

My habits and my attitude weren't doing a 180 overnight but Jesse got me really thinking down deep. I had a few people at work that I got along with, even joked with on occasion, so the next week I asked where people usually go to hang out or get a drink around here and a guy recommended this little pub only a five-minute drive away. It took a couple days to get up the nerve but that Saturday I hit the pub and within a half hour was getting to know a few of the regulars and my other co-workers. It was fun to talk to the living I joked to myself, giving me a little internal pat on the back. I always liked college football in the past and a preseason game was on the television as the whole bar got louder with a touchdown or hard tackle and I thought to myself man, I missed this.

I started going to the pub a couple times a week, drinking two drinks and ending with water every time. I'm no goody two shoes, I just had better things to do with the $7,000 or $8,000 a drunk driving would cost me. Things started loosening up at work as I think word was spreading that I was no longer the dude that only came out at night and never talked to anyone. I even noticed the nice boobs on our dispatcher one night and she noticed, but she also didn't turn around, and she smiled at me with the kind of smile that says, "hush! I won't tell if you don't."

With my spartan lifestyle I had saved a bit over the years and I'd always wanted a fast car so the next week I found a used

Dodge Charger RT with an eight cylinder and plenty of attitude left in it. I turned the key and that big rumble underneath me sparked something primal. Right then I knew Jesse was riding shotgun again but not interfering in my joy, just watching me build my groove again as I pulled out onto the road. I was off work for a couple days and all I wanted to do was cruise. I had a bad ass radio with GPS and cd player but at first all I needed to hear was the growl of my engine and the sound of life all around me. Eventually I found Jerry Lee Lewis on my Pandora and again, I got what Jessie was talking about. I hit the pub again that night and with the new clothes I'd splurged on my self-confidence was growing surprisingly quick. I didn't have my guard up anymore when I talked to women and weeded out the uptight ones fast, but the girls who just wanted to have fun seemed to gravitate to the new me. I didn't get any action at first, I was more confident but not quite ready to jump off the high dive anyway. I could sense Jesse shaking his head somewhere above me but I just thought give me time brother, give me time. The universe had a different plan, as it typically does, and the next time I was at the drinking hole I met a recently divorced red head who wasn't shy and wasn't taking no for an answer. I don't even remember her name now but I remember how she smelled and I remember her slightly wicked, soft laugh. It wasn't love but just one night, and that was good enough for me. I began dating a little, even getting confident enough to get a lady's phone number at the grocery store one afternoon, but commitment was not something I wanted or felt comfortable with just yet and honestly, I was enjoying finding myself again and began to believe in a new future.

I began wanting to feel better so I got a membership at a cheap local gym and started working out. Man, I thought, haven't hit the weights since high school and it felt good! I was going to do a bunch of things I hadn't done in a while, starting with giving a damn about how I looked. I grew my beard out and shaved my head bald, got my first tattoo, and expanded my new musical interest to up and comers like a local group the White Stripes and this chick named Sara Lugo who I really began to dig. Things were changing with my boss too, and one day he asked me to meet him for drinks after shift. Cool, I'll take a few free cocktails and who knows where this might go. It crossed my mind that he might be hitting on me but I dismissed it and met him that Saturday night at a new joint he liked called The Score. It was a crazy mix of college kids looking for cheap pitchers of beer, secretaries and divorcees and middle-aged dudes trying to get with them. He was already there when I showed up and ordered a bourbon and coke with lime as we got right down to business.

"You're good at what we do," he said, "and I get the feeling you know how to keep your mouth shut *and* be discreet."

I took a long pull off my whiskey and nodded my head slowly in agreement as he continued.

"There's big money in our business and the insurance companies make most of it, but we have an angle of our own to cash in on a little piece, and it's fairly flawless." Nothing is flawless I thought, especially when you combine people and money but I didn't interrupt as he went on.

There is a group of us that have formed our own little program on the side and we've established a growing network that can consistently supply those in need of our services. Hell, we are even doing a little business in Europe, but none of it works without reliable people, like you. So far I've got three other drivers in the company onboard but we need someone in this area and the group has been looking at you as that person. It won't happen immediately, but your side income will soon triple what you make now, if not more. Some of our people have even gone as far to open shell corporations in the Caribbean to hide and protect their action. It's serious money," he said sipping his drink, "and it's all under the table. We've got people at the harvest center and more wanting to get onboard. We've got doctors with private clinics and they all have doctor friends who want to get in on it. We've grown so much we've even hired an attorney and as he laughed, most of what we are doing isn't anything more than a misdemeanor. Can you believe that! We just need to keep being smart, and discreet. The business and the money is there for the taking."

We sat for a while, slipped a few more cocktails down and ordered burgers as we quietly watched the intoxicated, sexually motivated *carnival* going on around us.

I was curious that's for sure, but I always covered my ass and money had stopped being my only blind motivator. I asked more questions about the others involved, any background checks performed, and exactly how we got paid. Was it envelopes of cash like a drug pay off or something a little more professional which I preferred?

He explained that they actually spend about $5,000 on every potential prospect, background checks, thorough internet and municipality inquiries and even private detectives to look for things they might have missed. The preferred method of payment requiring each operator to create a small LLCs or s-corps for receiving funds. Most of them just listed their company as a supply services organization, keeping it pretty ambiguous and easy to pass outside inquiry. Once I opened my LLC they would deposit $5,000 into my account which I initially declined but he explained how for a number of reasons it was necessary and nonnegotiable.

"You draw off it, much like working as a car salesman," he said, "until you handle your first few transactions, which should put you even with the draw or slightly above. Like I said it won't be long until you will be making way more working with us than with the legitimate job but obviously you have to remain employed with them or you are of no further use to us. With that said, drugs or any other habits that can get you arrested are not acceptable, and yes we watch."

I had a pretty good buzz going from the conversation and had already changed to drinking ice water. Looking at my glass he nodded his head and said, "see, that is a big part of why we wanted to talk to you. You've got your habit and your thirst, but you're not an idiot about it. Up until recently you always drank in your apartment and you never drive if your intoxicated. Smart my friend, and that's the kind of qualities that we want in the people we work with."

I looked over and noticed he had switched to water right about the same time. We both grinned knowingly, raising our clear glasses made a toast after they clinked together. "To a profitable future," he smiled. "Yeah buddy," I thought, "this could get interesting."

Little did I know just how far it would go.

# FAME AND FATE

My next run threw me right into the mix when instead of my usual email I got called into the office. The situation was this, a local celebrity, a movie star who I never knew even lived in the area, was terminal and wanted to donate his organs, but he wasn't dead yet. Assisted suicide hadn't been legalized in our state and I wondered why he didn't just fly to one that had or go over to Scandinavia. Wasn't like he didn't have the money to do it. It was a one on one conversation with just me and my boss going over the details. The client would be given an I.V. of the necessary medications and would pass away at his own residence. I would be waiting with my truck already cooled in the driveway. The procedure would be performed at 3 am to avoid any press or nosy people. Once his personnel physician pronounced him dead the typical procedures would be engaged with the exception of drop off and harvest team. I would take him to the usual place but the facility had an onsite practice operating room that was normally only used for teaching. It was exactly like the other room that was typically used, with the same equipment, as if it were a legitimate harvest. A team from my new group would perform the procedures and a private jet would be on standby to fly the various organs to the predetermined recipients. I assumed they were all connected to the movie star somehow, rich, wealthy people that were in need and in the click. Not even close.

Other than the secrecy it would be the same old same old, the only exception being a $20k pay day my first gig! I understood the other runs would not pay anywhere near this but as was explained to me earlier the special considerations of this situation increased the cost to the client which he fully understood and had paid for in advance. I would come to find out that he had also paid for all costs in full, including post op recovery and any necessary short-term disability income to the recipients. I went home to get some sleep and at 4:04 am the next day I was rolling up on the highway, headed to Ann Arbor with my new friend John.

The sky was very light with a full moon making it seem much closer to sunrise than it actually was and I sipped on a cup of dark roast with cream and sugar as I scanned Pandora for an appropriate station for the drive.

"How about Kool and the Gang?" came from the seat beside me.

I smiled, took another sip of coffee and nodded my head as I tuned it in on the dash.

*Staying Alive* by the Bee Gee's was the first song to come up and I grinned again as the groove seemed somehow ironic and appropriate, even though I usually only heard it at a wedding.

"I always dug the funk," John said. "Got to have music with rhythm and some soul, if you know what I mean."

I thought that I, myself listened to pretty much every kind of music these days and while with my new attitude I was leaning towards more rock, I could roll with some R & B just fine. John asked me a little about me, the ending being different than it had been not long ago.

"So papa's got a brand new bag is what you're saying?" as he glanced over at me.

"Something like that," as I smiled and took another sip.

"What was it like being rich and famous?" I asked. Normally, due to professionalism, I wouldn't have asked but I already knew he could read my thoughts so why dick around.

"It isn't everything it's cracked up to be," he said. "It may sound cliché or like I'm whining, but not having any privacy gets real old, real quick. I actually enjoyed my career far more when I was starting out and struggling. I was hungry to actually act, not just become some polished half rate hack who's only remaining talent is that he sells seats at the box office. I think back to early on and we all wanted to change the world, our naiveté helping us to believe that we could. I did the small parts and commercials like everyone else, a few mid-budget plays, and then I got what I thought was my big break one day while on vacation out in California. A buddy of mine and I went to a party in Malibu and it got weird real quick, but in the middle of the chaos I actually clicked with this older woman who it turned out had connections. No sense sugar coating it, we fucked, and I was basically her boy toy for a year. But she introduced me to people who called the shots in the movie biz and before I knew it I got a leading role in a decent project. Along the way a ton of the typical Hollywood crap shook out; lots of cocaine, molly, X, dudes banging dudes and not wanting people to know about it. Me personally, I always thought *who cares* but it's still fairly taboo unless you're upfront about it and then you get a medal, metaphorically speaking. It was fun in the beginning but like anything else after a while what used to flip your switch is now more likely to turn you off. My career was solid by that point and Shelly and I had parted ways a while back. I considered her a friend but she was on to pursue more human trophies and I needed to remove myself from all of the plastic people and their chaos. I asked my agent to find me a gentleman's farm in the Great Lakes area and within a few months I had relocated to my little bit of heaven. My place had 120 acres with a nice stream flowing through it, the main house was a log cabin with two barns and a guest house that I turned into the farm manager's home. Ray kind of came with the property and knew the farming and agriculture thing more than I could have learned in a lifetime. I paid him more than he asked for but I'd learned long ago that you can't put a price tag on trust and I knew I could trust Ray from the minute I shook his hand.

He cleared and planted 10 acres of sweet cherries and together we built a gathering pavilion right in the middle of it with a full outdoor kitchen and both wood fired and gas ovens for cooking. We had a small in ground pool with waterfall and jacuzzi built into the side of a hill by the pavilion and a guest house that I actually preferred to live in during the fall to my own place. The second summer we talked about what we could do to benefit the local community and Ray had the idea of doing a couple gatherings to benefit charities in the area. I was still working in show business, although not as much, and it was fairly easy to get other entertainers to come and do an hour or so mingling with the guests, singing or performing short 15 minute plays that I usually performed in.

The next year we built a small stage with excellent lights and sound system and it became the favorite performance venue for myself and many of my acting associates along with some of our musician friends. We needed to build more guest quarters because once people got there, like me they didn't want to leave. I only made it big enough for four people and even at that we ended up needing to rein it in a tad as people loved it so much, both as performers and spectators, that it could have easily morphed into something I didn't want.

Financially I was able to pick and choose my scripts and started to work in roles I never could have previously. With money no longer a qualifying factor it was amazing to me how different my appetite became and we continued to do small performances at the ranch that would easily generate $100k from donations in an evening that all went to women's shelters, substance abuse centers, homeless shelters, etc. We would bring in local caterers from farm-to-table restaurants, with wines and cheeses both local and flown in. Several times we were contacted by nationally famous singers and bands that wanted to come have *the experience* as it was being called. Knowing how it would benefit so many people it was hard to refuse. Ray would build a large fire just before sun down and had run multi colored Christmas lights in all of the surrounding trees so with the stars above, the scents of fruit and wood smoke, lavender and sage from the surrounding fields, it was absolutely magical. I had never been so happy nor content in my life. I was in love with life in a way that I'd never even considered possible in the past, and then I met June.

I loved her name from the get-go, June always being my favorite month. It always felt like renewal to me. Winter is done-spring is in the thick of it-and summer is ready to jump. June had that air about her straight away and she also had no clue who I was or what I did for a living so we were able to avoid most of the usual hype and jitters that regular people get when they are around celebrities. June didn't know I was famous, and she didn't truly care one way or the other. We were able to fall in love solely based on us as human beings and nothing else, and our relationship blossomed like so many flowers in the fields of spring time. We stayed up late, sharing everything without reserve. We both had our past challenges but we focused on the good times and the future. Love has a way of doing that to you. He said this with a purity and warmth in his voice.

She loved the farm and I didn't want to be gone from her any longer than absolutely necessary, so I stuck to short films and local plays. I'd been secure financially for some time but never emotionally and June gave me that like no one I'd ever known. We had our minor spats but they were over stupid shit, mostly getting familiar with each other's quirks kind of stuff. The funny thing about it was that her oddities were the things I loved about her the most. The way she had to fold and tuck the towels into our old wooden cabinets just a certain way, the way she always added this or that to a dish she was cooking, the twitch of her lip when she read something emotional or the crinkle in her nose when she disagreed with what someone was saying. Brother, so many times I just sat back and watched her flow through life. I didn't need anything else.

The cancer came five years ago and I could afford the best doctors so we got it in check very quickly. While she was going through the chemo treatments Ray confided in me one day that he was more of a *farmer* than just fruit trees and crops, and he wanted to help because he loved her too. June had smoked weed in the past and obviously I had done my share back in the day so one early evening we all rode down to the pavilion, lit up the fire, and smoked a joint of Ray's home grown. After a few minutes I considered that maybe, with his talent, we were growing the wrong crops.

It became our night time ritual, Ray joining us sometimes, and sometimes not. I think he did it out of respect to our personal space and although I would have never asked it of him, I did appreciate it. We stocked the stainless-steel kitchen with every kind of sweet, snack, treat and healthy beverage you could imagine and when we got the munchies or cotton mouth from the smoke we had our own little convenience store to pick anything your mouth craved. June loved smores and one day while going through the grocery store I went wild buying every possible combination of smores stuff I could think of. It was complete overkill but it made her smile and that was all that mattered.

She lost a little weight and her hair came out but she was actually more beautiful to me than ever. Our relationship reached a depth premature of its age which was both a blessing and a curse. I used to sit and watch her while she took one of her many naps and while I felt blessed to have someone like June in my life, as my wife, I also considered what eventually comes to us all. I never dwelled on it, knowing she's have been both irritated and disappointed if I had, but I had come to realize that when you love someone as much as I loved my June you simply can't keep those thoughts from entering your head every now and then. In a way, even now, I consider it a blessing. I've seen so many people, *hell* even my own parents, not really, truly appreciating the gift of having real and honest love. I had it, and with it the uncertain certainty of what may come, but I had it and I would savor the good and the bad for as long as I could.

We wanted to slow the charity events down considerably but she wouldn't have it. June loved the gatherings as much as anyone but her strength wasn't always there so many times she would stay back at our place. I still enjoyed the music and the people, but it just wasn't the same when she wasn't there. I had completely stopped performing and she pushed me not to but I just couldn't be away from her. Maybe when she got better but not now. Her cancer was in remission but as is so common it came back. We beat it again twice but I could see it was wearing her down and one day just before bed she looked over at me, her green eyes faded with silver lining, and she said "I'm not strong enough to be me anymore and I need to let go."

I didn't quite understand at first but when it hit me I rushed to her side, burying my head in her soft cotton robe and as I gently nodded acceptance I couldn't quit crying. I thought we had more time, I thought my wealth and fame could buy it, but they couldn't. It wasn't long after and we buried her in our private cemetery on a hill overlooking the orchard and the pavilion. I kept the events going for a year after but every time I either stayed at our place as I thought man, June would have loved it tonight, but at least she has the best seat up on the hill. The problem was that I wasn't sitting next to her. When I got my diagnosis a few years after I actually took it with an unexpected calm. I was going to be with my June again and I was okay with that.

I hadn't lived a particularly long life, but I had lived a good life and I had true love, pure and honest love, and that was good enough. I asked about donating my organs and my private physician checked me out quite thoroughly, seeing no reason why I couldn't so I began searching for people that I could help live on with my gift who I knew would never have gotten to the front of the waiting list and would have died without it. I knew June would have been happy I made the decision I had and this also made my impending fate that much easier."

John's words got me thinking about my own life and as we drove I thought back to when I'd been married. You always say I love you to your spouse and people close to you but how true is it and how deep does it actually go? This man had something quite profound and he knew, recognized, and appreciated it. I still wasn't looking for what he had but more and more I was learning to appreciate the little things in life that I'd taken for granted so often in the past. When we pulled up I went to a different door and never called it in. Two attendants from the other team met me at my truck and told me the extraction would be about two hours and to hang out in the employee lounge while they worked. I was going to be bringing John's body back the same night so I just waited with my cold box running. Everything went as planned and a few days later his passing was in all of the newspapers with little details given.

Per his wishes he was buried next to his June on the hill overlooking the farm.

# TASTING THE FRUIT

After another six months of making runs, both above board and below, I decided it was time for a break. I had vacation time built up and plenty of cash so after clearing it with my boss I booked a trip and flew to Tortola in the British Virgin Islands for ten days away from the cold and the snow. The plane touched down just after noon and I caught a cab to my hotel, watching the tall palm trees and locals along the way. Upon arrival I was met by an enthusiastic concierge, Sidney who was quick to point out what to do, and what *not to do*. I smiled to myself as I thought I must have had the look of someone who could get into the bad action if left unchecked. Nice!

I was here to have fun and relax so I'd dropped a good chunk of money on a large suite overlooking the bay. It didn't disappoint and before I knew it room service was knocking on my door with a pitcher of Mai Tai's, a basket of fresh fruit, and a chilled silver tray with ice cold jumbo shrimp, crab claws and a couple of the small lobster tails that the islands are known for. The server set it on the bar on my outside patio and asked with a curvaceous smile and the body to match if I needed anything else? I palmed her a crisp $20 bill as gratuity and smiled back as I asked about where a fella could find some single women to mingle with?

I explained that I wasn't looking for prostitutes, just like-minded people wanting to enjoy their vacation. She wrote down a few local spots for eating, drinking, and dancing and with a firm handshake and a flirty smile she left. After sitting on the veranda for a couple hours drinking, eating, and watching the bikini clad tourists on the beach below I thought Hmm, I might have to run into that girl after work, but now the rum was making me mellow and it was time for a nap. When I woke up I took a long shower in the over-sized stone bathroom, put on a brand new tan linen suit that I'd bought in the states, and caught a taxi to a four star restaurant right on the water. The sun was beginning to set and the setting was intoxicating all of its own with calypso music wafting through the palm trees and beautiful people everywhere. One year ago I'd have never even gotten on the plane and now I was sitting here totally into the vibe and ready to taste. Man, I thought, life sure can get interesting if you can make it through the bullshit.

That night I enjoyed the company of an exotic light skinned woman from India, sleeping in late the next day at her cabana and waking to another romp in the hay. I half lied and told her I would call her later. She laughed and dismissed me like a schoolboy with a slight wave of her hand as she blew me a kiss. No games, no commitment, just live life and enjoy it. This was going to suit me well.

Over the next week I learned to shallow water scuba dive, went deep sea fishing with a couple I'd met in the bar and who were attempting to celebrate their anniversary with a threesome. I passed. I hired a guide and we tooled around the large island stopping for a beer and a light snack every few hours and met all kinds of interesting folks along the way. I figured I wouldn't be able to make the same money as I was now used to if I lived here but boy the fringe benefits of island life were hard to ignore. I was sitting in an outside tiki bar with two days left on my vacation when these two very attractive ladies sat down beside me. At first, I just glanced over occasionally and smiled, not wanting to look like a perv, but they had other ideas. They came here every year for girl's week, and I smiled again as I turned my bottle up and took a wild guess at what that might entail. We eventually ordered dinner and more drinks at the bar and chatted about life as I began to get one hell of a buzz. With the sun now going down, along with our inhibitions, the closest one too me leaned over and whispered a very naughty invitation into my ear. I was starting to question all of my recent sexual success, I mean I am not bad looking but I am by no means a stud. I guessed the island air and the rum makes even a slightly chubby middle-aged guy like me become interesting and again I thought back to my old friend Jesse and figured don't look a gift horse in the mouth so to speak, and just enjoy the ride.

The sweet smell of the young woman's French perfume wrapped any reservations I may have had quite tightly in its grip anyway and resistance was now futile. We walked a few short blocks to their hotel and went straight up to the top floor as first music and then more cocktails appeared. Is this heaven? I thought to myself. No one I'd transported ever described it like this but maybe heaven is different for each person. For right now this version was just fine and I danced with them both as we laughed and enjoyed the free energy of the moment. I took a seat on the wicker couch on the balcony and left them to whatever they had in mind, with or without me. A few minutes later they both appeared with only their panties on and presenting a mirror with what I assumed was cocaine drawn out in several long thin lines.

Damn!, I thought, and everything was going so well.

Setting my drink down I smiled again and shook my head as I looked at the coke, back at them, and said "Sorry, you ladies can if do what you like but it's just not my flavor."

They came and sat on both sides of me and tried very diligently I might add to convince me otherwise. They did all of the things a person might read about in the fantasy section of penthouse magazine, inviting me to join, but something inside of me told me to get out of there. As I got up to leave them to their own company I didn't have any regrets. This island was proving itself very open minded and I would be back. I grabbed my suit coat from the kitchen chair and as I began to walk out I heard a male voice say, "Congratulations, you passed."

Turning around I saw a face from 3,000 miles away that I had never expected to run into on my vacation. As it turns out they had set me up, wanting to see if I'd take the drugs when I thought no one would know. What they didn't realize was that hot girls or not, there was no way I would have done it. I came from a family of addicts and knew far too well the dangers of even trying the shit. My boss patted me on the back as the girls came into the room, smiling but still naked. I just agreed with him and complimented the girls saying they had made it incredibly challenging to resist.

"Enough chit chat," he said, "we've got a plane to catch."

I didn't argue as he was paying me a lot of money and I figured he had a good reason for what he was doing. He had a chauffeured suburban waiting outside at the curb with all of my stuff already packed in my suitcases in the back. We hopped in and took off at a fast clip to a waiting private jet on the far side of the island.

"The company is going to reimburse you for this trip but we've got another priority transfer happening and we need you home."

No problem, like I said, I will be back.

# THE LAST BITE
# OF CAKE

It was snowing when we landed and they gave me two hours to get home, unpack, and change into weather appropriate clothing before I would receive an email on my I phone with the particulars of this next run. It wasn't any unusual pick up spot, just the local morgue, but when I got there I had three federal agents waiting for me. Was I getting arrested? I wondered. What the fuck! I thought and then the lead agent stepped forward and introduced himself, explaining very little about the situation. I guessed it was one of those need to know things which was fine. I just wanted to do my job and get home but that was going to be a while.

Recently I'd been involved in some very interesting situations but the next 24 hours would soon top it all. The agents escorted me to the morgue where we carefully identified the body, prepped her for transport, and without calling it in, departed for Ann Arbor. They wanted one agent to ride with me but I refused, explaining to them that unless the top brass at my company had cleared it, no one, cop or not was riding in my truck. I'd lose my fucking job, and that wasn't going to happen. They rode behind me in an unmarked black SUV as we got on the road, not long after which Amanda introduced herself. She began to explain how this whole situation came to exist and as she spoke I thought to myself now I really have heard it all. She and her husband had owned a very popular local Italian trattoria or restaurant. They specialized in Sicilian cuisine as both his and her parents had come over from the old country and the family was very proud of both their heritage and their cooking skill. Everything was made from scratch, including the bread and pasta, and it was obvious they had put a lot of love into what they did. Unfortunately, her husband also had a secret gambling habit which eventually threatened both their livelihood and the business they had grown to cherish. It's funny how every spirit I'd come to know had a different and very distinct vibe or scent about them. Amanda's filled the small cab of my sprinter truck with a musky sensual blend of lavender, chamomile, and light smoke, and her energy was somewhat like a beautiful thunder storm coming in from the distant horizon with a powerful presence that couldn't be ignored, partnered with the expected and reassuring calm that follows after.

"They took my husband, but they paid the price," were the first words she had spoke and after listening to her I came to believe once again that karma truly is a bitch and in this case she was a short, smart, Italian woman with great patience and resolve.

"We had a good life you know, not complicated," she spoke. "Simple and at the same time extraordinary. I typically woke before Vincent and would have a pot of freshly ground coffee along with a plate of fresh fruit and rolls waiting for him. I was never a servant and he never made me feel like one, I just liked to show him I loved him with small things like that. I remember as I sat at the kitchen table reading the paper with the sun streaming in he would walk by me and bend down to kiss my forehead as he went past. I still remember the scent of his oily skin, the stubble of his unshaven face. It's the little things I miss the most. He often closed the restaurant so he slept later than I did but once he had coffee in him the world came alive. He was the most curious and passionate man I'd ever known. We would begin the day catching up on any necessary business affairs and then the conversation might head towards a video he had watched about a country he hadn't been to yet. His eyes would light up as he spoke about the food, the culture, and the people almost as if he had lived there his entire life. He loved to share with me this new invention or that, some of them his ideas or many he had just read about. Vincent had an insatiable curiosity about life and a huge heart. At Christmas he would be up cooking all night, not just prepping for our clients but as long as I could recall also making turkeys, mashed potatoes and all the side dishes to feed a hundred homeless people at the local mission. Even during our slower years, which were not that often, he would insist that we give back where we could. He was the first person to reach out when one of our customers had a tragedy in their lives and it wasn't just being nice, you could tell he meant it. Our business grew and we were able to buy a slightly nicer house although he wouldn't move out of the neighborhood simply smiling and saying this is our home. At Halloween he gave out little gift bags of Italian cookies and sweets to all the kids and when a local youth baseball team came in asking us to sponsor them he gleefully said Yes!

Vince loved kids and even though I couldn't give him any children of our own he never complained. I believe he just took the love he would have given to his own kids and shared it with the others. Everyone loved my husband, but like many of us he also had a secret. I wouldn't have known it but one night I had to go back to the trattoria, and I could hear some men arguing in the kitchen. I knew to stay out of it so I quietly kept to the ladies room by myself as I knew they would never come in. I couldn't hear everything but I heard enough to know this was trouble, for him and for our business. He never mentioned it but I began to notice more men coming in to eat and never getting a bill for their dinners. He always laughed it off and suggested they had done him a favor and he was just returning it, but I knew these were not the kind of people who did anything for free. After a while I began to think my husband had paid back whatever money he had owed but then one night the two brothers Johnny and Bobby who ran the local group came in later than usual and had Vince sit down with them for over an hour. When he got up and returned to the kitchen I had never before seen the look he had on his face. It was a combination of defeat and disbelief and in the weeks to follow two things happened, my husband had booze on his breath every moment of every day, and the restaurant began getting bills for things we had never ordered or received.

One night after getting a call from the bank earlier that our account was overdrawn, I finally had to confront him. I expected him to respond with anger but he didn't, just holding his head in his hands and softly crying as he said over and over, "what have I done, what have I done?"

As it turned out my husband had been under the gun to the local loan shark for over two years. He explained that at first he was able to pay it back with successful bets but as is the case with any gambler, his luck finally ran out. In desperation he upped his bets and his card playing, believing somewhere inside that with a few smart bets and a little luck he could fix it. His bets weren't smart, and luck never came. Before he knew it he was beyond any reasonable mark and on the day the brothers had made their visit to our place they came with an offer to settle his debt. He hadn't discussed it with me, he couldn't, and he knew what my answer would be. So very quickly the business that we had built and watched grow for the past 20 years became someone else's cow for slaughter. I suggested having me speak with them to try and work out some sort of payment plan but he said it would never work. He was in to them for over $300K and they weren't going to wait five years to get their money back. The only option was to bust out our business completely as it was called and run our credit up until we could get no more. In the end the bank would plan to auction off our trattoria, our equipment, and even try to take our home, but Vince wasn't going to let it happen. In the end my husband, the love of my life, got an insurance policy for $1 million and planned his own death.

He was in good health so obtaining the plan was not difficult. We were of an age where it was certainly plausible for a man to want to provide for his wife's future in the case of his untimely demise. It came back from underwriting in less than a week and I could only guess that they hadn't looked at our books or spoken with our accountant. The policy was issued and Vince knew the clock was ticking so one winter night just a week later, after closing our place for the last time, he got in his car sober as a judge and hit the I-90 at just over the speed limit. There is a turn in the road that was well known for slide offs during inclement weather and with Frank Sinatra playing *My Way*, my dearest Vincent drove his four-door sedan straight over the cliff.

I could only imagine my husband, all alone, driving straight into his own end. His last action being to protect me like the caring and compassionate man that he was, but he could never have dreamed how his decision would change me. He had left me a last letter explaining his decision and apologizing for what he felt was his only option. What he never considered or even asked me about was that I didn't care about losing the fucking restaurant if it meant we could still be together. Let the bank have it, let the brothers burn the damn place to the ground, at least I would have still had my husband, but now he was gone and in his place was a cold fury and an appetite for revenge that I had never even considered myself capable of."

As I listened to her I felt an understanding for her loss. I thought back to the days before when my life was fine. I lived the right way, was a good father and an honest husband and then one day through no fault of mine my entire world was turned upside down. I had been in the military as a young man, performing law enforcement and investigative duty. When I got out I had continued as an investigator and eventually working in executive security but babysitting rich people wasn't my gig and I ended up going to college and getting my EMT certification. I worked the night shift for the first couple years, just like every rookie ambulance driver does, and it put a strain on my marriage as it does with pretty much everyone. I just thought that my marriage could survive it but when the accident happened and our daughter died it didn't. To some degree I think my wife had blamed me for not saving Chloe, I was after all an emergency medical technician, but I wasn't God, and our daughter had died. By now you know my story in the years after but you probably didn't know my background is what got me recruited to be a donor driver in the first place. It isn't like you go on craigslist for this type of position and the companies that operate these groups need to employ people that have their shit together. As you can tell I did not, but I could fake it like a pro and I had a solid resume that would come to help me in a way I never could have fathomed before tonight.

Amanda continued on, sharing the plan she had for her little payback and all I could think about how really glad I hadn't been the one to piss this woman off as she continued sharing her story.

"After the typical investigation the insurance company issued the check. The business had accrued just over $160K in debt but with cash in the bank I was able to settle it for sixty cents on the dollar, paid in full. You might think I was afraid of approaching the two mob brothers, but I wasn't. In fact, two weeks after the funeral they approached me. I remember how at first they tried to sweet talk me but it didn't take long for them to get to the business end of it. The oldest one Johnny explained that my Vincent had a substantial debt to them for matters undisclosed. I asked him if it was a business loan, because I had no knowledge of it and I was the sole owner now.

He shifted slightly, tapping his finger nervously on the white linen table cloth.

"I don't know how to say this honey, but your Vincie liked to gamble, and he owes us a lot of dough."

"Owed," I replied.

"What?" Johnny answered without much confidence.

"Owed, past tense. My husband is dead and your debt was with him, not me."

The whole time his younger brother Bobby kept trying to sneak a look at the cleavage on my blouse. What a fucking creep. Johnny tried to back pedal but I knew he had bosses to answer to. Still I played the grieving, dumb widow.

"I hate to come to you with this, but the debt has to be settled. I got people that expect to get paid and they aren't going to just let it go, even with Vince gone," Johnny said.

I began to fake cry as I shouted at them, "you bastards, you fucking bastards, you sit here and look me in my face, knowing my husband is dead, and you have the balls to try and shake me down! His fucking body isn't even cold in the grave yet!"
I actually spit on the floor of my own place as I called them both *disgraziatcy*. I put on quite a little show and in the end they were even more amicable than the creditors. I assumed they didn't want the word spread that they had harassed a grieving widow and they settled for less than half what Vincent had owed them and I made them agree to a payment plan on top of it with no juice on the note.

They began to frequent our place less but Bobby always hit on me when they did and I decided that his lack of control would be the first step in my revenge. They also loved my almond mascarpone cake, and this would also be valuable to me in the end. I was making my payments and building the business back up when one Wednesday afternoon a couple of feds decided to wreck my day. They approached me soft but it didn't take long to figure out that this was going to be another shakedown, the only difference being the badges on their cheap polyester suits and not wanting to get in my pants. The lead agent quickly came to the point that they knew the mob frequented my restaurant and they wanted my permission to bug the joint. Of course I could refuse but it was possible then that I might have some new problems with the local health department and my past tax returns might also require another look. Fucking pricks, but I could fit them into my little plan and maybe have some fun doing it so after a staged protest, I agreed.

I let them plant their devices, even directing them to the tables the Capos usually preferred. At the same time I allowed myself to get slightly more cordial with the brothers and with Johnny's cousin having a 40th birthday coming up I asked if he was planning a celebration, suggesting catering it at his home in the suburbs. He had a beautiful place from what I'd been told and sitting on ten acres. It was secluded enough where interruption would be less of a factor. Over the next couple of months I nurtured both relationships as they all became foolishly comfortable in my presence. The agents never ate at my place but when Johnny and Bobby came by I would stroke their egos and entice the younger brother with a bit of encouragement, casually touching his shoulder as I stood by their table and laughing at his immature sense of humor. One night just before closing he cornered me by the hostess station and decided to make his play as he suggested getting together at his place for a drink. As he stood over me, glaring down at my breasts, he picked up the thick glass globe I kept on display. It was one of those that snows when you turn it upside down and shake it. Vince had given it to me a few winters back when we were in Vermont skiing for a rare weekend alone. Bobby shook it to see how it worked and then abruptly clunked it down as he got back to the business of trying to fuck me. It turned my stomach that this cretin piece of garbage had even touched it but I kept my focus and allowed him to continue his assumed dominance over me. I declined the drink but suggested another time as he prodded a bit more but eventually shifted his desire to one of our waitresses that he knew would be easy entertainment for the night. My plan was going smoothly.

As it got closer to the cousin's birthday Johnny took me up on my suggestion of a catered gig at his place, asking what I thought for a menu and what I needed for deposit. I knew they loved my cannelloni with meat sauce so I suggested that as a main course with antipasti, both hot and cold, before dinner and my famous almond cake with coffee and sambuca after. Of course we would have breads, olives and wine and perhaps some kind of vegetable although truth be told I don't think I had ever seen any of these mob guys so much as touch a leaf of lettuce the whole time they had dined with me. Johnny tried to get me to comp it out with the discount they'd given me on Vincent's debt but I smiled as I told him this was a separate deal, not to be confused with the other, and he reluctantly gave me $400 cash as a deposit as the date was set. It would be him, his brother Bobby, the guest of honor and his top two lieutenants. I didn't think any women would attend as some business talk was sure to occur at some point, but I would cook for them too if need be. The next Monday the feds stopped by to fill me in on the upcoming indictments and arrests, sharing with me that I would now be called as a witness.

"A witness?" I asked. "No one ever said anything about being a witness, you know they will put a button on my back if I testify!"

"Yea well things changed," was all the lead agent would say and again if I refused there would be consequences.

I had expected and prepared for this long ago but again I needed to protest to sell it to them completely. Fucking men I thought, egos and dicks rule their lives, but the plan was going just as scheduled.

Bobby liked to stop by late for dinner on Wednesday night before heading off to gamble in the city as he often did on the weekends. You would think anyone in his line of work would vary their routines so they couldn't be easily hit by a rival group but as it so often common, arrogance had made him believe he was untouchable. It also made him fairly predictable and one hour before closing he came in alone as I sat him in one of the secluded rear sections and brought him a Johnny Walker blue on the rocks with a little something extra in it."

As I was listening to Amanda's plan for her revenge the agent's vehicle behind me starting flashing their lights rapidly to signal me. I slowed and pulled off on the shoulder of the highway and before I could get out one of them ran up to my door, huffing and puffing, telling me he thought his partner was having a heart attack. I jumped out and ran back to find the other agent slumped against the passenger side door and not breathing. I checked his pulse, nothing. I couldn't drag him out onto the side of the busy and frozen highway to do CPR and I needed to think quick or this dude was going to die. My mind was racing and the words Fuck, Fuck, Fuck! were all I could muster and then I remembered a 24-hour super market just off the next exit as I told the driver to follow me and I ran back to my truck. We pulled up right by the exit and left our vehicles running as we dragged the unconscious man right through the front door and laid him on the floor. I scanned frantically around as I told the agent to call 911 and then I saw it. I remembered from my days as an EMT that all modern supermarkets now had electronic defibrillators or AED's as I ripped open the glass door, pulled out the machine, and raced over to the agent laying on the ground. Tearing open his shirt I quickly peeled the tabs off the adhesive pads and slapped them on his chest as I waited for the light on the small yellow box to show green. His chest surged up as I hit the send button and I checked his breathing and pulse again. Nothing.

Boom, I shocked him again.

Nothing, Fuck!

I hit him again, and then again as his eyes remained closed and his chest lifted violently on every turn, and then I got a pulse. His partner knew CPR so I had him start breathing for the man. After a few minutes the ambulance pulled up and they got him stabilized with oxygen and an EKG to monitor his heart. They didn't have time to waste and I told the agent to go with them to the hospital. I had run a hundred bodies and his partner needed him. I didn't. He hesitated as he pondered the repercussions of abandoning protocol but in the end loyalty won out and off he went.

I got back on the highway, my hands still shaking and after a few minutes Amanda continued her story as a blizzard that could match her fury started to roll in.

"I made sure to let the help out early and by the time the alcohol with the Vicodin in it had kicked in it was just me and Bobby in the place," she said. "I sat with him at the secluded booth after setting a plate of fried calamari with lemon and capers in front of him. He played with it a bit, not able to hide his true appetite as I smiled and laughed easily. He got very comfortable and as he did I decided it was time to wrap this thing up if I was going to get it done. I enticed him with the suggestion of watching me prepare his entree in the kitchen as I picked up my glass of wine and headed towards the back of the house, never questioning if he would follow. From behind the stainless-steel counter I watched him half stumble through the swinging doors as he looked around the large kitchen with a half-witted grin, arrogantly believing he knew what was about to happen. He didn't have a clue. I waved him to join me on the back line as I had a veal scaloppini sizzling in white wine, cream and butter waiting just for him. I plated it, tossing a handful of linguine with oil and garlic on the plate right next to it and held a fork in my right hand demanding he taste it. He took the fork, bent over the plate with a sideways grin and took a bite.

"God damn Amanda, this is amazing," as he greedily took another large forkful of the homemade pasta. When he bent over the plate one more time I swung the glass globe that my husband had bought me, wrapped in a white restaurant towel, against the side of his head. The hard, thick glass didn't break as I feared, but his head did and he dropped cold to the red tile floor. I hit him again to make sure and then I went about checking all of our doors to make sure I was completely alone to do what I needed to do next. When I was sure I wouldn't be disturbed I put on the disposable jump suit I had bought off Amazon, employed the research I had done over the past few months, and most of Bobby *the ladies' man* disappeared that night.

The feds visited me again the following week as did Johnny, both asking if I'd seen Bobby. I told them both that he was in and mentioned going to gamble in the city with a new lady friend of his but I didn't know anything else. The feds shook their heads with irritation, his older brother just smiled and said, "I just hope he makes it to his own cousins party."

The event was planned for that coming Sunday and although it was pushing it a little with Bobby being missing the entire week I knew with his reputation for booze, dope, and broads, no one would be sending out the national guard. That Friday the lead agent informed me that the bust would be going down after the birthday party. They would wait until I was gone and would then arrest them all coming out, figuring that having plenty of alcohol and food in them they would be easily surprised. I couldn't help but think, oh yes, you are all going to get quite a surprise as I made the final preparations in my mind. They had gotten a warrant to bug the place and gave me a panic word of "claustrophobia" if things went south and that worked perfectly into my little plan as we briefly went over what they expected from my testimony and I confidently nodded in agreement, the two of them looming over me like they had just bagged a trophy buck. Dicks and egos, yes sir.

Sunday afternoon I showed up at 5 pm sharp and started unloading the prepared dishes, keeping the hot food hot with sterno chafing pans. Johnny had splurged on some good wine and they all enjoyed themselves as they laughed, bragged, and gorged on the free food. Dinner took the better part of two hours and when they asked for dessert. I quickly prepared a silver urn of Italian coffee and began to serve grappa and sambuca to go with it. Johnny made a toast to his cousin, followed by a sarcastic joke about his brother Bobby not being there as I began to place slices of my almond cake in front of them. I watched them get half way through my special cake and then said I'd like to make a toast if I may. Johnny raised his glass and said, "go ahead," as the rest of his guests lifted their own glasses and cups.

"I'll be brief, as you don't have much time." They all looked curiously at each other as I continued.

You know a while back I lost my husband Vincent. He was a good man but like many of us he made a mistake. He liked to gamble and his so called *friends* obliged his habit, as I looked around the table at each of them. He got in too deep and as a man he always looked out for his family so he did what he had to do in order to provide for me after he was gone. You see, my husband killed himself to keep you bastards from taking his restaurant and making us destitute. What you didn't know is that I knew. I knew everything and tonight I get my revenge. Johnny you mentioned Bobby not being here and how good my cannelloni was, well guess what Johnny tonight you are as close to your baby brother as you will ever be.

With a confused and angry look he stood on legs that were becoming unsure of themselves as he asked me what the hell I was talking about?

Smiling and lifting my own glass I walked up close to him, letting my lavender perfume soften the air as I tilted my head up and whispered in his ear, "because my friend, your little brother is the meat for the *meat* sauce in that pasta you just ate. He isn't missing or gambling, he is dead and I'm the one who took his miserable life." The mob boss fell back into his chair with a bewildered look on his face.

"I see the almond cake is doing its job," as I slowly walked around the table of panicked and incapacitated men. Not wanting to draw this out any longer nor wanting to suffer breathing the same air as these pigs I said aloud, "you know this whole thing is giving me a bit of claustrophobia," as moments later the front door burst open with agents in tactical gear quickly filling the house.

"You bitch!" were the last words Johnny said to me as they stood him up and slapped the cuffs on him.

He went off like some sort of wild man, telling the feds they needed to arrest me for the murder of his brother but they all laughed him off as I smiled and shook my head, packing up my stuff and leaving quite peacefully as I drove directly to the hospital. I had already placed myself on the donor register and after registering with the ER nurse for stomach pain I sat down and enjoyed one last piece of my unlaced dessert as I thought of my dear Vincent and looked forward to joining him in the near future. We never had much family so my funeral would not be of any size or substance which I preferred.

I had sold the business to my employees on Friday and when I did I gave little explanation as we all had a drink, cried a little and talked of all of our years working together. They earned it and they deserved to have a chance to build their futures and I always knew that their hearts were in it and they would take it to the next level. I took most of the money from the sale and formed a small scholarship for culinary school at the local junior college, the rest, along with my savings I split between prepaying for my funeral and donating to our local dog park.

Once I was convinced everything that needed to be done had been done I excused myself to go the restroom and with a very calm and deliberate motion, drew the single edge razor blade upward vertically on my wrists so that they could not be repaired. As the blood drained out of my veins I thought of those prick cops patting themselves on the back. I hoped they would lose their jobs over not keeping their star witness alive but just knowing I'd played them was quite satisfying all on its own. As it turned out they had followed me to the hospital and eventually found out that I had taken my own life. They preferred to keep my death secret as they planned to threaten my testimony to get the other perps to roll over. Like I said before, dicks and egos.

You know some people might think I was crazy for ending my life but in truth my life, the life I wanted, ended when my husband died and I cried myself to sleep every night since. That's just no way to live but I kept myself going with my motivation for revenge. We had no children of our own which I think is the main reason some widows or widowers don't end it and I had achieved everything I'd wanted out of this life. I never really wanted anything more than to deeply love the man I married, and I had that, so for me when I fell to the ground of that bathroom, realizing that the men who had killed my husband would go to prison for a very long time and pulling the nurse button as I did, I had no regrets."

I dropped Amanda off with the morgue attendant as I called it in and just shook my head and smiled at the lengths people will go too to get payback for lost love. I had to hand it to her though, this little lady was smart, patient, and willing to wait. In the end she settled the score and she did it quietly. Two weeks later I received a phone call requesting my presence at the office of the honorable Judge Henry Holmes. I had no idea what it was about but you don't say no to a federal judge so I put on the only sport jacket and tie I owned and drove on over. It was quite casual from the minute I walked in and the judge came out shortly after I arrived, giving me a firm handshake and ushering me into his office, asking his admin to please hold all calls.

"Do you know who I am?" he inquired.

Shaking my head slightly I answered that I had no idea.

"Well mister, my son is the agent who had the heart attack during your transport a few weeks ago, and you saved his life."

Not sure how to respond I simply said that I was glad I was able to help, the judge never looked away from my gaze as he sized me up out of professional habit I guessed.

"I did a little digging, and always one to return a favor I need to let you know that the little enterprise your company is doing in the dark is not *unknown* to the law if you get my drift."

Now I physically tightened up and I knew he could see it as I just didn't answer him. Sometimes saying or doing nothing is your best move and I kept my mouth shut.

"Look, I have way bigger fish to fry so your afterhours body parts business isn't of any real concern to me, but you saved my son's life and I wanted to give you a heads up. What you do with the information is up to you," as he pulled his personal card from a small silver case on the desk. He wrote *give this man special consideration* on the back, signed it and handed it to me.

'It won't get you off a murder wrap so don't push it, but like I said I always return favors and I'm guessing in your line of work this may come in handy someday."

The air kept still between us as I let it sink in and then following his lead I stood up, shook his large and firm hand once more, and walked out.

# THE FAMILY MAN

Over the next several months we were busy as usual, with suicides becoming more and more common so I was actually glad when I got the message to go pick up an average Joe with a normal death from a hospital up north. I was never happy to get any of my calls but the circumstances of my client's demise were beginning to weigh on me and I pondered the need for another vacation as I pulled up to the security booth and showed my paperwork. I was soon to learn once again that in this world there was nothing normal anymore, even with supposedly normal people.

Jimmy was still laying in the triage room when I walked in. Normally they sent dead bodies straight to the ice box but for some reason this little hospital in this remote burg of the north had decided to leave him out on the operating table. They hadn't even covered him up and all he had on was a bright yellow pair of smiley face boxer shorts and black *old white guy* socks. Not cool, but I had a job to do as I got the unsure nurses to help me bag him up. I was slightly irritated at the whole situation and I asked the one lady jokingly if this was her first dead body. She replied with a shudder that it was and I rolled my eyes as I thought great.

He still had an IV needle stuck in his leg and they weren't sure what to do as I reached into my bag and pulled out a pair of pliers. It took a good tug but I pulled it out of the bone it was imbedded in with a pop as the youngest nurse looked about to faint. They all looked like they were ready to bolt or throw-up and I figured I'd save us all the uncomfortable scene as I said, "it's okay, I can take it from here."

That was all they needed as they couldn't get out of that room quick enough as I started bagging the donor. It took a little finagling, as he was a large man of substantial appetites, but I got him secured on the gurney and into my truck as I called it in and headed back out on the road. He may have looked like your ordinary-middle aged-white guy who had died from an all too common heart attack, but I was soon to find out there was nothing ordinary about Big Jim.

"Man, I could use a cold one," was my introduction to his world.

I don't remember laughing much during my past spirit conversations but Jimmy was a different duck and chock full of personality even as a stiff. During our little road trip he made me chuckle more than once and I thought that I would have liked to have him as a friend when he was among the living. He owned a party store, a bar, and a campground on a nice little lake and he loved life. He had four kids, little Jim, Rocky, Tim, and Isabelle, and a buxom woman who was his bride of 20 years just this month. I felt bad about that and Jim said, "don't, I had a great life." I had almost forgotten about the whole mind reading thing until now. To look at him from the outside or on paper you would see one picture, but the truth was far more interesting as Jimmy had always had to hustle to make a living and wasn't afraid to chase a buck, even if it was down a dark and sometimes dangerous road.

"Growing up in the Upper Peninsula of Michigan no one had any dough and even as kids you learned to find ways to get extra," Jim began to explain."

"My first grab was going to the local supermarket and checking for unlocked car doors. I was only eight but the hustle was in my blood from both genetics and necessity and we could usually find something to sell either in the car, the backs of

DANIEL LEE SILVERTHORNE

trucks, or if we had time, the trunk. The best spot, as I would
soon find out, was a small casino parking lot that the local
tribe operated. The tourists were pretty lax or drinking and
we found plenty of unlocked cars and RV's to take from. We
had to be a little careful as they had cameras in the lot but
even if they caught us they didn't do much. We were just kids
and they were making plenty off the gambling so other than
an occasional smack upside the head they left us alone. Sometimes I thought they actually enjoyed us clipping the white
people a little. Lord knows the Indians were taking them to
the cleaners in what they jokingly referred to as the red man'
revenge. As I got older I graduated to hitting the local truck
stops, liquor store and massage parlor parking lots, and when
Wal-Mart came to town that was like Christmas for the first
couple of years. I got my CDL when I was old enough and
started driving truck. It wasn't long before I hooked up with
a local guy who had weed, pills, liquor and smokes coming
in from Canada and then the real money started flowing. I
got popped once coming across the border with untaxed cigarettes so the Canucks wouldn't let me in anymore but there
was plenty of cash from running in-state. I think my guy was
hooked up with some Albanians from Windsor and we started
to have other stuff get packed into the truck. They always
hid it halfway back in the load figuring the cops were pretty
lazy and unless they thought they were getting a big drug bust
nobody was going to get cold and wet over something that
would never advance their career like booze, cigarettes or
electronics. A few times I had my suspicions about them hiding a fugitive in the load but I didn't need any hassles and I just
made my runs, made my money and shut up.

I ran back and forth seven days a week with merch coming in
from both the north and the south and I was smart enough to
do my job without asking questions. I knew we weren't big in
the dope business, mainly because the players above us made
it clear that it was theirs and theirs alone. We had some small

96

timers try and break into the trade on occasion but even up in our no man's land it was made clear to leave the big hustles alone. A friend of mine who liked to test fate even as we were kids was running coke and X for a minute but one day they burned his van in the middle of the night to send a message. He was greedy and foolish and wouldn't quit. When I went to the funeral it was a closed casket and if there was ever any doubt it became crystal clear to me not to mess with the big boys. It wasn't really necessary anyway. I made great money driving truck and if your boss pissed you off you could tell him to go fuck himself and find another driving gig before sun set the same day plus, I was always able to run a little extra goodies on the load and it paid cash, no questions asked so again I was content with what I had and left any query otherwise alone.

As I got older and came to meet my wife I realized that I needed to start playing it a little safe. With a baby on the way I wanted to give my family the stability I'd never had and by watching my expenses and working 12's I put away enough for a down payment on a house on a small local lake that had a rundown commercial building up front by the road and 20 acres. I had friends that could build and do electric and plumbing so after a little legal finagling, which pretty much involved hiring a lawyer to get my record expunged, I turned the building into a liquor store. I was really surprised no one had thought of it before, I mean hell it was the main thorough-fare to get from our small town to the highway and to me it seemed like a perfect fit.

I was still driving truck and my wife ran the store, with limited hours. She hired her nieces to help during the crazy summer months but we closed on Christmas Eve every year and reopened March 15. My wife figured there was no sense paying for utilities and staff when there was nothing but wind, snow, and darkness for company that time of the year and we more than made up for it in the rest of the time. After a while I got the idea to run a blind pig-*back room bar*- just for the locals but my wife told me I was an idiot for even considering it as she convinced me to go through the lengthy process of getting a legal liquor license. Like many other times I was glad I'd listened to her and after we got approved that September my friends and I spent the winter putting up another building three times the size of the store. My wife was a heck of a cook and her family learned quick so pretty soon we had people driving from an hour away just to eat her food. Before I knew it I was able to pick up another 200 acres around me and the next spring we opened our campground. We had a captive audience with the people already coming to or through the area in summer and the locals kept the bar busy year-round so it turned into a pretty sweet gig. I give my wife all the credit for our success but I always had that wild hustler side of me and with one stupid decision on my part I was about to threaten everything we had worked so hard to build."

Hearing Jim talk about his life and his wife made me think back to my own prior marriage. I had loved my daughter as much as I knew he loved his kids, but I could never recall the reverence and passion he held for his bride. My wife wasn't a bad person but, as I have already said, ours turned out more to be a marriage of convenience and obligation and not the closely held and cherished kind of love I had come to see in many of my clients. What was it that made some people have this kind of fire? I still wasn't sure but I was learning more and more about what love was, and perhaps even more, what it was not. The stories I had heard all held loss and pain, but they also kept unbreakable commitment and a tenacity to go on regardless of anything life threw at them. I heard in their voices the occasional anger and borderline contempt they occasionally held for the actions of their partners, but never, not once, did I hear any inflection of giving up. When I thought back again I couldn't recall ever having that kind of fuck the world devotion to my wife, nor she for me. I was starting to wonder if it was even possible for someone like me but as I looked over at the form of Big Jim I thought to myself that if he can have it maybe I can too.

"Absolutely," Jim replied as he continued on again.

"You know I had a great life, I mean really, a great life. Nobody in my family accomplished what I had and I don't mean money. My wife and kids will be set but what in retrospect I am most proud of is the husband I was, and the dad I was. I loved every breath my wife took, even when she was mad at me over my stupid shit, and my kids, man my kids were my world. I wish I hadn't eaten so many burgers or drank so many beers, but that's just me. My body may have given out on me in the end but what I gave my family in love will never die. I hardly remember any family time with my own mom and dad but I made damn sure my kids and my wife had plenty of great memories after I was gone. We had our usual end of summer barbeque at the campground and we really threw down the on the meal ticket as our way of both saying thanks to our customers and having them remember us for next year. We cooked for two days to get ready and I ran the large barbeque pit I had built as we prepared two pigs, ten briskets, a hundred chickens and thirty pounds of sausage. My wife and the girls whipping up all of the sides and desserts to go with. Yes sir, it was quite the feast.!

About half way through our party a local boy who was a bit of a computer whiz approached me as I was sitting by myself overlooking the festivities. He kept it to small talk at first but eventually told me how he worked for the state and saw some interesting stuff on occasion. I wasn't sure what he meant and didn't much care, my belly was full and I was doing one of my favorite things just watching my kids play, but he kept on.

He worked in some department that handled surplus, claims, and lost money, which I assumed was a fairly large chunk of change. I had no idea how big until he told me and when he did I took my eyes off my children and he had my full attention. Any government agency has waste and things that get grid locked in bureaucracy or *lost in the shuffle* as people like to say. Our state was no different and this young buck drinking a beer with me had figured out how to drain some off the top without anyone noticing. There were a number of angles we could approach but most of it would only add up to chump change. There was merchandise that could disappear, materials that could be scrapped, even industrial equipment that could be sold to buyers out of state with never a trace if you simply altered the inventory records. I asked him how he knew all this and he explained how when he had been in the Army he and some trusted friends had figured out the same situation existed in the military, only on a much larger scale, with more oversight. The big difference here was that at the state level everyone was mainly trying not to lose their jobs to departmental cuts and just make it too retirement. How they got there was flexible and everyone was going to keep their mouths shut and their heads down along the way, which left a wide open market for fraud.

As he went on I calculated risk reward as I always had in the past. The big difference was that when I was running hustles before I was a young dude with nothing to lose. Now I was in my early 50s with a family, property and investments, still the excitement of the game was hard to resist and I let him go on. I was ruling much of it out already as I listened and considered the logistics of turning the surplus or other items into cash. Any physical materials or products we had to sell would accelerate the risk significantly as it does anytime you have more than one or two people involved and I could only see it working with a minimum of two more dudes on the team. He had a few other ideas but quick inner analysis ruled them out as well, and then he mentioned the graveyard bank.

In any government agency you have money that doesn't go anywhere. It can be refunds that were never collected, allotments that were never dispersed, settlements never claimed, the list goes on for a while and we found one that seemed bulletproof in the form of a growing fund of money from a variety of sources that the state couldn't keep, but they also couldn't find the people it was supposed to go to. They actually had formed a website to let people know about it but between pessimism or not being aware it even existed most of it never got claimed, and my new friend could access the list. He explained the way it worked was fairly basic as you went on the website, typed in your name, and if you had money that you were entitled to you moved forward in verifying your information and claiming it, then they sent you a check. The angle he found was that it didn't need to exactly be *you* that claimed it. They had a process for a person you had designated as your agent to request it for you and there were actually companies you could hire to search the entire United States for money you had ownership to but never knew about. With the consideration that people die, get divorced, and move, there was literally millions of dollars every year that no one ever went after, but we were about to. I did some more research on the idea and vetted my new partner as much as I could. By the next weekend I was convinced it was definitely doable, and the plan began.

The first thing we did was set up post office boxes in ten different post offices within 50 miles of us. Next, I was given a list of all in state claims above $3k. We didn't want to mess around with the nickel dime crap and multiple scores at $3k and above could add up quickly and quietly. I went online and searched for the addresses of the claimants, finding many of them who had died or no longer lived there anymore. I figured if it was this hard for me to find them no way in hell some suit behind a government desk was going to take the time to pursue them, and my partner was the guy who authorized the settlements anyway so he wasn't going to challenge any of them. The following Monday I was able to submit phony agent documents for seven people. Two weeks later the first checks started coming in and by Friday I had deposited $22,522.82 into the account of Liberty Asset Services, a local company that I was now the president of and my friend the CFO. In the next year we brought in over $400k and we never lifted so much as a single box or delivered one shipment of anything illegal to do it.

Things were running smooth all around and I was just sitting at the bar one afternoon, considering some interesting other options, when a guy in a suit walked in and asked for the owner. With a hand shake I introduced myself as a partner and asked how could I help him but he was keeping his cards close to his vest from the get-go and I could clearly see it.

"We just have a few questions about your business," was all he said as he proceeded to begin asking vaguely about a bunch of things that had nothing to do with either the bar, the store, or the campground. My sixth sense was tingling like when you get pulled over by a cop with a smashed out joint in the ashtray and a case of empty beer bottles in the back but I kept it cool as I tried keeping my answers as basic as I could. He didn't stay long and you would think it would be a relief that he didn't but I'd been around enough cops and crooks in my life where I knew this was just the beginning as I felt my chest hurt for the first time, dismissing it as aches from my age or too much spicy food. I poured myself a cold draft from the tap and sat back down to think as I chewed on all of the possible angles he'd come at me with. I took another sip and grinned to myself because I truly enjoyed the game but I didn't smile too long as the thought of having to explain it to my wife entered my thick head.

The next week he came in again. I had given him my business

card and told him to call anytime but these guys like to surprise you and courtesy isn't exactly tops on their list of priorities. He filled 45 minutes with more vague questions and I couldn't really pin him down on the direction he was going but I had figured he had already run a check on me and even minimal digging would throw up a few flags about my past. Our liquor business was always kept straight and tight as was the bar, heck I wasn't even running anything out the back door for over three years now and I knew he didn't know about the state cash fund scam; or did he? I got no answer to any of it as once again he departed without so much as a single smile or so much as a comment about sports or life as most guys will eventually do.

"Jesus, how the hell was I getting looked at by such a tight ass? " Was all I could think and this time I wasn't ready for a cold beer, and my chest hurt again.

Over the next week I didn't hear anything back from him but one of my bartenders asked why cops were asking him questions and that night my wife asked me the same thing. I kept my cool as I told them both I had no idea but I was starting to get nervous and I told my partner we needed to shut our action off until this things sorted itself out. We had plenty in the business account so he didn't flinch and I think he was ready for a little break too as I made the suggestion of him taking a vacation. He had 62 days saved up and with the state you are on a use it or lose it system so after approval from his supervisor he flew off to spend a month with family on the west coast. He hadn't been approached yet and I wanted to keep it that way but I still drove to Grand Rapids and placed a retainer with a top level criminal attorney that specialized in dealing with the feds. I had been making cash withdrawals for the past several months of under $10k each to avoid the IRS reporting from the banks and had brought just over $100k in cash with me to secure my rainy day fund in case anything happened. It wasn't raining yet but I could smell the clouds as I spent the following afternoon driving around town and purchasing the ten 10 ounce Credit Swiss gold bars from multiple gold stores I had called two weeks prior and arranged for. I had spread my purchases out again as not to draw un-needed attention to myself and that night I drove home, stashed the gold in the small side wall under the sink of an old pop up camper we never used anymore and finally able to relax, had a nice steak dinner with my wife and kids at our restaurant.

The following week I took the family up north to a water park resort with plenty of activities and beaches to hang out at as I explained that we hadn't had a family vacation in a while, and it was the truth, so it was easy to sell. At night after the kids went off to bed my wife and I had more quality time than I could remember in years and as her head lay on my bare chest she again asked me what was going on with the cops. I tried not to ever lie to her but I knew this would blow over so with a white lie I whispered that there was nothing to worry about and she accepted my answer. We had a great weekend and I spent my time just really wanting nothing but to cherish the kids and my wife like I'd never have it again. We went big lake fishing, rode the sand dunes on a huge and loud dune scooter, and on Friday night they shot fireworks off to top it all. I didn't know this would be our last vacation but in retrospect I'm glad it was. It was pure and honest, other than my fib, and I can't really explain it but I just knew with all of the laughter and great times together in the hot summer sun it would remain vibrant in my children's memory the rest of their lives and that brought me a great deal of inner satisfaction regardless of whatever might come down the pike after we returned home.

When we got back all was quiet for a few days but then Barney Fife, the curious cop just had to come back and when he did I was in no mood. He started off with his round about questions again and I'd had enough so I told him I thought it was time for me to hire an attorney as this was beginning to feel like harassment. He asked why I thought that I might need legal representation and I chuckled lightly as I told him that while I may have been born at night, I wasn't born *last* night and this is the third time he'd come to my business without really telling me exactly what the hell he wanted. He didn't flinch, but he did smile. The son of a bitch was enjoying this, I thought and I also thought of knocking the grin right off of his face but assaulting an officer wasn't something I needed on my record. I had already hired a lawyer but he didn't need to know it and without answering me, or shaking my hand, he left. Now I was getting nervous and I'm pretty sure it showed.

A month went by, I always thought purposely so, and then as I was driving down local route 101 one beautiful afternoon my friend the annoying cop pulled me over in his unmarked car.

As he walked up I rolled down my window and when I saw who it was I got pissed. I'd had enough of his pestering me without letting me know what was going on and I told him so. My face was getting red and I started dropping F bombs left and right as I was completely sick of his shit, and then my chest and my head starting hurting again, I started having a hard time breathing, and that was it.

He called an ambulance and I was still alive when they got me to the hospital 10 miles away but by then the damage was done. They brought me back three times but that was all they could do and at 2:34 pm I entered the big saloon in the sky. My wife came to the hospital but I never regained consciousness and I just wish I could have told her how much she and the kids meant to me and how sorry I was, but done is done and all she could do was hold my cold hand and stroke my cold forehead as the tears flowed down her face. I always told her I wanted my organs to go to help someone else when I died so they called you guys. The next day she filed a lawsuit and a federal complaint against that dickhead cop who would lose both his job and his pension over it. The messed-up part of it all was that he was never even investigating me, my wife, or our business. He had gotten a tip that one of our bartenders was running dope at a pretty good pace and we were his first stop. Me eventually getting sick of it and giving him an earful got him thinking that maybe he should dig a little further but he never got anything and if I'd have kept my temper and my mouth shut during his last visit he was going to close the case as unsubstantiated and we would have never seen him again. Damn!

As I drove my truck up to the harvest center and called in my arrival I could hear Bob Dylan singing *Knocking on Heaven's Door* somewhere in the air and I pulled in and shut it down as I completed Big Jim's final ride. The funny part of it all was when five months later Jimmy's wife had sold that old pop up camper to some strangers from Indiana. She said it had too many memories and they never used it anyway but those nice people from Indiana must have gotten one heck of a surprise when the water line to the sink began to leak and they had to rip it out and replace it. Jimmy's wife never heard from them again, but they did buy a much nicer camper that fall and rumor has it they paid cash.

# I MAKE A FRIEND

The next months were filled too many young suicides for my liking but I had a job to do and I just had to keep my head down and keep on working. Still the clients taking their own lives who should have been getting ready for prom night or college weighed heavily on my mind. Someone upstairs must have been looking out for me when I had the chance one night to spend a few hours with a Croatian woman who would come to change me in a way I didn't even know I needed. Kata was a lab technician at the harvest center where she worked the night shift, attending college full time during the day as she worked to finish her schooling. After taking several years off she was now trying to become an MD and I was amazed that she could both work full time on the midnights and go to school but I would come to learn that facing challenges was not something my new friend was unaccustomed to. I didn't know much about her country before I met her. I knew about the Serbian war crimes and the hatred by them for non-Serbs but I had no idea the level of depravity for human life that had been demonstrated until I spent some time with a woman who had lived through it. I had just dropped off a client who was slated to be an extensive harvest but who would be returning to a funeral home afterward, so they made me wait for the procedures to be completed. We weren't under any emergency protocol so I was going to drive over to a local coffee shop to wait. Kata was finishing her shift and asked if I could give her a ride, which typically we weren't allowed to do but I'd been here so long that I knew it wouldn't be an issue and no one was going to report me so I said sure. I backed the truck in and finished up some paperwork as I told her I would join her inside in just a few minutes. As we waited for our drinks to come, I immediately felt very relaxed around her. It wasn't a sexual attraction, not that she wasn't attractive, it was just more of a friend feeling than anything else and that suited us both just fine. It was appealing to think I might make a female friend with no other attachments or luggage to deal with. Not that having friends with benefits was a bad thing, I just needed something more right now. After a brief conversation she shared the same thought about me and it allowed the subject matter to flow more freely without having to have your guard up or calculate your words. Nice!

We went back and forth at first with the usual where are you from, how long have you worked here stuff but our comfort level with each other was equal and we dove into the deeper end far quicker than either of us had imagined. She had a small tattoo of a purple flower on her inner left wrist and I was going to leave it alone but she caught my flickering gaze towards it and explained with a smile that it was called born of lightning in Croatia. She said it was a national flower that grew wild in the mountains around her village in springtime and it reminded her of both where she came from, and where she intended to go. As a young girl she would walk in the hills with her grandfather as they foraged for wild herbs, plants, and vegetables to bring home. As they walked, dug, and picked he shared with her many things about their culture and the flower she had on her wrist was named for the story of how the locals believed the places it grew had been struck by lightning from the ancient gods of the skies. In early spring the area was filled with the light purple flowers and it was quite beautiful to behold. Her grandfather died when she was just ten years old but every time after when she and her siblings would go to the forest, she thought of him and she knew he was in heaven now looking down on her family and protecting them. Life was simple but blissful as she and her family lived together in the stone house her grandfather's father had built many years ago. They had a two sided open fireplace that heated both the kitchen from one side and the small living room on the other and it had an iron arm that swung outward which allowed you to hang a large cast iron kettle on to cook the delicious stews and dishes her mother would make over the aromatic oak embers. Many nights after dinner her mother would read to them and I asked about her father and grandmother, but she only said her father was a stoic man with a desire for the bottle more than his family and her grandmother had passed when she was a toddler. Still, her memories with her family were good ones, that is until the war began.

Her first memory of it was the sound of what she believed to be thunder in the distance. She remembered the worried looks on the adults faces but they lied as they agreed with her that it was thunder as war was something to protect children from, in mind and body, for as long as they could. She thought it strange that the thunder lasted for days and when she looked up she could never see any lighting or storm clouds but she did notice her family begin to pack things into old wooden boxes as father seemed to inspect the family's old truck more often than ever before. He checked the oil and worn tires, starting it twice each day as the engine purred and he gazed cautiously off towards the mountains of the east. She didn't have to go to school which surprised her and her mother kept her busy in the kitchen as they preserved vegetables, fruits, and pickles in glass jars. She didn't mind as she always enjoyed working with her mother but didn't they usually do this in the fall she asked. Her mother lied again and told her they were starting early this year, but she didn't sing while they cooked which also surprised Kata and she began to realize that something was not right.

Three nights later the thunder seemed closer than ever before and it scared her so she was awake at 3 am when her mom came into her room and told her and her sister to get up and get dressed. Bags that they normally only used when the family would travel to the seaside for holiday had already been packed and she could hear hurried voices outside her window. The truck was already running and when she came down her father was standing in the gravel driveway with a rifle in his arms as he scanned the rode in both directions.

"We loaded quickly into the waiting truck with my uncle and his family joining us," she said. "My father headed east as a frightening silence engulfed our group, even the children knowing something evil and very dangerous was after us. My father knew of a place 80 kilometers away where he and his friends went to hunt deer and wild boar in the past and he assumed we would be safe for a while from whatever it was we were running from. It was very deep in the woods and although I could still hear the sporadic sound of thunder it was distant, and with it, not as threatening to me. The adults put up an old army tent that was large enough for us all to sleep in and they put a portable wood stove in the corner to cook with. We slept on the ground but by then we were so exhausted it didn't matter and I slept soundly as two of the men kept watch in the woods outside.

The next morning I asked what was going on but no one would answer me and my mother solemnly handed me a bowl of porridge with dried fruit in it, but no cream. As I ate I watched the men clean and oil their rifles, sharpening their knives and checking the truck again. They stayed by the edge of the woods and nervously smoked their cigarettes with worried looks and I noticed that none of them ate anything much for days. The thunder eventually got closer again and we packed up and drove further east, avoiding the main roads and trying to remain in the woods of the mountains as we traveled. We found another place to camp by a river and for the first time in a week I was able to wash as a man with a rifle stood on the cliff above the water keeping watch. We all took turns bathing and cleaning our clothes in the cold, clean water and that night they made a small fire outside of the tent and the men drank coffee and very small amounts of a homemade liquor of honey and herbs that we always had in our basement. They ate some slices of dried meat and fresh bread that my mother had made but still the look of fear never left their face. We survived hidden in the woods for almost a month but one day as we drove to find a new camp we came around a bend in the road to find military trucks blocking it and they were not Croatian. The soldiers wore brown uniforms and black balaclavas on their faces as they motioned with their rifles for us to all get out. I was very scared but my mother told me everything would be okay as she wrapped her arm around my shoulders and smiled as best she could. The leader walked up and wore a very angry look as he spoke quiet but angry to my uncle, asking questions about where we were from and where we were going, and then he pulled his pistol and shot my uncle in the head.

I cried as I saw him fall to the ground and they in turn began to shoot my father, my cousins, and my mother in rapid succession. When the shooting stopped I could smell the burnt air from the gunfire and my entire family was dead. I was in shock as the older man approached me and asked my name telling me that I was pretty for a Croat woman and if I did what I was told they would not harm me. I didn't answer but if I knew then what they intended to do I'd have grabbed his gun and killed myself.

One of the soldiers walked me roughly to one of their trucks and we drove to their camp. The first night they gave me food and allowed me to wash again, and then the captain raped me in his tent. This went on every night for many months and I was only thankful I didn't get pregnant from it but what I learned later was that at my young age, with his rough and demented sexual appetite, damage was done to my insides and

I would never be able to have children. The war raged for the next several months or years, in my mental state I couldn't tell the difference, but we moved camps several times and at the last camp I formed my plan to escape.

I was afraid but I knew if I stayed I would either eventually be killed or worse. One evening I saw a map that had been left out and I could see from the notes on it that we were only eight kilometers from enemy lines. With my freedom only a short drive away I felt a fire in my stomach to survive and I thought back to how my mom had always told me that I was very cunning when I chose to be and if I put my mind to it, I could accomplish anything. I wasn't going to let her confidence in me or her memory die and I began to meticulously coordinate every angle I could think of with my pending escape. The captain had been promoted to colonel and began to treat me more and more as a possession and not a human being, his arrogance growing and his sexual savagery along with it. He would make me go into the woods to forage for fresh herbs and plants and one evening after he complained of stomach pain I shared with him that I could make a tea from a flower in the hills that would help. The next afternoon he had a soldier escort me up into the woods to find it and that night I mashed the flowers and roots into a pot with a little sugar and water and it gave him great relief. I repeated this several times over the coming week and as I knew he would readily accept the offering I began to work his ailment into my little scheme.

He bragged about an upcoming dinner party very near the front lines and I thought that it was their militaries way of waving their occupation in the face of the enemy but that was not my concern, it was simply another gift to aid in my escape. One day just before the occasion he brought me a cheap red dress and I knew he planned to show me off to his friends like some prime livestock. As he preened around the camp with his smoking pipe and his tall jack boots I could only imagine what would happen if any of his comrades expressed interest in me but I wasn't going to let it get to that point. The night of the party, as expected, he asked for a cup of tea just before we were to leave and I diligently performed my duty for him as I always had before, the only difference being the flower I used to make it. When I was a little girl learning the herbs and plants of the hills there was one that my mother had warned me about that we called the black lamb. It looked very much like the flower I used to make the tea but it was poisonous and would cause anyone who consumed it to stop breathing one hour after ingesting it. Death was a given.

It took a short time to put him out and at first the driver hadn't noticed but as we rode along the country road towards the party he sensed something was amiss as he asked me what was wrong and instructed me to wake the colonel. I explained that I didn't know and that perhaps he was napping but the driver didn't buy it and pulled off the road to investigate. He turned his head backwards towards us as he repeatedly asked his boss if he was okay. Getting no response he reached for his own door handle and the second he took his eyes off from us I stabbed him several times as quickly as I could in the right side of his neck. The colonel had insisted I wear a broach for the party that had a sturdy four-inch pointed piece of metal to hold it in place. I had taken it out of my hair minutes before and held it tight in my palm as I waited for my chance. Once the driver took his eyes off of me I knew I had mere seconds to try and kill or incapacitate him and I stabbed him with a ferocity and a fear that made me strong and my efforts effective. As he reached up to his neck it was too late as the blood from his artery sprayed the inside of the car, painting it with the rouge stickiness of his last minutes on earth. He managed to exit the vehicle as in desperation he tried to stop the bleeding with his hat but biology was not on his side. He stared through the side window like a frightened child who had realized something very bad had happened to him but for him I had no sympathy and I waited patiently as he fell to his back, his breath becoming shallower.

He and the others had allowed me to be brutalized by their leader for longer than my mind would allow me to recognize and as he lay near death on the side of a lonely dirt road I stepped out of the long car as in my native language I smiled down at him and told him to enjoy the journey to hell. I drug his body down the hill and covered it with brush, walking over to a small brook and washing as much of the blood spatters from my dress and my skin as I could. I got back in the car and although I wasn't a good driver I did know how to drive as I pointed the large green vehicle towards the border and my new life. The colonel was propped up leaning back in the seat and looked like he was sleeping when I pulled up to a road block. I had to stop and explained that we were going to the party, the driver had taken ill and was left behind, and the colonel was taking his usual nap as I demanded that he not be disturbed. I don't think they really believed that another driver would not have replaced the usual one but the guard was far too busy looking at my breasts and they all drank on duty anyway so he wasn't the sharpest as he looked at my cleavage hungrily saying that the colonel is a lucky man and waved me through. I drove past the building I was supposed to park at and kept on west as cold sweat broke from my forehead and my hands began to tremble. There was another road block 200 meters before the line that divided the allied forces and the enemy and I had to decide if I could lie again or just take my chances with determination and fate. As my stomach tightened into a knot I put the accelerator to the floor and smashed through the wood and sandbag blockade, watching the soldiers jump to the left and the right as they avoided the thundering hunk of steel violently plowing through the former security of their crudely constructed road block. They began shooting and I expected this but I had imagined that once I made it to the other side I would be safe. What I hadn't had time to either consider or plan for was that with me driving a clearly marked enemy vehicle the allies thought I was a suicide bomber and they began shooting too.

One of the bullets hit my right shoulder and as I had only seconds to choose, knowing I would never live to give an explanation, I turned the steering wheel sharply to the left and plunged down the short embankment to the river below. I now had bullets coming from both sides and somehow managed to keep the car upright but the pain in my shoulder wasn't helping me think straight and even with the vehicle now stopped I kept the gas pedal to the floor as I continued to hear the ping of bullets hitting all around me. The glass on my window had shattered from the gunfire and all I could think of was to climb out and try to swim as far as I could. The water was fast and I could only steer my path with my good arm but I put distance between me and the gunfire quickly and eventually washed up downstream. How far I had traveled I didn't know but it was now very quiet in the darkness of the deep woods and I dragged myself up to a small cave in the side of the hill to hide. I didn't know if I was in allied territory or not but the bleeding had stopped and stuffing a medicinal tree moss into the wound I covered myself with pine branches to insulate against detection as the cold and trauma engulfed me and I fell into a deep sleep. I woke with the sun warming the front of my hideaway and at first I didn't dare move at all. I listened for any movement or voices and hearing none I slowly stuck my head out just far enough to look around. I waited like this for over an hour and deciding it was safe to investigate further, smeared my red dress with black dirt for concealment as I began to move up the hill through the dense brush. When I got to the top of the hill I could hear road traffic in the distance but I didn't know who or what from as I cautiously moved forward. I would have waited longer but I knew that between the years of abuse and the gunshot my condition was not good. It took me half the day but I eventually arrived at the top of a hillside overlooking a field of soldiers and with great relief I could identify their uniforms and vehicles as allied forces as my relief overcame me and I stood up on bare feet, sobbing and stumbling down the hill towards them. I only remember the first uniformed man looking at me in bewilderment as I'm sure I looked far more like a frightened and injured animal than a 15 year-old girl.

I don't recall much of the first few days as the trauma and shock continued to rule my body. Later a doctor suggested to me that it was possible my mind had shut off its own ability to recollect the recent events in an act of self-preservation as sometimes happens in combat or trauma situations. I don't know why my brain did what it did, I'm just glad it did as I had seen many, many things I never wanted to remember ever again.

When Kata stopped talking I realized I still held the paper coffee cup in my hand, the contents now cool, as I digested the story of her young life. How the fuck can people do what they do to other people was my first thought, and then how the fuck did a 15 year-old woman survive what she had survived was my second thought. She touched the top of my hand as she said, "I know, it's very difficult for people to process. It even is for me after all of this time, but I had to go on, and I did." She filled in the blanks between then and now, being grateful for the people who had helped her along the way as she revealed that now her mission was to help others and the fear or shock of seeing dead bodies had left her as a child so now she used what had happened to her as the odd *gift* that she now perceived it as. Not everyone can do what we do, and see what we see, without it messing them up inside but the world was full of needy recipients and people are always going to die whether we like it or not. The choice is what to do with the situation and putting a person in the grave when you could save a life with their body parts seemed irreverent towards the gift of life, at the very least.

She shared with me her goal and dream to become a doctor and be able to do transplants in underserved countries around the world. I asked if she planned to ever return to Croatia and she told me she had gone back once but what relatives she still had were either impossible to find or like her parents had been killed. Either way she had no desire to go in reverse and relive the past so now her focus, like mine, was on moving forward and making a new life. I could tell after dropping her at her apartment that I had just made a new true friend, something that had been as foreign to me as speaking Chinese for as long as I could remember, but like the other new and scary things I'd opened myself to as of late I was okay with it

# TIME FOR A CHANGE

Over the next year I did my runs and grabbed coffee with Kata whenever I could, discussing some of our pasts but typically leaning towards fun stuff like food, travel, music, and even sex. We weren't looking to hook up with each other but we had some laugh out loud moments about of our past trysts and agreed completely that the living were far more complicated than our clients.

Nothing ever lasts forever, I knew that, and one day when I pulled in to the parking lot of our offices I could see people I didn't recognize walking out with boxes and computers. I paused as I considered how to best approach it but direct was in my mind the best approach and I walked through the front door like nothing was wrong. My supervisor was sitting at his desk answering questions from some hard ass in a blue FBI jacket and neither of them looked in a good mood. I asked what was going on and the admin just looked around with a very worried look on her face as she pointed towards my boss and said, "ask him." I decided to just let trouble come to me and after a few minutes with raised voices coming from his offices, Jerry came out with his hands secured behind his back, looked me straight, and said, "get a lawyer and keep your mouth shut," as two of the agents now focused on me, asked for my ID, and after getting no response to their inquiry, placed me in handcuffs as they walked me to a waiting and un-marked car.

When we arrived at their office they hit me heavy, saying they knew everything already and if I wanted any leniency I would cooperate. I thought back to when I had first met my wife and one afternoon her grandfather had invited the family to a bar-beque at his home in the country. He was an ethical man but also a damn good attorney and that evening while sitting by the stone fire pit on his palatial back veranda we had a brief man to man about me, my background, and my plans for the future. He listened intently as he sipped the 12 year-old sin-gle malt in his glass, nodding and smiling but just listening as I could tell he was sizing me up as the potential suitor of his granddaughter. After I apparently passed whatever test he'd constructed he asked if I'd ever been in trouble with the law? I had not and I replied so. Taking another sip he set his glass down, leaned forward to emphasize what he was about to share, and said, "well young man I'm about to give you a very valuable piece of advice if you ever are." He smiled like the wise old barrister that he was and said, "I don't care if the cops kick the door in, the gun is still smoking in your hand, and the body is falling to the floor. Drop the gun, deny everything, and don't say one word to them without an attorney."

I was confused and as he sat back in his chair, he further ex-plained that the whole line about anything you say or do, can, and will be used against you wasn't a fairy tale. The cops' job is to put you in jail and the majority of the time it's people's own big mouth or arrogance that helps them do it, so keep your mouth shut. I don't care if they want to know your eye color, tell them to read it off your driver's license and don't say shit until your lawyer shows up. I thought back to that after-noon as the FBI guys kept busting my balls, telling me they had everything they needed to put me away for ten years. I asked for an attorney, a glass of water, and heeding the advice from my past, kept my mouth shut.

They kept on me for another hour and they rattled me slightly when one of them said that my girlfriend was going down with me but I didn't have a girlfriend. They meant Kata and

I figured that out by what they revealed without ever giving them a clue so I now knew who they were referring to. She lived two hours away but I also knew she was both tough and smart and I thought back to having shared the conversation about my wife's grandfather in one of our chats about life. I now sat easy in my chair as I knew that at that same moment Kata was doing exactly what I had with the police now in front of her. I was arraigned, along with seven others from our company that afternoon. Once they figured out that Kata actually was not involved they kicked her loose so at least I could put that worry to rest. The bail was low, being a non-violent crime, and I easily posted the 10% required to be set free. I didn't know what they had or did not have but I knew in spite of my dislike for them, federal agents and cops in general were not dumb asses so I needed to have a plan.

As it turned out one of the newer techs looking to get whatever accolade or fame would come from turning us upside down had been the one to rat us out. He ended up getting a brief talk show career out of it afterwards but nowhere near the money I think he assumed he would get. In reality, if he'd have stayed on our side, he would have made substantially more than he got for throwing us under the bus. The reason it got any attention at all was that the client he used to jam us up was some senator's wife who had donated her organs. It wasn't my run so I knew little about the case but what I did know was that she herself, while among the living, had been a black market recipient for a kidney. She had an odd blood type and her time had been running out so her hubby who had plenty of cash had procured our services to save his type one diabetic wife. In the end her body rejected the transplant anyway and her other kidney wasn't far behind. I felt bad for her and her family but it was too bad some glory seeking dickhead had used her for his own agenda. Such is life I guess.

The next week I spoke at length with my attorney and it

turned out the feds actually had a pretty strong case. I wasn't looking at the ten years they bragged about but I was definitely going to jail. If it had been an average Joe we would have gotten probation and a hefty fine along with never being able to work in the industry again, but this being a senator's wife they wanted the press and a few people needed to hang. I and my colleagues were the low hanging fruit so the people above us easily cut a deal to save their own skin and we were looking at a vacation with no beach drinks or room service. I started looking at my smartest options and they seemed few, but then Kata had a thought and made a phone call. It seems she had a girlfriend who was also Croatian and she had some serious computer skills. Not that she owed Kata anything but neither of them had any family left so they had a bond of nationality and orphanage if nothing else. The next day they met for coffee. I was asked not to attend and that was fine with me. Sometimes in this life the less you know the better and Kata figured this was one of those times. With what they were planning, and a jail sentence already hanging over my head, she didn't feel it smart to involve me in yet another crime. I couldn't have helped them in it anyway, being pretty much computer illiterate except for my phone and basic shit like Facebook. Their plan was simple but required a certain genius to create. Her friend the computer chick would create a virus that could be uploaded by any wireless system unaware of its existence. The police ran everything in their precinct on such a system and while their techs were certainly proactive against viruses and internet threats and also smart, Kata's friend was a hell of a lot smarter. Implantable chips, much like what they used for dogs, had become available for human use. They could be programmed with all of a person's personal information, the intended use for medical or security use, but they could also be programmed with a virus and that is just what the ladies did. Her friend had another friend who didn't mind being in constant contact with the law and not on the friendly side. The dude was a bit of a drifter and occasional poet which is what everyone had nicknamed him and had no affection for authority of any type. He went to jail on a regular basis for petty crimes like disorderly conduct and public intoxication. The cops knew him quite well and if he got pinched and hauled into jail it would be just another day in their life. The only difference was that this time he would be walking through their door with a micro-sized chip implanted in his right wrist. Again, I don't know hardly jack about how all this works but according to the ladies the plan was that when he got booked into the jail, they put a bracelet just like at the hospital, on his wrist. The first scan would be performed by the facilities nurse when she performed the routine intake exam and when she did the scan the virus that was in the embedded chip directly beneath where the bracelet was would upload automatically into the police network infecting everything it came into contact with and they would have no idea where it had come from.

He got himself popped on a sunny Friday afternoon and by the time he had been processed in central booking, changed into jail clothes, and given the standard medical check the entire system had begun to freeze up. The Poet just sat on the hard, plastic bench with a huge grin at the little coup d'état he was now a part of, watching the frustrated faces of the guards as their computer systems went completely haywire and nobody had a fucking clue what to do.

Score one for the little man I guess and we should have been in the clear unfortunately, they still had enough that had been hand written about our case to move forward. The next week I got our preliminary hearing date and I started to worry. I was sweating like a hooker in church. I had money but I couldn't run. I had information to share but I wasn't a rat and they weren't asking anyway. I was fucked and was not looking forward to being locked up if even for a week. Then I remembered the card I kept in my wallet and I made a phone call.

The judge was a little hesitant, I guessed because of the political connection, and my request to spring myself wrinkled him a bit but in the end I had saved his son's life and he took care of me. My first class get out of jail ticket was cashed in and they made a deal to cook the two people next up the ladder instead. Like I said somebody had to hang, I just made sure it wasn't me. After settling my affairs I decided it was time for a road trip somewhere sunny to clear my head. Kata still had a year of school left so she stayed put but we promised to keep in touch once I got wherever it was I was going. As it turned out a little city on the north side of Lake Pontchartrain by New Orleans would become my next home and the easy ways, warm temps and southern cooking of Slidell, Louisiana suited me just fine.

# RED HEADS ALWAYS WERE MY DOWNFALL

I had plenty in my savings account and property in this part of the south was very reasonable, so I purchased a small two bedroom that needed some work, spending the next few months either working on my house or getting acquainted with the culture. I gambled a little at the riverboat and met a few women my age who came to the Big Easy on vacation looking for an adventure. I only had two neighbors, one a bible thumper who wanted nothing to do with any Yankees, the other a retired female marine drill instructor who lived with her lover and raised show dogs. I didn't have much in the way of tools or experience and one afternoon after watching me fumble about she strolled over and introduced herself. She introduced her female friend and I made the mistake of hesitating a split second before their relationship dawned on me for which I was bluntly rebuked with a very direct you got a problem with that?

In fact I did not and I liked direct people which I revealed to them with a smirk, so we got along just fine. I wasn't a very good cook, and they were, so at least two nights each week I joined them for supper or lunch. I always asked if I could bring anything which they politely declined. I knew they liked good wine so I got acquainted with the clerk at a local liquor store as I didn't know shit about wine either. It all just worked. We quickly developed a comfortable relationship as our always interesting conversations ran the gamut from my former line of work and the stories I'd collected, to the bitchy politics as they called it of the pro-dog world and some interesting stuff from 25 years as a dyke (her words, not mine) in the Corps. It was the week of Christmas and at dinner I thought back to my daughter for the first time in a while. I hate to admit it but eventually life does go on and the memories of our loved and lost can get caught up in our pursuit of the future. Still, I felt guilty and I promised myself to keep her in my thoughts more, even if I couldn't clearly label the benefit to me of doing so.

It was a lazy Wednesday afternoon and I was sitting at a local raw bar in the French Quarter downing a dozen and a couple of pints of Abita when this attractive redhead sat at the bar a few stools down from me. After ordering she smiled and complimented me on the Hawaiian shirt I was wearing, leaning over to shake my hand and introduce herself. She was from Iowa or that's what she told me and was here for a little fun as she offered to buy my next round. Women down here were mighty friendly and hospitable, and I accepted the offer as I moved to the stool next to her. The next hour or so was spent with conversation about the usual who, what, and where you from as we put away a couple more drinks each and snacked on some fried alligator bites with a wonderful remoulade for dipping. Pretty soon "the question" came up and she suggested the privacy of my place. With my beer buzz and her ample cleavage, I agreed, settled the tab, and walked with her to my parked car. It was late afternoon and the middle of the week so the roads were clear, still I had a few in me and had no intention of inviting a roadside conversation with the local PD so I kept it at the speed limit and used my turn signals every time. After we crossed the bridge she asked if there was a local watering hole in Slidell that we could grab a quick one at before our private party. I liked a place called Barnacle Barneys and it was only half a mile from my place so I pulled into the dirt parking lot and we grabbed a small table on the patio out back as the waitress brought us menus. We ordered drinks and it was time for me to hit the head as they say in the Navy so I left my new friend to hold down the fort. When I got back our drinks had arrived and she raised her glass to toast the day as we both took a healthy swig off the cold beer. We weren't hungry so we just finished the cold ones and paid the tab, her treat this time and I thought man do I like women who aren't afraid to take charge. It was refreshing to say the least and as we made the short drive to my place I began to have some wicked thoughts about the next few hours. I knew I had an open minded and willing partner and I had been enjoying living on the wild side with some of my recent friends but it was funny, all of a sudden my head started getting light and I didn't feel so good. I suggested a shower, thinking that would get the party going and wash off whatever it was that was hitting me but she said she had a quick call to make and she would join me in a minute. Maybe I'd gotten some bad oysters but it wasn't getting better and by the time I got to the couch I was feeling like a zombie. This was not good and I watched as the redhead dialed a number on her cell phone. As she looked over at me I could hardly move and as she lit up a cigarette from a gold metal case, with the smile of a hungry vixen she spoke to whoever was on the other end all set, bring the van.

From here I had no sense of time and hardly any memory but my next-door neighbor, Sarge filled me in the next day when I came to. My neighbors had seen me pull in with my lady friend and this on its own didn't raise any red flags but when the van pulled in 20 minutes later and a dude in a grey jumpsuit carrying a duffle bag walked into my place they knew something was up. The man and woman had picked me up and lain me out on my long kitchen table, a white surgical cloth under me as they readied me for the next step of their plan. When the neighbors walked through the slider off my living room they were quiet and my house guests didn't hear a thing until Sarge asked, "what you folks up to?" the 12-gauge Benelli shotgun she'd received as a retirement gift leveled at the man's chest.

The red head started to slowly reach towards her hip and my other neighbor pointed a nine millimeter Beretta at her as she looked her dead in the eyes with an unquestionable conviction and said, "honey, I wouldn't do that."

Apparently, the dude had a hearing problem and went for his piece as Sarge opening his chest up like a bucket of tomatoes with a single blast. Red as it turned out was on the run from the law and decided to take her chances. She also got answered with one in the chest and one in the forehead. Unknown to me prior to this, my neighbors were also competition shooters and getting into a standoff with two untrained body part snatchers wasn't even a fair fight as they dispatched the two without a second thought or a wasted motion. It was certainly nice to have neighbors that looked out for you and when I finally came to you wouldn't have known the whole thing had even happened.

My memory was foggy at best and as they pointed out I would not have made a reliable witness so in the absence of my being able to make a conscious choice they had made it for me. They pointed out that if they had called the police it would more than likely have opened up a shit storm, can of worms that none of us, and certainly not the dead folks would benefit from one bit so they handled it. They just handled it.

There was blood to wash up but I had wood floors which they cleaned, stripped, bleached, and spot refinished in the course of four hours. It would pass the luminol test if one ever happened and then they proceeded to dispose of the bodies. They had some distant cousins who came over from the panhandle of Florida, packed up the two bodies, and drove them and the van off to never-never land. As requested, they made a few random calls from each of the dead people's cell phones as they headed east, which would throw a wrench in the works of anybody tracking towers and looking for their missing friends.

When we discussed it Sarge laughed as she said, "well the alligators need to eat, and scrap metal is at a good price," and that was all she ever said about it.

We went back to our weekly dinners and no one ever talked about it anymore, but I wanted to thank them both for saving my butt and we never drank a bottle of wine that cost under 50 bucks ever again.

# THE HUSTLER AND
# THE JERRY INCIDENT

I wondered if I even wanted to go back to running bodies but one evening I got a call from one of the people I used to work with up north and after the typical small talk they asked if I was working. I wasn't and I wasn't really looking to get back in that game anyway but after hearing where I was living they told me that a new company was forming out of a college in Baton Rouge and they were looking for drivers.

New Orleans by default produced a significant number of donors and with me already living there and being a trained operator, it would only be a phone call to get things going again. I expressed my concern over the bust but all had been forgiven or forgotten and business was business. This business happened to generate a ton of money and as is always the case, money smoothed the path for putting me back on the road talking to the dead. Heat was obviously more of a factor down here and all of our trucks had two a/c units, one main and one for back up. We also had an oversized horse trough as I called it in the holding area of the sprinter van in case both of your units broke down. It never happened but if it had you could just lower the client into it with a winch system installed above, go to a convenience store and buy 20 bags of ice, and after covering the body, keep everything nice and cold for the trip. Sometimes it just comes down to keeping it simple and I like simple.

Working in the south had some pros and some cons, just like

anywhere. It seemed like there was more poverty and inadequate schooling, much of it bred out of basic necessity as children still got put to work down here much sooner that was common in other parts of the country. Folks had to eat and if your momma or your daddy got sick or died the kids were expected to step up. My next client, Brady, was such a case and had been feeding his family since he was only nine years old. His Paw Paw as he referred to the man, had gotten himself dead from a back-alley craps fight gone bad and Maw Maw was never much help as she preferred drinking and strange men to her own kids. He saw her occasionally in the morning when he was making breakfast for his younger sister and brother but after two every afternoon she was nowhere around.

I was picking up his body from one of the most notorious prisons in the south and from the minute I pulled my truck to the guard station I could tell that every person here, convict or employee, were to be taken with serious regard and the rules adhered to. The warden of Wurther Hill state penitentiary had been successfully running the place for over a decade and while regarded as a fair man, was again not a person to be trifled with on any level. His law rippled through every person here and it was obvious. From the first guard I met with his dark grey uniform and shiny black sunglasses, to the last one who cleared me to leave, it was understood that all I needed to do was respect them and their rules and I wouldn't have any problem. I did just that.

They inspected my vehicle thoroughly, running dogs around and inside of every inch of it sniffing for contraband and dope. After the dogs, they put my sprinter van up on an outdoor lift, much like in a service garage, and walked slowly under the vehicle as they looked in every nook for hidden cargo or compartments to carry drugs. They searched me personally and my briefcase and repeated it when I walked through the main entry to the morgue. They searched my gurney and even had a machine to x-ray it all, my briefcase and even my boots. It didn't bother me because I was clean not that my feelings one way or the other meant shit to any of them. What did matter is what would happen if they let something get through that shouldn't have. I read in the paper later that two of the guards had gotten caught smuggling in ecstasy, cocaine, and fake weed a few years back. They were now guests of their former employer and they now wore orange instead of grey and so nobody, I mean nobody, messed around when it came to an inspection. Brady had been taken off life support early that morning, so we had the standard 24 to harvest but I was wondering already if we'd make the cut-off. I had been here two hours already and they hadn't even cleared the body, or the paperwork. Once I identified him and matched it to the documents needed they inspected the body itself. I was surprised at this and slightly taken back but the lead guard looked over at me and said, "we got to do this, motherfuckers will hide shit in places you can't even imagine. Hell, I seen bodies with letters going to gang bangers on the outside jammed up their ass." Just then I looked over and sure enough the morgue attendant, wearing a rubber glove, was inspecting the rectum and then throat of my client.

"Don't worry," the guard smirked, "going ass to mouth like that it ain't like he's going to need a tic tac," as he and the technician both laughed out loud.

I smiled, kept my head down and my mouth shut, thinking please, just get me the fuck out of here. Two hours later me and Brady were on the road and I began to hear one of the most cunning, gut wrenching, and even funny stories I had ever heard.

As I mentioned earlier my client had become the bread winner for his family at a very young age. He started out being a watch dog for a moonshine still out in the swamp. The hours were long, unreliable and mosquito filled, but he was paid in cash. Early on he witnessed that the whiskey makers liked to sample their own product when they were done, always leaving a few quarts or so in the cooling vat. It was quite literally the bottom of the barrel, but it was still 120 proof and when the men fell off into a slumber he ran it into a plastic jug, diluted it half and half with water and could later easily sell the two gallons of hooch for a good price. He considered it his bonus plan and truth be told the shiners came to know about his side profit but he was a reliable worker and was feeding his family all on his own so they never mentioned it. Drugs, particularly meth and the other hard stuff, were creeping in and he never wanted any part of it. Weed was common and grew easily in the heat and humidity of the back country. He had even run bales of it a couple of times with a friend who owned a flat boat and knew the waterways but it just always seemed like bad business to him. The penalties were substantially higher for drugs and people would always like their liquor so he had a sense of job security which half the men that were twice his age didn't have.

The temperature outside my truck was hitting 86 degrees and I stopped at a local quick and go to top off my fuel and get a cold drink. People down here referred to soda as either a Coke regardless of what it was, Seven-Up, Dr. Pepper, etc., or a cold drink. They also seemed to sweeten the hell out of everything and while I liked good iced tea I didn't take it with sugar which caused people to give me an odd look on more than one occasion. As I filled my large styrofoam cup with ice and unsweetened tea the man next to me gave me the usual weird stare. I thought to myself that if he knew what I was carrying in the back of my rig he'd really get a look on his face but that was never going to happen so I just paid for my stuff, got my receipt, and headed back on the road with 17 hours left on the body clock and three hours to get my client delivered. No sweat, right?

Wrong.

My new cell phone and my truck both had GPS and they notified me of a brush fire up ahead that was taking over five miles
of highway and growing fast. Part of the qualification for my
job was being able to think on your feet and always get the client in on time. People's lives depended on it and today was no
exception. Before I had even left for the pick up I mapped out
my primary route and several secondary routes just in case.
In the north we dealt with snow storms and traffic accidents,
wildfire was a new one for me but I had a solid handle on my re-
route as I punched in the new coordinates and steered off the
highway onto old US 33 which would add 20 minutes to my
run but should avoid the fire and the traffic chaos it had created. I was back on track without any other vehicles in sight
when I came around a bend in the road and drove straight into
hell. The fire had apparently jumped and with the wind kicking up had raced north, far from what any GPS was currently
reporting. The entire right side of the forest was lit up and I
saw a tractor trailer stalled on the side of the road ahead of
me, not 30 feet from the tidal wave of flame headed right at
it. Whoever was driving it had not placed the red triangles for
caution on the pavement in front and behind the long semi
and I assumed the driver had just abandoned it out of common
sense, but I had to be sure.

I quickly got out of my cab and grabbing the emergency entry
tool I always carried, ran up to the driver's side to make sure it
was indeed empty but when I climbed up I could see the driver
frantically trying to unbuckle his seatbelt with no success. He
looked at me and then he looked at the flames that were now
setting the asphalt a blaze right beside him. We didn't have
much time and we both knew it so without warning I smashed
his window.

"The fucking belt won't release!" he yelled and I could hear the fiberglass on the outside of his cab begin to crackle with the heat. Reaching inside I took the cutting part of my entry tool and with two pulls sliced directly through the hard strips of reinforced fabric holding him in. The god damn door wouldn't open and as I pulled him through the window his pants came off but this was no time for a delicate disposition as me and Joe Boxer shorts ran our chubby middle aged asses back to my vehicle and put that girl in reverse. The fire caught hold of his entire rig and hit the fuel tank just as I turned my truck around and all I saw in the rear-view mirror was a big old fireball coming out of the now fully engulfed remains of what I assumed had been around a $100k dollars' worth of highway transportation. He must have been thinking the same thing as he said, "fucking foreign shit, stalled on me at the worst possible time but I guess that's what insurance is for," as we both let out a nervous laugh pondering just how close this had come to a barbeque no one wanted to attend.

"Buddy I owe you my damn life!" as he reached over to shake my hand.

I couldn't think of anything to say and just said, "okay."

"No, I am serious as a damn heart attack, I owe you and I owe you major league!"

"My names Jerry," and handing me his business card he said, "I won't forget it, and I always pay my debts."

Again, I didn't know what to say other than I was glad we made it out safe as I looked at my GPS for a new route.

Glancing towards the rear he asked, "what you hauling?"

Glancing over I told him, "can't tell you, and trust me, you probably don't want to know."

Being a truck driver his entire life, with the common sense and real world understanding of people and situations that comes with it he just smiled and said, "say no more, but I still owe you," as he began to relax a bit.

"You wouldn't happen to have anything to drink would you?" and all I could offer him was a pull off my iced tea.

Taking a sip he choked briefly and stopped, looked at me, and said, "mister, you ain't got no sugar in this tea. How in the hell can you drink tea without sweetener?"

"I'm from the north, hardly anyone puts sugar in their iced tea where I'm from."

Handing me back my drink he thanked me just the same and shaking his head said, "no sugar, man you northerners sure got some strange tastes. Tell you what, you got to come by my place sometime and at least let my missus fix you up some proper Cajun food. My cousin has a band and we can make a party of it. I want my family and my boys to meet the Yankee who saved my butt from becoming roasted Jerry. You tell me when and we will set it up and I ain't taking no for an answer either."

I liked music, I liked good cooking, and I liked my new friend Jerry so I promised to call him in a couple of weeks. As we pulled into a large truck stop he took my hand firm in his again and getting slightly choked up said, "mister no one's ever saved my life before and when I tell my old lady what you done she is going to want to thank you too, so please don't forget my offer." As he climbed down from the cab of my truck I began to appreciate the no bullshit ways of the people I was meeting in my new home, but Brady had places to go and people to save so it was time to get back to business.

A mile on down the road the faint sound of *Your Cheating Heart* began radiating in my ears and not long after Brady showed up.

"Man, you boys almost joined me back there when that rig took fire. You sure move quicker than you look," the first words that came out of his mouth.

I had to smile at the humor of the dead, remembering they had an above the arena view, both mentally and physically, of what went on here on earth.

"Well you do what you have to when you have to," I answered him back.

"That I can relate to, heck that right there is my life story," and Brady began to filled me in.

"I can never remember not having to struggle to live. Seems like not long after I came out of my momma the world put me on notice that this here weren't no free fair. With daddy gone and hardly any of his kin living near I got belly hungry sooner than any child should have known. Before the moonshine gig I mainly had to steal to supplement our grocery. I'd lift what I could from my momma or the men who had passed out next to her in that old ratty bed of hers. At first, I made the mistake of taking all of the money out of a man's wallet and I got the shit slapped out of me when he woke up. I learned my first lesson right there, steal a little from someone and you can do it a long time. You get greedy and the well gets shut down and you likely get an ass whippin' or worse. From there forward I nicked them for only a quarter of what they had on them and no more. I would also lift a few of their cigarettes and after I had a bundle I'd head down to Ricker Street to sell or trade with the bums and the winos. At first they tried to work me down or rip me off, I reckon because of my age, but I was scared and prepared so I'd brung me an old ice pick that I found in the garage and I only had to stick one old boy in the leg before word got out not to try me. Another lesson I learned, nobody gives a damn about your age when it come to them getting what they want. Me and my friends put this to work a few years later when the railroad company shut down the old track that used to run on the outskirts of town.

I'd been watching the stills and hustling what I could on the side and wouldn't you know it the rail road folks up and left one of those box cars right where they disconnected it. The track was no longer in use and one day I was walking back through the woods and happened upon it, my first thought being to try and cut it up and sell it to the scrap yard but even a fool could see that was a futile endeavor at best. I must have walked by that box car 20 times before it struck me, it was really just a big room on steel wheels. I recalled a farm not too far from it and after striking a deal with the farmer we run a single electric line through the trees right up to our new watering hole. I got my buddy Clyde to help me, cutting him in on the action at 20 percent for his time, labor, and fighting ability. He was four years older than me and all Clyde liked to do was fish, fight, and sweet talk the girls. He didn't hardly care none about eating and he never touched liquor. He was strange, but he was loyal and I knew I could trust him. It took us better part of a month but we whipped us up a pretty slick little bar in the middle of nowhere and once word got out we started pulling it in hand over fist. We built a crude wooden serving bar along one of the ends with old tables and chairs scattered throughout. We built stairs that went up to the sliding side door on the one side and I intentionally put railing along only one half of it so if we had to roust a drunk we could just throw him off and the hard rocks below would knock the fight right out of him for us. It was only a four-foot drop from the side car to the ground but it did the trick, even with the big boys. We ran five card tables and took a small cut from every pot, we had watered down corn whiskey and bottled beer that was hard to keep cool but no one complained. Our customers were mainly roughnecks and drifters, the city folk preferring something more civilized I imagine, but we had plenty to keep us busy and it was literally bulletproof so on the rare occasion that anybody pulled a pistol we'd just brake him over the head with a piece of pipe or a club, throw his ass out the door and slide it close. Most of the time the fella would decide he'd had enough trouble for the night but a couple times they opened up on the box car and we could hear the bullets pinging off the half inch steel sides, which always made us laugh, until one idiot ended our whole program and put us in front of the county judge.

The night had been going smooth and everyone was drinking, losing money, and generally enjoying themselves when this one old boy that carried a chip on his shoulder started running his jaws about being cheated at the card table. Clyde was on him quicker than jack rabbit and I thought it was handled but when Clyde walked away the dude sucker punched him in the back of the head and the mood went foul straight on. Clyde was a hard one and I'd seen him get hit a hell of a lot harder before, with items way harder than a fist. I was standing behind the bar pouring a whiskey and I saw my friend turn around with a grin on his face telling me he was going to thoroughly enjoy the ass kicking he was about to lay on this fella. He let the man hit him again just for fun and it was a solid punch that knocked out a tooth. Strangely enough all this seemed to do was make Clyde happier and madder at the same time, if that's possible. I don't know, Clyde was a good friend and a solid partner, but he was also crazier than an outhouse rat and like I mentioned, Clyde *loved* to fight. He could have easily thrown that man off the boxcar but I think he kind of wanted to play with him a little before he did him in, like a barn cat does with a mouse that he's slapped around for five minutes before biting him. The man could barely stand but I give him this, he could take a lickin'. My friend beat him six days to Sunday and when he had to hold the man up to keep hitting him he had enough and dragged the dude over and threw him off. We slid the door half close and figured the man would just lay there until he woke up or wised up, and that would be the end of it. We had no such luck.

The angry drunk had a small 32 in his pocket and when the dumb SOB tried to shoot at us through the opening the bullet hit steel, ricocheted back, and dropped that fool dead. What are the fucking odds of that? I've asked myself that question a hundred times and I still can't come up with it. It was trouble and nobody wanted it, but figuring he wasn't going to be missed and not wanting to deal with the sheriff either, we buried him in the woods. It was only me, Clyde, and one of our regulars who even knew it had happened. Me and Clyde weren't going to say shit and the other man had been kicked out of every bar in our town that would have him so we were his last resort if he wanted to keep on drinking and carousing. Everyone else was too busy throwing back whiskey and gambling to care plus it was midweek and our numbers were low, but wouldn't you know it just one month later that man who we figured on keeping his mouth shut got himself in some trouble and trying to save his own ass, turned us in.

He lead the sheriff back in the trees to the body, and I heard it was a terrible sight as the local wildlife had gotten their own fill before the worms and such. I'm pretty sure the photo of the corpse that they showed the jury and the judge is what hit the nail to our coffins right on the head. We didn't even know we was in trouble until the cops dragged me and Clyde from what had been a blissful sleep. Getting down to the station they kept us in separate cells but being a very small place we could talk just the same and we both figured somebody's wife had turned us in or maybe one of the card players who couldn't find luck if he had a shovel had run off at the mouth. Either way I figured on a big fine, maybe a couple weeks of bad food and looking at bars, and that would be that. Man was I wrong.

The worst part being when the trial come up, that derelict, rat bastard that turned us in said we had shot the man. He couldn't say exactly who, he had just heard the shot, but either way it didn't take them long to come back with a guilty charge on second degree murder. They had given us each some court appointed hack of a lawyer and we told them the truth but both of them laughed in our faces and advised us to keep that little ditty to ourselves for fear it would piss the prosecutor off even more than he already was and he'd be pushing for first degree which would get both of our necks stretched. Me and Clyde were both white trash, dirt billies and every soul in that court room looked down on us with that label in mind as the judge cracked his gavel hard like a thunder bolt and sent us both upstate for 30 years. Our attorneys said we were damn lucky, with the tough southern laws on killing a man it could have been a life sentence quicker than you could blink, but I didn't feel lucky. I was just turned 22 and giving up 30 years would be the better part of my young life.

Old Clyde sent them cops off with a gift before they put us back in handcuffs. He looked over at me with that crazy grin of his and with three court officers standing around him he let off with fists a flying, feet a kicking and teeth a biting. It took three more to get him restrained and when he was done two of them would be riding to the hospital and the rest would never, ever, forget my friend Clyde. They gave him another five years for assaulting an officer and they beat the tar out of him, but like he said later, "I'm pretty much doing life already, what the hell does five more years matter?" The beating put him down for a couple weeks but he had nowhere to go, it wasn't his first time being on the south end of the ass whipping stick, and he always liked fighting anyway so he figured he might as well head off with a bang. My brother took me going away as well as you could expect okay but my sister was a wreck. She had always been the nervous kind and looking back I was probably the only person in the wide world that she ever really trusted. The prison was an hour and 45 minutes away and we all knew that whatever visits they could manage would be basically holidays and special occasions if there can be such a thing in prison. I had learned how to make shine a couple years back and had gotten my baby brother in so he had a skill and he could take up where I'd left off I reckoned but my little sister's well-being stayed on my mind and would eventually be used against me."

I had plenty of questions running through my mind but listening to Brady talk about his life I was at a loss for words, and just drove as he kept talking.

"When I got to the joint it wasn't much of a shock to me. Many of my customers from the boxcar bar had done time, most of it soft as they called it for things like theft, assault, and minor infractions just bad enough to qualify you for the state penitentiary. I'd heard storied about pretty near every prison in the south with people I'd known having spent time in Louisiana, Mississippi, Arkansas, and Texas. Each institution had its pluses and minuses, food being a big one mainly because when you are locked up you haven't got much to look forward to and if you had a decent kitchen it made the time just a little bit easier. A few of the wardens were pretty smart about in my opinion and had made sure their cooks took pride in what they put out. It had nothing to do with coddling the inmates or giving a damn about their diets, it helped to keep the peace and that was a big deal if and when you could pull it off.

I got jumped a couple times the first few months with men trying to see if I was a punk or would allow them sexual favors. I was small and I knew not to fight back, but I wasn't a punk and I wasn't going to be one so I would fall to the concrete and curl up in a ball when they set upon me. Eventually they would get bored with it and move on to other targets who might fight back which is a large part of what they were looking for anyway. Rape does happen in prison but truth be told some of the inmates are homosexuals and they can trade for special consideration, protection, or items from the commissary. They were only doing something that outside the wall they do anyway so they figured why not get something out of it, plus it kept the predators minds on somebody else.

After a while the con who ran the commissary offered me a job but, as I already knew, nothing is free in this life and not long after I took the job he started trying to get sweet on me with his behavior getting more and more aggressive every day. I was small and young and I think he figured me a pushover as one day he cornered me in the supply room and tried to force himself on me. One-on-one I could handle myself and I fought him off but I took a light beating because of it. When I got back to my cell wearing a black eye my cell mate asked me what had happened. I didn't want to talk about it, mainly out of embarrassment but it kept happening and finally I told him.

Theodore or Teddy Rawls was a five foot ten inch, solidly built brother from Nacogdoches, Texas and he spent most of his out time in the yard lifting weights or playing hoops with the other black inmates. The different races pretty much keep to they selves in prison but Teddy and me was cool and after seeing me having trouble he offered to speak on my behalf to my boss. Again, nothing is free in this world, and damn sure not when you're locked up, so I asked how much it was going to cost me hoping Theo wasn't looking to get sweet too. He had a taste for those prepackaged Honey Buns that we sold in the prison store for a dollar each or five for four bucks and we struck us a deal for me to give him five of them for his help. It seemed a fair price.

A day later I was sitting on my bunk when the lockdown sirens went off and when my cell mate came back neither one of us said shit as he laid back on his bed reading a book like nothing was going on at all. He wasn't raised book smart but one of the things he liked to do was to read and learn new words which I always respected. A man should always try to better himself when he could, no matter where he was at.

They brought me in for questioning, and him too. I had no idea what they wanted but they told me that someone had beat my former supervisor to death and they wanted to know what I knew about it. I told them I didn't know anything, had no problem with the man, and that was that. Obviously, Teddy said the same and less.

The following week I finally broached the subject when we were alone, and he shared with me that he had indeed gone to speak to the man on my behalf but his request to leave me be was ill received. He wasn't going to give me a play-by-play, prison talk just wasn't that way, but he confided that the man had told him to go fuck himself and it hadn't gone well from there.

"No racist, rapist, is going to call me a boy and a nigger and not pay the price," was all Theo told me as he barely looked up from the magazine in his lap.

He had beaten the man to death with only his bare hands and while I had expected a fight when he went to the dude, I never thought it would end up as a killing. My next thought, and my question to him, was the cost. We had agreed on five Honey Buns for the talking to, but now the man was dead and I had to assume my cost had risen with it.

"Naa," he said as he looked up with a grin.

"Deals a deal, and I kilt that old boy of my own volition so I ain't gonna make you pay extra for it," and that was that.

# THE HUSTLER-
# PART DEAUX

Funny how things can work out in your favor and with my boss dead it created an employment opportunity when the junior warden told me to take his position. I knew how the place ran, I knew ordering and inventory control, and I also had a solid relationship with the kitchen supervisor Cookie so it came to me that maybe I could put some of my old skills to work and make my prison time a little easier. I was right about the first bit but unpredictably wrong about the second and my grand plan would eventually become the death of me.

Most people don't know it but you can make alcohol out of dang near any plant, fruit or vegetable. You just need water, yeast, and somewhere to let it ferment. In the joint guys made bathroom hooch that they kept in the reservoir of their toilets inside a bag that they hung until it was ready to drink. They use potato peelings, corn, fruit or whatever they can get their hands on and then just a pinch of yeast and the rest is water. It usually tastes like crap but it will give you a buzz and that's all anyone on the block is looking to get.

I had access to our supply of goods at the commissary and the kitchen had all the sugar, yeast, and fruit scraps we'd ever want so me and Cookie struck us a deal. I hired another con to work with me and two shifts each week I started to go to the kitchen and whip up a large vat of mash that we would eventually cook off. The kitchen made three meals a day for over 1,000 men so no one was going to miss the stuff we were stealing to make shine as I used one of the big 100-gallon soup cookers they had in the back to make our brew. We didn't have access to much ice so me and one of the guys who had mechanical skills figured out a makeshift condensing coil that was just copper tube running through a big sink full of cold water. We drilled a hole in the side of the sink and installed a removable spigot that we could plug when we weren't using it and after a couple test batches we got our system down pretty tight. After a while we started making different booze, you know give people a few choices and even though I was livin' locked up I started livin' pretty comfortable once again.

Another thing I know is if you got a good thing going eventually word gets out and someone is gonna knock on your door wanting in. My door got two knocks in the same week and it was going to be like trying to dance with two pissed off ex-girlfriends at once; nobody is gonna enjoy it, toes will get stepped on, and eventually one or the other is going to want the dance all for themselves.

The problem I had was that the first knock was from the head of one of the stronger gangs, the second from the assistant warden himself. I was really in a jam, the warden obviously wasn't taking a back seat to a bunch of cons under his rule, not that I ever told him, and the cons sure as hell weren't going to back off from a lucrative money maker like ours. The one thing I had on my side was the numbers, I knew 'em and they didn't. The warden had control of the budget but no idea how much shit was going out for legit purposes and how much wasn't and we weren't the only ones taking candy from the jar I assure you of that. The cons didn't know how much liquor we were making or how much cash it was bringing in so I negotiated a figure that I knew would make them happy, watered the product down a bit more, and things worked out for a while.

We went on like this for a good two years but eventually people get greedy as they always do and the leader of the gang started shaking me down for more and more. I had discussed it with my partner in the kitchen and we agreed that giving up part of our own was better than getting killed or beaten on a regular basis and the warden wasn't going to take a cut in his action so it made an easy decision all on its own. We tried forming an alliance with one of the other gang leaders but they simply weren't powerful enough to take the role and everybody knew it, so we left it as it was.

Brother Lightning had started as a small group of WW II vets who enjoyed riding and working on their motorcycles. When they got home from fighting the Germans and the Japs they wanted freedom and to be among brothers that had shared the same horror stories that they had all witnessed during the war. They also didn't care much for people telling them what to do and early on came to realize the many financial opportunities available if you weren't afraid to take them *and* were willing to kill anyone that got in your way. I don't know everything they did as I was never a proby or a patch wearer but even before I got locked up anybody with half an ounce of common sense knew to steer clear. Even the cops in our little dust heap of a town left them alone. The group owned a large Quonset hut of a building on the outskirts and if you weren't wearing their rocker on your back, or hadn't been invited, you best mind your business. I had heard tell they ran dope, chopped cars, and gave protection or insurance to select businesses and they were smart about their endeavors so they were to a large extent bullet proof. If anybody ever got popped and thought about flipping on them they knew what would happen and these former soldiers had absolutely zero aversion to blood or violence. You want me to tell you what happened to informants? Just use your imagination.

Giving the gang greater profit I assumed they would stay peaceful and satisfied but again I never underestimate human greed and me being the guy who actually knew how to make the product they cornered me in the yard one day to once again renegotiate. That was the worst day of my prison life and it set in order a chain of events that would both end the liquor business, and me, as I took a beating I would never forget. They wanted a new deal that would have had me making it for free, and I explained that I had to get something out of it but my portfolio was not of their concern and they beat the hell out of me.

I wasn't going back to being prison poor, if only on principle alone, but all they cared about was lining their own pockets and they weren't at all concerned with how that happened. Being the short-sited checker players they were they didn't stop to think that with me laid up in the infirmary no booze would be made but the warden sure noticed and he tried to find out who had put it on me. I wanted to tell him but I knew that if I snitched the whipping I had took would pale in comparison to what came later. I also knew that no matter if I did, he'd only lock them in the hole for so long and eventually they'd get out. When they did I'd be a dead man, if not before. I never told and I was just going to accept it all, but then they went and did something I couldn't ignore and word got back to me that my little sister had gotten a visit.

She was always only half okay mentally at best and when some friends of the biker gang stopped by our shack they put the fear of God into her. They roughed her up a bit and threatened to do much worse but they knew they wouldn't have to. Sure we have the law but the law is only gonna do so much, particularly with helping dirt poor nobodies like us and if you've never gotten a face to face with real outlaws let me tell you they get their point across effectively, often without having to lift a finger. The mistake they made was never having read Machiavelli. If they had I think they would have sought middle ground even with someone of my small stature. Inside I read a lot and after I read *The Prince* I learned certain things, among them many concepts which I had lived my entire life and just never knew what to call them. One of the greatest lessons the book preached was that a) you never fuck with someone's land, their livelihood, or the people they love and b) if you back someone into a corner with no escape you've most likely created a situation where both sides are gonna sustain losses. Compromise was always smart business. Most of your organized crime groups understood this and the fact that violence isn't good for business but the top bull of the prison gang, a large and imposing man named Henry or Hank as he preferred, was more of a blunt instrument. Effective to a large extent, but his black and white methods left little room for bargaining.

Hank was a hard man, cold and indifferent by design, and his life wasn't far from mine in the events that characterized it. He had bounced from foster home to foster home, killing his first man at the young age of 13. He couldn't be prosecuted as an adult so at 18 he'd been unleashed on the world and spent more of the years to follow inside a cell than he did outside. His sheet grew with every crime under the sun ranging from aggravated assault and burglary; all the way to extortion and murder . His last killing is what finally put him away for good and that was the one crime he didn't really talk about. I wasn't sure if it was from the embarrassment of finally getting done in by Johnny law but I'd also heard tell it was because of a family he had murdered; a young boy getting killed during his violent rampage. Even killers can sometimes have emotion and I believe that the boy's death turned Henry into Hank and the leftover was permanently damaged goods, wrecking whatever good might have been still in him. Apparently, he'd been enjoying the afternoon company of a local farmer's wife and her husband had come in early from the fields one late afternoon, catching his bride in the embrace of a very large tattooed guest. As it goes the man was no stranger to violence, having served in the war himself, but Hank was carrying a pistol and without hesitation had fired two bullets, one striking the man and one striking his young son in the next room. The woman was in hysterics over the bloodshed and instantaneous loss of her family and quickly assessing his options Hank looked his lover straight in the eyes and with no emotion or apology given, shot her dead.

He enjoyed the notoriety of his criminal history, with that one exception, and had no hesitation to share his past exploits with those who inquired but he hated rapists and was proud of the fact that his violent and sociopathic tendencies notwithstanding, he had never had to physically take sex. He had no taste for men so the homosexuals were safe, at least from Hank. The other mistake he had made with me was underestimating his adversary, his ego failing to even allow recognition that a threat of any substance could even exist. I did what they told me to at first, making sure I appeared compliant. They now received all profits of the shine business, minus the assistant warden's cut, so there was no reason to threaten or harass me any further. In fact, I was now under their protection which allowed me certain liberties and affiliations I doubt I'd have had without. People think that prison is strict and that the guards and wardens control it with a tight fist. Yes, it had rules and regulations, and penalties when they are broken, but just based on numbers alone and the ratio of cons to guards there is no way to monitor or regulate it at all times. You may have heard it before and it's true, the guards hold the keys to the doors but the inmates run everything inside and that's the way it has always been.

I had to make side money so I added a few other businesses to my enterprise and this got me back in the position of having something to trade. I made a deal with the guys that delivered meals, reading materials, and mail to the men on death row and in solitary. My cellmate was now the head of the laundry facility and they brought in the dirty clothes from St. Agnes

Women's Correctional a few miles up the road to be cleaned along with our stuff. It was basic and also nasty, but the men doing long time or in the hole needed something to help them enjoy themselves and magazine only went so far. We began stealing soiled ladies' panties and even though they weren't Victoria's Secret they did the trick. We sealed them in Ziploc baggies and sold them for $5 each to the cons. I'm guessing I don't need to explain to you their intended use but they weren't for dressing up I can tell you that."

By now I was both completely amazed at Brady's ingenuity and at the same time perplexed at why they would put the panties in plastic baggies so I asked him.

"Dude, seriously? Smart man like you and you can't figure it out?"

I could sense the sarcasm in his voice, that is if a spirit can have such a thing, but I kept driving, and listening.

"It enhances the experience brother," was his reply.

I was still not there but he went on to explain that the men used them to stimulate their thoughts as they satisfied themselves personally. I wondered how often this occurred and once again reading my thoughts he said, "what the fuck else you got to do with all of that alone time?"

I still didn't understand having to seal them up and he laughed as he said, "the smell baby, the smell. Some brothers tell me the dirtier the better and I guess to each their own. I just wanted that money and they were willing to pay it," he explained.

I finally got the picture and in one last boy scout moment asked him why they couldn't simply use their imagination?

"Dude, no offense but what kind of white bread life have you lived? If you been locked up and down hard for 10 or 20, your imagination is gone and the ONLY thing you can count on is animal instinct, if the time hasn't taken that too."

I was literally shaking my head at the thought of it all but I guess inside you do what you got to do to survive, and again, that was that as Brady continued.

"The bikers and I were getting along fine just so long as they got their weekly and I made sure it happened. The assistant warden shipped all his out but Bro Lighting drank almost as much as they sold and with Hank's birthday coming up it was almost time for my little payback but something else was in the wind and it wasn't good. As you probably guessed many of my fellow inmates had nobody or next to nobody on the outside. If they had family they most likely stopped giving a damn about them long ago and went on with their own lives. This created an opportunity for the warden that I never would have thought him capable of, being a church going fellow and such, but again I never underestimated human greed and I eventually got let in on the biggest and most lethal hustle going on inside those walls, and the cons weren't running it.

You always have fights, that's just part of being locked up. Most times it was just fists and feet but if it was serious or a hit people got stabbed or beat with a lock in a sock or piece of metal pipe that someone got out in the yard. Either way it was always bloody and when it broke out you best stay to yourself and keep your fucking head down. The past year though I noticed more fellows getting shanked, sent to the infirmary and not coming back. Most times in a hit they come in straight on or directly behind and would stab you as many times as quickly as they could with weapons that resembled an ice pick more than anything else. They were easier to make and far more effective as you could stab the guy four or five times in just a few seconds and then walk away before anyone even knew what had happened. If you wanted to kill someone you went for center chest or lower back where the kidneys were, but lately people were getting hit in either the upper or lower arteries so they would most certainly die, but not before they got to the prison doctor. Sometimes they might last a couple days but with that kind of blood loss brain damage was a given and the families didn't need much prodding to pull the plug. I'm sure for many of them, if not most, it was a welcome phone call that meant no more drives to the prison, no more security checks to go through, and no more foul-smelling visiting rooms with men they had in truth written off long ago. Knowing the warden like I did I realized that all of this came into his mind as he had concocted his grand plan. I just knew to steer clear, make my shine and mind my own business.

Dudes kept getting hit in the same way with a couple exceptions, legitimate beefs within the cons, but still way more unusual deaths than ever before. My partner in the kitchen was the one who spelled it out for me one night when we were tasting our own product and I now wish he hadn't. He had gotten a little more relaxed in the mouth than usual with half a jar in his belly in short time. He laughed nervously as he started talking and I wish I'd have had the sense to tell him to shut the fuck up, but I didn't. It was almost like he had to make some sort of confession, him being a devout Baptist before he got himself locked up, and I was the one he decided needed to hear it."

"Man," he smiled as he took another sip from the mason jar, "you ever notice we got more late day trucks going out than ever before. They all refrigerator trucks too, got to keep stuff cold."

I hadn't noticed but let him go on.

"Yes sir, we shipping more meat then we eatin'."

The prison had its own livestock, crop fields, and such and this served two purposes. First it fed the cons, but it also gave them jobs which kept them out of trouble to a certain degree.

The warden had a motto that he wanted us all too tired at the end of the day to get into trouble and by in large it worked. They had always sold the extras and it was good, grass fed black angus so we never had to look for customers. The pigs and chickens was the same and old Hank was the chicken farm boss, but it's funny how on slaughtering day he would not work. He couldn't stand seeing the birds killed. Humans dying didn't mean shit, but for some reason chickens did. Weird right?

I still didn't know what Cookie was talking about but he kept drinking and he kept talking.

"All them boys getting bled out from being stabbed in the neck or leg, the warden is selling they body parts on the black market. I hear tell they got a damn waiting list and someplace over in Georgia is buying it up fast as he can supply it. The doc is in on it, he has a list, a goddamn *list* if you can believe it of what is needed so when they turn the lights off on them boys he goes in and carves them up like he ready to make a mother fuckin' Frankenstein or some shit," as he took another long pull to wash the vision from his own mind.

"Come here," he said, motioning me to the back storage room.

"You see them white Styrofoam coolers that we supposed to be shipping beef in?"

I looked over and sure enough he had four stacks of six coolers each up against the back wall.

"We put a blue star on the ones with parts in them so the drivers knows what to pick out."

"They gettin' 40 large for a heart, 30 for a set of lungs, kidneys the same money, so at the end of the day, when they got these boys skinned out, you talkin' bout over a $100k and ain't nobody ever gonna look inside the body, shit they probably end up with a prison funeral and a paupers grave anyway. If they family takes them outside the wall they sure as fuck ain't gonna drop no good money on an autopsy and you know they ain't spending top dollar on the casket and a bunch of flowers so them people at the funeral home don't give a fuck neither, long as they gets paid."

As I stared at the boxes my stomach ached at the thought of it all, I mean I knew people could do pretty fucked up stuff, but this? Man! this was something all on its own. Now I needed a drink as I cracked another jar and he kept on.

"They take what they need and sew 'em back up like stuffed animals and shit. I hear tell they take damn near anything including the eyes, but at least they don't take they dicks. Least they leave them some dignity but man, what kind of person can up a butcher another dude like that, you tell me?"

I recalled right then that I myself was a body donor and was just glad to know that whenever my time came my sausage and biscuits would be left intact, that is unless they developed a dick market before I died.

Brady kept talking.

"We sat back and put a dent in another jar as we both chewed on what Cookie had just revealed.

"Man, you can't tell nobody I told you this," he said.

Spitting up part of my drink I said, "are you fucking kidding me, I don't even want to know what I know, and you best keep your fucking mouth shut on it or we will both be heading to Georgia packed on ice with a blue star, like a damn Christmas roast."

This must have sunk in and he didn't say another word as we finished the jar and locked up for the day. With Hank's birthday coming up I put up a couple pints of apple pie shine, knowing he had a sweet tooth. The only difference being I added a little something to the two jars I'd be giving him. It had been well over a year with our new business arrangement so he had no reason to tread cautious around me. Still I kept tight when he came for his pick up and after some small talk about business and baseball, off he went. That weekend he and two of his boys tore it up, with steak supper from the kitchen, some decent weed that got smuggled in, and two mason jars of my apple pie moonshine for dessert. I heard tell around 10 was when they started to figure out something weren't right. The LSD I'd put in the whiskey showed itself and came in with a nasty head, filling their minds with hallucinations and terror. Cons a whole cell block over could hear them screaming at the shit going through their thoughts and when the ethanol hit and they could no longer see, it all came down.

The next morning the wood alcohol had taken their vision permanent to one degree or another and none of them would ever be right in the head again from the intentional overdose of acid. I figured early on that I'd never be able to kill them. I was too small and there was too many of them, but blind and crazy for the rest of their lives was even better in my opinion for messing with my little sister and once again, that was that.

I kept my guard up as I knew they or someone in their crew might figure it out but a month later still nothing had happened. I was heating mash in the back of the kitchen when Cookie come up and started talking with me. Again, it was just small talk, food, how his kids were doing and such, and I never suspected a thing. I had my back to him as I stirred the vat and I heard him say sorry brother as the steel shank punctured the right side of my lower back four times in rapid succession. I spun around to face him, a look of complete surprise on my face, and the damage to my kidney was already making me feel light headed as I dropped to the floor. Man, I expected to get hit or beaten, but Cookie was the last dude I expected it from and that's why it worked.

I was still conscious and he bent down to share with me that it wasn't even the bikers who ordered the hit. It was the warden, just cleaning up a bit. Cookie had been drinking more and more and one day the warden come down and confronted him about things. He was actually there about inventory shortages but god damn Cookie, with the fear of our conversation still running around in him, had spilled the beans and blurted out that he had not meant to tell me, it just happened. Obviously, the warden wasn't one to leave loose ends so my days were officially numbered but the chef hadn't reckoned on something else. He smiled arrogantly as he also told me that he himself would be taking over my booze business. He'd been working with and watching me and could now run batches without my help so he figured he was the man.

He still had that smile on his fat face and I was fading fast but right then I saw the two dudes come up behind him and he didn't. Between running his mouth and being my friend and business partner for so long he was in for the long haul as far as anyone considered and nobody with any sense leaves loose ends. Not sure really if it was the bikers or the warden who hit him but I knew two things; god may forgive but Bro Lightning doesn't, and the warden was always a thorough man.

The last half hour of the run Brady was silent and no song of any kind echoed in the cab. It was more of a melancholy energy than I'd had with any of the other clients, even those who had taken their own lives, and it caused me to drift back in reflection over my own life. I had worked hard to grow and get on with my living but certain emotions in others will trigger pause and I recognized it. Brady was born with the deck stacked against him but he did the right thing for those he loved. I can't really say my life was particularly bad, or even that challenging until my daughter had died. What happened afterward I now realized was more choice than chance as I was the one who locked myself away, and I was the one who lay in the bottom of the bottle as the world kept on breathing around me. This young man I was about to drop off could have chosen many other options, he could have only taken care of himself and let his siblings go into foster care, he could have lived his life off the system, but instead he found a way. Illegal or not, he found a way, and I respected the hell out of that.

The new harvest bank was similar in system as I pulled up in my rig and called it in. I had two trucks in front of me so keeping it running I caught up paperwork and processed again where I had been, where I was, and where I intended to go in my life. Realizing fully that so many times man plans and god laughs, but I had a plan and that was more than many people have. Finally, the big door raised up and I pulled in. Opening the rear of my sprinter I rolled the gurney out with Brady secured on top and began to push up the ramp to the central morgue, but the damn thing didn't seem to move as easily as it normally did. Not that rolling one 183 pounds of dead weight is ever easy but this time it was peculiarly challenging and I stopped for a moment.

"I don't want to go," whispered in the air.

"I don't want to go, not yet," again I heard it.

Thank god no one was around and I looked side to side, back and forth just to confirm.

"What, why?" is all I could say very quietly, not wanting to explain if one of the others overheard me.

I was new to the area and no one was going to get me out if I got locked up in a mental hospital for talking to a dead body.

"I'm too young brother, I'm too god damn young, and I got stuff I wanted to do," he answered.

Fuck, we just came off a three hour plus ride, why couldn't we have done counseling on the road, in private? I thought.

"I wasn't ready to talk about it," he replied.

"Is everything okay?" came from behind me as one of the techs came walking in.

"Yeah, wheel on the gurney is just stuck, I'll get it figured out," was the only thing I could think of as I was starting to panic a little.

"Okay," the dude said as he walked past. "Let me know if you want to swap the body onto another cart. We need to keep this area clear."

Nodding in agreement I let him leave the room as I thought hard on what to say next to Brady.

"Believe it or not I somewhat understand how you feel, unfortunately you can't stick around brother, not in this life."

"Why?"

"I don't make the rules kid, just the way it is. Do you believe in reincarnation Brady?"

"Never did read much, so not sure about it one way or another, " he replied.

"Well I do, and I don't believe you deserved the life you were given in this body. I think that there very well may be another, better world, somewhere out there and that my friend is what is waiting for you. You did what you could here on earth to protect the people you cared about but the universe has a next plan waiting for you. You just need to trust me and trust that better things are yet to come."

It was kind of bullshit, but not completely and maybe that's why I could sell it.

Panic can make you get creative and I could hear another truck pulling in outside so this gurney needed to get moving.

After another few seconds pause the words, "okay, I lived a life of not trusting most people, but I'm gonna trust you, let's roll," came out and that gurney with 183 pounds on it pushed right up the grey cement ramp as easy as a sailboat with a full head of wind behind it. If you can believe it the damn thing almost pushed itself if that's even possible, as Brady and I parted company.

# THE PROFESSOR

This new harvest location was going to take a minute to get busy so my work was slightly sporadic at first which suited me fine. I worked on my house, had dinner with the neighbors, and started learning to paint which I'd wanted to do for a while now. I took an intro class at the community college in New Orleans and really began to enjoy both the class and the people. I remembered back to my first client, Tabor telling me about his life growing up here and I listened many afternoons to the duct tape musicians and crooners he had talked about. It was certainly a place of great splendor and crime and poverty, just as he had shared, but like so many people I got hooked. I could sit at an outdoor cafe or coffee shop for hours without pause as I watched and met people from every walk and every place, having conversations that revealed more from a living person that I'd ever heard before but maybe it was the alcohol talking. I started bringing my little painters kit to the square and worked on my new skill with stimulation swirling all around. I met a man who had been an art professor in England for several years and for the price of a beer and lunch he offered to give me private lessons. James wasn't gay just a tad lonely and I was always open to making a new friend so I got to expand my limited talent and he was able to fill some previously unfilled hours sharing tales of his country and his life.

He had served the queen at the tail end of the war and for many years after and had seen his share of both pain and courage. He lied about his age, enlisting at the very young age of only 15. He spoke of the rationing of food and the night time bombing raids that had them sleeping in the cellars and underground train stations when he was just a boy. He had lost many family members and friends to the fighting but was very proud of the fact that his countrymen had refused to give in, even when the fight seemed futile and the impending odds insurmountable. He loved the food and the art scene in his new home and regaled in the appreciation for it that bloomed everywhere around him. James became a very good friend and eventually a dinner companion where he would converse into the late hours of the night with my neighbor lady friends as they shared and debated the various points of war, history, the military, and the psychology of those engaged in them all.

I worked when I was needed, staying out of the black market end of it for now, and continued to spend many afternoons eagerly learning about the nefarious past of the local pirates and hustlers, the ghost inhabited mansions that still held the unsettled spirits of yesteryear and the many times mother nature had tried to end it all to no avail. They had an unwritten rule here that basically said do what you want, as long as you don't hurt anyone else while doing it. With my new outlook on life I fit right in.

I got a call from up north one day that Kata had graduated and was coming to visit. On the drive out to the airport I was giddy with excitement and couldn't wait to share with her what I'd experienced in my new home. After getting her bags we headed to a family place in the French Quarter for lunch. Antoine's had been here or over 50 years and had survived Katrina and everything else you could throw at it. They specialized in Creole and Cajun with a little French and Italian cooking tossed in to keep it a solid mix. We started off with dessert, a huge slice of chocolate and ricotta cake that was big enough for four people. I ordered a very nice bottle of white to wash down what was coming next as we ate oysters Rockefeller, antipasto, a light salad, and then the main course of sole meunière that was simple but amazing. We finished with strong New Orleans coffee and brandy and headed over to Pat Obrien's to grab drinks and catch up some more on life. As our tall rum drinks appeared she caught me up on her life post-Me, having gotten a couple visits from a pesky detective who thought he could shake something new out but that storm had passed and wisely she had kept her mouth shut. She had applied to a couple places around the area and was hoping to move down closer to me all along. I felt like a little boy on the playground who had just received a handmade valentine's card from a girl he was sweet on but hadn't had the courage to tell her, and for some reason, as a full-grown man, I still didn't. We had always kept sex out of it and both valued our friendship so much I doubted that was going to change but life always has maybes in it right? After listening for hours it felt like we were back in Ann Arbor except no winter, and no snow. Finally, I told her I had some news too, my twin sister was coming down next month to visit.

The visit was a double-edged sword for me. I looked forward to seeing my sister but I also knew that along with the stories of our life some old wounds were sure to be scraped. What I had endured couldn't compare to what Kata had faced but the uncertainty of how she might react to my family's long history of drama and dysfunction weighed heavily on my mind. Never-the-less I filled her in.

My dad was an economics teacher at the local high school, my mom a bank teller. They had adopted us right after birth and the peculiars of that in itself always made me cringe a little. They never said if it was dad or mom who couldn't donate to the family situation and I never cared. We had a family and that's all any kid wants. My mom had been at the bank for ten years and one day they got robbed. The man pointed a pistol at her head as he screamed to give him the god damn money which brought out a fear she had never experienced. My mom herself came from a pretty fucked up family and with what she had seen and known as a young woman, furniture throwing at Christmas, etc., I wouldn't have thought a gun to her face would do much but piss her off but she had lived such a sedate and peaceful life with my dad that the threat of violence brought her back to her past and she snapped. After the robbery she went to counseling and popped valiums but the damage was done and she lived the rest of her adult life with a PTSD diagnosis, tranquilizers and cigarettes. She was never a smoker before but she picked it up after the trauma. With her monthly check and my father's salary we lived comfortably. I don't recall any excess as a child but I don't recall anything lacking either.

We had a normal life with normal problems until my junior year of high school. I had my father as one of my teachers and was attending his class when the local police showed up with a warrant for his arrest. They took him out in handcuffs like some kind of outlaw and a bunch of my buddies thought it was cool. I didn't. That night when I got home he had been released and I knew not to ask any questions. My dad, while a relatively calm man, was never one to communicate. My entire life I don't remember him ever telling any of us that he loved us. Not me, my mom, or my sister, not once. He provided for us and I believe in his mind that was all he owed any of us. He had tenure and after arbitration by the union he received a severance package from the school with a non-disclosure agreement. We went on a two-week vacation to see the national parks out west and when we got home he took a position at the local junior college. Nothing more was ever said about what he got arrested for but years later I found out that the cops had been running a sting in a local massage parlor and my quiet and humble father apparently had a little freak in him and got popped. I knew he and mom didn't have much of a sex life after the robbery and I sincerely doubted they had much of one before it so in my mind I cut him some slack. It wasn't my marriage anyway, with nothing to gain by prodding, and I left it alone. Later I found out more about our adoption and here is where it got really trippy for me.

My dad's older brother Ron had been fooling around with a younger woman years earlier and had a kid out of wedlock. Her parents didn't much care for him and the fact that he was married put the old nail in the coffin on the two of them ever being together. Her family moved three states away and he never heard from her again until 16 years later. She was in love with my uncle even after all that time and one day she looked him up. As it turns out she had given birth to a girl and that girl was now pregnant with twins. This lady still held a fire for my uncle along with a grudge with her parents from being pulled from the man she loved. When it eventually came up that my mom and dad were looking to adopt she convinced her impressionable young daughter to allow her former lover's brother to adopt the twins. They drew up the paperwork without ever letting her own mom and dad in on the plan. Three months later me and my sister came into the world and the two people who were technically our third cousins became our parents. The grandparents to be on the other side were furious but I guess payback is a bitch and to this day we have never met either one of them. It was weird but it wasn't like incest or anything so no one on our side made a big deal out of it and we lived like any other family and went about life. My sister went to state college and on to law school where she received her degree to practice corporate law. She graduated high up and was offered a cushy position at some firm in New York. I was already working midnights as an EMT so the first couple years after she moved I hardly heard from her, or she from me.

Judy quickly moved up to partner and one night she met a real honest to goodness NY fire fighter who quickly swept her off her feet. I never much cared for Ted but he seemed to make my sister happy and I learned to accept his arrogant ways. The fact that they lived 800 miles from me made it easy and when we had the occasional visit at their end of the country or ours I had avoided him or took a few extra barley waters to ease the pain. I will give the old boy one thing, he was one of the first responders during 9/11 and I always respected him for that. I'm not sure I would have had the stones to do what those men and women did but it fucked Ted up in the head and I genuinely felt sympathy for him. He took an early retirement but got bored so when he called me years later I connected him with our company out east and he started running bodies. I wouldn't have done it but he approached me and not the other way around. I figured with what he had already experienced hauling dead people would be the last thing he'd want but apparently one on ones he could handle. We talked about the whole thing over some good bourbon one rare Thanksgiving after my divorce and I asked him how he was able to come back after what he had seen and done, carrying so many dead and dying at the Trade Centers.

As he took another drink he explained that seeing that much all at once is what broke him, but after years of pills and therapy he was flat out getting bored and he liked the fact that his clients wouldn't be chatting him up like everyone around him now. I took the hint and another swig off my bourbon as a slight curl lifted my right lip. Smiling to myself over his last statement I thought man, you sure as hell don't want to know what I know about the dead, but as usual I kept it to myself and it was time for dinner anyway.

Ted and Judy did alright for a long time, had two great kids and with her clearing a solid six figures lived the good life, but as of late it was all beginning to unfold and she needed to be with family. My parents were no one to turn to, just like when my daughter had died my dad was a closed ear and mom a walking mental eunuch who followed the old man's lead, good or bad, so I guess I was it. It felt good to have her need me and I looked forward to seeing her as in my head I loosely planned out our itinerary for the week. Ted was an east coast dead head with a man bun, way before the millennials took up the movement, and decided one day that he needed to revisit his youthful ways. His latest adventure including a weekend diet of molly, magic mushrooms, and chicks young enough to be his daughter so my sister's sympathy over his past experiences at ground zero finally gave way to self-respect and she sent him packing. The man bun alone would have kept me from ever talking to him in the first place if I were a woman let alone giving him any action, but about fucking time is all I thought.

When I met her at the gate she looked worn out but I know first-hand what divorce can do so I just gave her a big hug and told her it was really great to see her. It was. I knew she wanted to see the city but that could wait. As her twin brother and part time protector I also knew she needed rest so we headed to my place to hole up, catch up, and go from there. I listened as she told painted a portrait of the last couple years, she and Ted talking less and less, the kids growing older and more distant, work becoming just work. When she started sobbing I moved over and held her, knowing right now words wouldn't fix anything. I allowed her to cry it out and as expected, the conversation turned to a target. That target was me.

Why did I get him into my line of work?

Didn't I know what it could do to him?

Couldn't I have refused?

He had after all been the one to call me but I knew full well that wasn't going to make any difference, not right know anyway so I just let he talk. Most of it was emotion based blind bias and no way I was going to win any battles with her in this state of mind so it was best just to let her keep speaking without trying to engage or argue. Later I could speak with her rationally and she would listen, right now I poured her another glass of wine, sat back, and took my lumps. I tucked her in later and sat in the bedside chair watching over as she drifted off. I hoped only that in her dreams she had peace. I knew what it was like to live without it and I loved my sister. I wanted her to have peace. The next morning she woke me with a gentle nudge on my shoulder. I was still in the chair and had been there all night in some sort of self-imposed vigil but the day was upon us and as she grabbed a shower I got coffee, scrambled eggs and toast prepared for two. Judy was never a person of passion. She followed my mom this way, or at least that's what I had always thought, but when we got into the Quarter she came alive with a wonder and curiosity I had never known. I watched contently as she seemed to glide along the worn cobblestone and brick walkways, the whirling smells of dark coffee, trees in bloom, and last night's debauchery all hanging in the humid air. My sister glowed in it all and couldn't seem to get enough of the street art, musicians and the tourists from every part of the world. I may have slept in a chair last night but seeing her this way healed me in a place I didn't recognize was still broken and we stretched our adventure into the early hours of the next day. We repeated the scene many times in different places along the gulf coast over the long weekend as we openly talked about everything you could imagine. The only exception being my line of work, which was cool with me. The evening before she had to go back home Professor James insisted on throwing a dinner party, also insisting that I bring my neighbor lady friends along. He had asked me to invite Kata but she hadn't been feeling well lately, perhaps next time she had said and I nodded as I agreed. When we arrived I could smell wonderful aromas coming from the small kitchen in the professor's flat and I'd had no idea the man could even cook. The professor would prove to be full of surprises that evening as we opened several bottles of both red and white wine and everyone introduced themselves. My neighbors Carol and Seville, Judy, myself, the professor, and two of his own neighbors were hitting it off quite famously as the food, the wine and the conversation flowed for several hours and broached almost every imaginable topic and opinion. I was truly enjoying it all until Arroqe, one of the prof's neighbors, and also a very braggadocious bisexual, began to get a tad surly. He had an opinion about everything, even things he held no experience or knowledge of, and his opinion increasingly leaned towards confrontation and anger. I assumed it might just be the wine but when he turned his intoxicated wrath towards my sister I was no longer having fun and neither was anyone else.

The professor, being both a gentleman who had been smitten with Judy from the first handshake nor one to tolerate rude behavior, addressed his impolite guest quite directly.

"Arroqe, it would seem the libation has caused you to forget your grace in my home. I ask to please refrain from any further aggression, apologize, or leave."

The tension grew thick as the other man stood and taking another drink looked James dead in the eye and said, "why don't you go fuck yourself you closet fairy," as he and he alone smiled at the insult.

"I believe I was clear on your options sir, and that was not one of them," as the older man stood.

Fuck sakes I didn't need or want to see a fight, and I sure as heck didn't want my sister's last night to involve one either. We left that shit behind long ago and I intended to keep it that way as I got to my feet. The professor acknowledged me and motioned with an open hand to remain where I was, saying confidently, "it's no worry, I assure you I can handle this."

Arroqe burst out in a lecherous laugh as he took another drink, set his glass down and taking a half step forward said, "sure you can old man," as he began to move aggressively back and forth from one foot to the other.

"Now my friend," the professor spoke, "we don't really want to continue this do we? I invited you for your company and wit, certainly not to in anyway offend or provoke you, but you do need to apologize or as I expressed already you need to leave. Perhaps a good night's rest is all that's needed and we can discuss it further in the morning, what say you?"

I was amazed at James candor, knowing full well at least four people in that room wanted to see Arroqe get his ass kicked but my friend kept smiling as he himself took a sip from the glass of scotch in his left hand, his steely gaze never leaving the man in front of him. I noticed his right was in the pocket of the cardigan sweater he wore but didn't take it to consideration as the intoxicated man continued to provoke.

"You, you fucking wanna be aristocrat with your fancy lesbian friends, your suck up art student, I guessed he meant me, and this cunt lawyer who thinks her shit doesn't stink can all go screw yourselves. How's that for an apology old boy?"

I wasn't expecting what happened next, none of us were, as the Prof produced a small British pistol from the pocket of his sweater, drawing it up quickly and accurately as he leveled the sight directly at Arroqe's chest.

"Now, I believe I've shown great restraint and amicability with regard to our present situation, but I simply cannot abide your conduct any further. I have known you as a cad and a scoundrel both and have at times reveled in the amusement of it but the actions of a boring and petulant child I won't have put upon me or my guests any longer. Your last chance sir, please apologize to the lady and my guests that you have offended with arrogance and drunkenness and do it now."

I figured anyone with any degree of common sense or self-

169

preservation would finally admit to himself that he needed to, at minimum shut the hell up and leave. Arroqe had neither and afterwards I assumed it some kind of macho Latin bullshit, but he just smiled again took a step closer to the gun and said, "fuck you."

"No my friend, fuck you," the old man whispered as the bullet from the small pistol punched a very small hole in the left chest of his aggressor, a small wisp of smoke curling out of the blue steel barrel as Arroqe, his face reflecting both horror and surprise, grabbed his heart and fell to the rug covered floor. Classic fucking Shakespeare was honestly the first thought that I had but then blood began to run out of him and everyone's buzz, except professor James, quickly vanished as the seriousness of what just happened settled in. I was expecting to have to smack the dude or escort him out, watching him take a bullet had never occurred as we all thought what the fuck just happened?

The old man calmly placed the automatic back in his pocket, walked over to a large reading chair, took another sip of scotch and dialed the police from the only land line telephone I'd seen in years. He was oddly calm as he dialed, speaking without either emotion or excitement to the sergeant on the other end, first giving his address and then proclaiming somewhat boastfully, "yes, I've just killed a man. Could you please send an officer, and I believe a medical examiner will be in order, as well. No, he is quite dead I assure you. How can I be so sure? Well that's easy, I intended to murder him and I'm a very capable marksman. I have no intention of harming anyone else. Yes, I have guests in my home at the present, but I assure you they are in complete safety," as he took another drink and smiled at us as he affirmed the comment with a raised glass in our direction.

"The door will be unlocked and the pistol has been unloaded and placed in the kitchen sink so please assure your officers

170

that no harm will come to them from my home. Yes dear, thanks much. I'll be here," as he repeated his address.

Hanging up the phone he stood and did exactly what he had said he would with the small gun. When he returned the room enjoyed an unexpected calm as he offered his most sincere apologies, particularly to my sister, as he took her trembling hand in his, clasping his other hand over the top for sincerity and looking her straight in her deep blue eyes as he said, "I am a gentleman dear lady, and I simply could not abide this man's insult to you. Please forgive me," as he shook her clasped hand for confidence and then let it go.

I heard the sirens far off in the distance and James approached me as he asked that I join him briefly in the parlor. I looked back at the dead body on the floor but really no one except Judy seemed much affected by it and just waited on the authorities to show up as they continued drinking wine. I myself obviously had no quandary over death or dead people, the dude was an asshole anyway, and the cops would bag him soon enough so no one would have to look at him any further so I just thought, fuck it, as I followed my friend and former art teacher into the adjacent room. As he poured us two short snifters of Benedictine we sat facing each other in the tall backed, leather chairs and I could not help but think to myself that he sure had a pair of stones for someone in his mid-90s. Taking a sip he smelled the air and proclaimed, "wonderful isn't it? I've never been much a fan of the French but they make some damn fine cognac I must admit."

He began to educate me on the origins and history of the liquor in our glass and I didn't want to be rude but I had to interrupt.

"Prof, no offense but we have the law pulling up pretty quick so whatever it is you want to tell me you need to get to it. No offense."

"None taken I assure you, you're a fine fellow and I wish I could have known you longer but such is life," as he downed the contents and set the empty glass on the small table beside him.

"The police are coming and we know they will be taking me away." Reaching into a drawer on his desk he took out a pad of paper and began writing a bank account number, the name and number of his attorney, and another name and address that I didn't recognize. Next, he produced a power of attorney agreement and a will that he had previously signed and notarized, both making me his legal executor.

"I had considered you for this position for some time now, although I never expected to propose the request under these circumstances. I do apologize and I hope you accept." I did and after a brief read of them, signed the documents.

"Good, now the police will arraign me tomorrow. Contact my attorney and he will handle my criminal matters from there. I would ask that you post my bail as I can't fathom the thought of being caged with these dregs of the earth any longer than I absolutely must."

I must have looked troubled at the thought and he said with a laugh. "My good man, certainly you don't presume I am asking you to personally make the funds available? Good heavens no. I am a man of a modest lifestyle but trust me I have acquired sufficient means over my years to accommodate any financial request necessary."

He went on to explain that not only did he own the four unit flat that we were in, you couldn't have touched it for under a half a million, he also maintained rental properties of equal value in several parts of the city as well as Florida and Texas. He had a few stocks and bonds and a few patents that brought him enough residual income to provide a very comfortable living all on their own. The professor may have thought himself a man of modest lifestyle but he was one savvy investor, and a hell of a cook. I listened as he filled me in further and I knew it wasn't anything I couldn't handle, I just wondered who the name on the sheet of paper was and looked out the window as the first police car rolled up.

"The name on the paper is my daughter, the address her last known in Britain. I need you to contact her and money is no object. I am dying and I need to speak with her before I pass."

I heard the front door open abruptly as the professor lifted his hands and his head to say, "we are in here officers and we are unarmed so do act with restraint won't you."

The police came in, guns drawn as expected, but when they saw who it was relaxed slightly. The professor was an established and well-known citizen and would be afforded a courtesy uncommon to most people who had just shot a man. They had to place him in handcuffs and he cordially obliged as they interviewed him with quiet reserve. He repeated the exact events of the night and when he was done they escorted him to a waiting squad car as the crime scene techs finished taking photos and packed up. My neighbor friends had been interviewed and left, taking my sister with them as I explained that I had some of James' affairs to attend to and would be home later. He wouldn't be arraigned until morning so after cleaning up the blood, wrapping the rug in heavy plastic and putting it in my trunk to drop off at the cleaners later, I headed home. Judy was asleep when I got there, a couple of Valiums helping her head into dream land. I was awake the next morning before she was and over coffee and croissants, we discussed the past evening. I gave her the reader's digest version of what would follow and after grabbing a shower she packed up and was ready to go back home; I assumed in more ways than one. We had still enjoyed most of our time and I had no personal regret over how it ended but hoped it wouldn't keep her from ever visiting again.

# MANGO, MARIE, AND A LITTLE MORE INSPIRATION

I got the Prof out on bail, the standing judge only setting it at two hundred thousand with 20% cash to make it happen. Twenty grand to kill a dude? Well it always depends on who it is doing the killing but you already knew that right? I met his attorney and wondered to myself why he couldn't do the search for the daughter but James explained it was a delicate matter at best and required a great degree of decorum in its execution if it was to be successful. I asked if he had any contacts in the private investigations world which he didn't but after a brief Google search and some investigation of my own I found three local candidates. After arranging interviews with each of them for the following week I headed to a local bar that also served one of the best inexpensive breakfasts in town. Finding parking wasn't too difficult this time of the year and I popped quarters in the meter right out front as the smell of fried bacon and chicory coffee grabbed my nose. Mango and Marie's- Lunch box and Libation the sign over the back-alley door read and I thought to myself, "this city has its share of bizarre people and happenings, but they sure have some damn good food!" I found myself a corner booth to sit in and ordered a cafe au-lait with a shot of Jameson's, purely for medicinal purposes as the professor liked to say. I was finally able to digest everything that I'd experienced in the past couple days but truth be told none of it rattled me. I knew the same couldn't be said for Judy but somehow I thrived on the pulse of this vibrant place. My life in the north had been so dark and sedate that even watching an asshole get shot had its degree of entertainment value as I ordered scrambled eggs, fried potatoes and grits, country ham, and a warm basket of fresh baked biscuits served with a small jar of local peach preserves. I loved this town but If I didn't watch it I was going to pack on 20 pounds before I knew it. Still I finished everything in front of me as I considered that enjoying food is a treat only reserved for the living and I could exercise later.

Mango, the chef and part owner to his wife Marie came over with his ever-present grin and said hello. I motioned him to sit if he pleased and the ever-present scent of marijuana sat down with him. Manfred Mango Timbers was a ranger-special forces vet, an amputee, and a well-read man who could work a flat grill with his left hook of an arm quicker than anything you ever saw. He had lost the lower part of his arm to infection from a gunshot during a firefight in Somalia, where he had gotten the nickname as well. He never explained what it meant but I assumed it was just cooler than Manfred and at some point had just stuck. He was a medic as his primary but also a sniper and had traveled extensively to places like Africa, South America, and the Middle East. As with most combat vets talking to non-vets he never spoke on what he had seen or done but we easily filled the air with talk of music, food and history whenever I ate here. He used weed to replace the plethora of pills the military had given him without regard for addiction or side effects and he was now a very vocal promoter of the benefits of the plant. I myself was just never a fan of the stuff but I recognized the medicinal value and I had immense respect for my one-armed friend so I listened many afternoons as he educated me to the various uses. He was also a third-generation descendant of locally owned slaves and his family owned 40 acres of good land upriver where he hoped to grow hemp and marijuana someday if the state of Louisiana ever got around to legalizing them. His wife was a petite and quiet woman with a strong head for business. Being raised in a bar and restaurant herself she knew how to run one, and she knew the most important part, how not to get ripped off. They served amazing home cooked food and strong drinks until midnight but only four days each week and they opened at six am for a very brisk breakfast crowd Wednesday, Thursday, Friday and Saturday excluding holidays. They ran a limited menu and turned a tidy profit which, combined with Mango's disability checks allowed them a far better livelihood than any bar owners I had known. They kept the hours limited so they didn't get burned out and it also allowed Mango to volunteer with numerous vet groups and Marie the inner city kids. They were great people and I was proud to call them my friends.

\* \* \* \* \*

When I got the email for Paddy or Patrick which was his full legal name, I looked forward to getting back on the road. He had passed in a small hospital only 20 minutes away so I gave my ETA as 14:30, started my truck, turned on the refrigeration unit for the rear box, and went back inside to get my uniform on as I poured a traveler mug of iced tea. I checked in at the front of the hospital and waited briefly for the morgue attendant to escort me down to the basement as the scene of Arroqe getting shot popped in to my head again. He had it coming was my only opinion so I let it pass. When the lady showed up in her white lab coat and hair pulled up into a bun I was slightly taken back by her beauty and I must have shown it as she gave me a look much like when a woman knows a man is slightly unconfident talking with her. This gal was a raven beauty and I figured she was accustomed to men falling on themselves just like I had but I recovered and we were able to do what needed to be done. I was kicking myself inside, what the fuck, are you

I 16 again? but I followed her down to load up my client. The body bag was misshapen, and I must have revealed curiosity on my face as she explained that Paddy had been wheelchair bound and rigor mortis had begun to make him curl in the form of his usual position. It looked like someone laying on their side with legs drawn up in the fetal position inside a six mm plastic bag. He wasn't very big and after strapping him in I was confident I could transport him to my truck without the fear of tipping over en-route. We tried to use every considerable measure of respect and consideration when moving a body and I still remembered back to an operator up north who had dumped a client in the middle of a hospital hallway right at lunch time. As the story goes when the body hit the concrete floor the poor lady inside broke through the heavy zipper of the plastic bag and her head and upper torso were quickly on display for all to see. It happened right by the cafeteria, at the dinner hour. All I knew was that I was glad I wasn't that guy who lost his job over it as I double checked all of my straps one more time and started to roll my gurney back to the truck.

Calling everything in I got on my way and very quickly heard *What a Wonderful World* begin to hum in the air. It was the version sung by the large Hawaiian man and not Louise Armstrong but it was still very nice as the bright image of a young man with flaming red hair began to form in the seat next to mine. I had never wondered this before, mainly because most of our body runs were during the night, but could other people see what I saw came to mind.

With a laugh Paddy said, "man, that would sure freak some folks out wouldn't it! Don't worry, you're the only one who can see me," and that was a relief.

"It was funny seeing you get all embarrassed when you met that hot lab lady," he chuckled.

Damn it! I thought, these dead people seem to hear and know everything but I wasn't uncomfortable. In fact, I felt incredibly peaceful in Paddy's presence. He just had that way about him and I believe that he was just the same when he was alive.

"Dude no worries, I think any red blooded man would have caved a bit being around a smoker like her. All that beautiful black hair, and what a set of knockers! Come on dude just because I'm disabled doesn't mean my dick doesn't get hard, especially over a looker like that. Heck even dead I think I got a stiffy."

I spit out my coffee and choked as I almost had to stop the truck from laughing so hard.

"You're one funny guy, ever think of doing stand -up when you were still breathing?"

"It would be a tad difficult," he answered, "seeing how I can't actually stand up."

Touché Paddy, touché.

This was going to be a short run for me but I wanted to know this young man's story, my first question being how someone with his disability had such an amazing energy about him, even in death.

"I'd talk you out of a cigarette if I was still able to smoke, but here's my story," as he began.

"My first accident, the one that took my legs, happened when I was ten. I had a small tumor near one of my lower vertebrae and the surgery was supposed to be of a routine nature. With my Irish luck and my surgeon's drinking habit the surgery didn't fare well for me. Dude showed up that morning with the shakes if you can imagine that from a fucking neurosurgeon, but he did. Anyway, when he was removing the thing he actually sneezed and in half a second cut a nerve in my back that paralyzed me for the rest of my life. The thing that sucked so much for me was not being able to run anymore. Man, I loved to run. I played every sport I could and I was good at all of them."

I was completely confounded as I thought to myself, he sneezed. Paddy chuckled and continued, "yup, a friggin' sneeze took away my legs," as he continued once more.

"Obviously, my parents got a lawyer and the hospital not wanting any publicity quietly settled. With the money they bought a brand new van with wheel chair access and had our home made handicap friendly. My mom assured me that we had enough to cover any possible bills for the rest of my life, even taking into account if I ever got married, got my own house and had kids. It still sucked but I always considered it could have been much worse and I had plenty of living in front of me. I got into wheelchair basketball and made some great friends. I went to normal school and had a happy life but I could see how much it weighed on my dad and that bothered me. One day we were watching Alabama play Clemson in the living room and I could see him looking away from the television to someplace only he was in. I didn't want to push him but it worried me and I asked him what was wrong. His eyes were red and he started crying as he looked at me and said, "it's not fair, it's just not fucking fair," and I knew he was talking about me. He went on to share how he had looked forward to watching me play football and baseball in college, driving my first car, going to prom and having to wait up all night hoping that I didn't drink and get in a car crash.

He went on to tell me about the many times he had watched me play t-ball and the time I caught my first fish. He had always wanted a son and although they were only able to produce me that was enough. We were a small family but we were tight, and then I could no longer walk. It was hard on my mom at first but she was a trooper and kept both her and my pop propped up as she always said, "it could have been much worse. We still have our boy and I thank God for that."

"Mom and dad were not particularly religious but after the accident she started going on a more regular basis. My dad went at first but I've come to think that he was mad at the Lord for letting me get hurt and he stopped going shortly after. They both had so many questions, why did it happen to me? Had they done something wrong and was this the penalty? Even I knew it didn't work like that but I also learned that we all have to find our own answers in life and life is not fair. A young kid can't fix his parents problems but that day in our living room I just told my dad with a laugh that my life was far from over and I could still fish. He smiled but only his face. His eyes still showed the hurt and that hurt me too.

Without so many teenage distractions I spent way more time on my school work than I think I would have. I dated a few girls but even though they were all nice to me I never found one that wouldn't eventually succumb to the reality of my situation. I never held any anger towards them over it and I knew in my heart that someday I would find the right girl. It may take some time but I wasn't going anywhere and time was something I had plenty of. I ended up going to a local college. I had solid grades and had gotten scholarship offers to a couple great schools but they were too far away and realistically the thought of having to hire someone to help me the way my parents did was not something I wanted to do. We had put an addition on our place with a wheelchair ramp when I was 18. I learned how to drive and could manage my own shopping, going to the coffee shops to hang out and most of your normal stuff but doing it two hours away would have made my mom sick with worry and besides, the local college had everything I wanted anyway. I was studying to be a doctor, planning on proctology as my specialty, when I met *the* girl."

Interrupting I said, "Proctology? You mean an ass doctor?" I asked, slightly startled

"Yes sir, I wanted to be an ass doctor."

"Why, of all the things you could get into why that?" I challenged him.

With a laugh Paddy said that it was partly just simple physics. Being in a wheel chair he was already on the same level as a person's southern parts, but he had always been fascinated with the rectal system. I thought to myself that I've been curious, interested if you will in many things, but buttholes was never one of them. To each their own I guess.

"Exactly," Paddy replied.

"Anyway, one day I was shopping for groceries and I met Ann. I couldn't reach something on a high shelf and she got it for me. We started talking and I don't know, we just hit it off. She attended the same school as me and we started off as study buddies but within weeks she kissed me for the first time and I fell like a rock. The thing was she never pitied me and I had to have that for us to survive. It was honest and I knew I'd never build any kind of relationship I wanted with any false thought or action mixed into the foundation. I was in a wheelchair and that wasn't going away, but I was also smart, motivated, and capable of many things and that was what I needed people to focus on. Ann wasn't a dick but she would never allow me to wallow in self-pity and she'd always call me on my bullshit if I was being a jerk which didn't happen often, but like any relationship it did happen. We had sex too but we always wore condoms as neither of us were ready for a family. On football game days we decked ourselves and my chair out in our school colors and I even got my mom and dad to join us occasionally. Their relationship was not doing well, not sure if it was because of my situation or just people growing apart, but when we were all together I didn't look a gift horse in the mouth and enjoyed our time. Eventually my dad moved out and with graduation coming up I didn't see him as much as I'd have liked to. Ann and I were planning on getting married and in fairness to her she wanted to start with our own home even though my mom wanted us to live with her. Neither one of us thought that would be a healthy start to a new marriage and we found a place not far from either my mom or dad but after I moved out mom sold the place and got an apartment.

It was all so weird for me, and scary. This being a grown-up stuff threw me off a bit and I started drinking on the weekends more than I probably should have. Like I said before Ann would always call me on my crap and one day she said I was over doing it in the drinking department and that it needed to stop. I don't know why, it wasn't the booze, but we had an absolute blowout over her suggestion. I think in hind sight I was just mad over my parents breaking up and I was scared at the prospect of being a husband and potentially, a father. She yelled, I yelled back, it was our first and only fight, and it gutted me. I grabbed my car keys and told her I was going for a drive as I rolled out in a heated anger. I got in my minivan and just drove. I don't remember how far I went, I was in a hostility fueled daze and not paying attention. I blew through a red light, a semi hit me broadside, and the rest is history.

I never woke up but they were able to keep me alive long enough for anyone who wanted to say their goodbyes. I can't tell you what it felt like to know the pain my decision was causing the people who loved me so much. I wasn't sure my dad was even going to make it, and Ann blamed herself for my death which was complete bullshit. I was the pissed off idiot who wasn't paying attention and got in the wreck, not her. I don't have many regrets in my life but man I wish I could have told them all how sorry I was, that I appreciated beyond what words could possibly say, all the love they had given me in my life, and that it wasn't their fault. I just wish I could do that, but I can't. I'm dead."

Paddy and I didn't speak anymore after that and I guess some things you just needed to let lay. It did make me go back to thoughts I'd had after my own daughter died in the crash. I remember feeling like Paddy's father had, with many of the same regrets over what had been taken and what could have been but I had also learned that often we just need to do what we can with what's left and go on with our lives.

I wanted to reach out to his family and fiancé and tell them what he had told me but how the hell would anyone believe some guy saying, "Hey, I've got a message from your dead son." This wasn't the movie Ghost and I'm not Whoopi Goldberg. Even still didn't believe at times that I can talk with spirits but it bugged the shit out of me just the same and the week after my run I mailed an anonymous letter to his dad. I had to decide who might receive it the best and with the religious situation of his mom I knew she might just toss it in the trash. The fiancé was too young and too hurt in my opinion to truly consider what I might say, but the dad in his deeply damaged state might just be the one to take it to heart so I sent it.

> *Dear Richard,*
>
> *First let me say how sorry I am for the loss of your son Patrick or Paddy as he preferred to be called. I realize full well that what I am about to share with you might seem like some oddly fabricated lie with an agenda. I promise you it is not. I have nothing to gain and I will ask nothing of you, only that you consider what I have to tell you as honest and true.*
>
> *Your son came to me recently in a dream. I don't know why and cannot explain it to either you or myself, but he shared with me his thoughts and I can only hope they give you and your family a small measure of comfort at this incredibly challenging time.*
>
> *First, he is so incredibly sorry that he wasn't paying attention*

*and got in the wreck that took his life. He wants you to know that it was his fault and his alone. He lived a life of obvious challenge in some regard but he also lived a life of incredible and un-faltering love from both you and your wife. It is a debt he could never repay but had hoped to give that same love to his wife and his kids someday. He says he had a great example from you both and he knows it was not easy at times. He also asked that when the time is right you share this letter with Ann. She was the one and he looked forward to spending his life with her but when enough time has passed he sincerely hopes she will be open to finding love again. She is far too young to give up, she is an amazing, kind, smart and beautiful lady and she has much to offer another man.*

*He also hopes that you and your wife can heal from everything you have gone through and maybe someday realize all that it was, all that it was not, and that again none of it was anyone but the surgeon's fault.*

*He wants you to know you were a great dad and he will always remember the times you played t-ball and the day he caught his first fish, and that he also felt so bad for you that day you both talked about it while watching football in the living room. It was only you and him in that room and he hopes this will convince you that everything I just wrote is the truth and came from your loving son Paddy.*

*I hope you find peace,*

*An anonymous friend*

# THE MAN OF FEW WORDS

As with every client I'd conversed with I gained something from Paddy. The kid had been dealt a shitty hand of luck at a young age but he worked with what he had and didn't focus on his problems or pity himself over what he didn't have. That ladies and gents is a lesson for us all and it inspired me like my conversation with Jesse to keep the rock and roll in my every breath.

I'd made appointments with three private investigators the week before and quickly weeded out two of them after a cursory interview, the second guy having nun-chucks and a bunch of martial arts shit hanging all over his office. Unprofessional as hell in my opinion and I needed someone found not beaten to death. I was getting a little frustrated by the time I had my third appointment but the lettering on the entrance set a good tone with me as I opened the worn walnut door with the frosted glass insert.

L.C. Wrigley-Inquiries and Investigation

He had no assistant and as he got up from his desk walked directly towards me with confidence and a balanced gait. I would come to learn that he had studied with the Israelis in self-defense and was a very capable individual on all levels of his profession but was simply never one that felt the need to advertise or brag. We went over the particulars of the case and he calmly took notes as he interrupted me periodically for further clarification. After he had what he needed to begin I interviewed him on his qualifications. He hadn't agreed yet, nor offered a fee, which I liked. The first guy I'd met with was far more interested in what I could pay than what he could do and I could tell that L.C. was quite the opposite as he filled me in on his past.

"I retired from the agency six years ago," he began. I worked mainly European theatre but dabbled a bit in South and Central America when required. I'm fluent in several languages which always helped. I started out in the marines and after four years of intelligence work I was recruited to make a lateral move into anti-terrorist ops at Langley. I think my language skills were part of it but I also have no family so getting a higher level security clearance wasn't difficult. I was involved in a few missions I can't speak on for obvious reasons and you don't want to know about, but it suffices to say that I am discreet and I am confident enough in my abilities that if I agree to take on your case you can be assured that it is because I believe will be successful. I have no desire to waste your money, or my time. Do you have any questions?" he asked as he looked across the polished wood desk, his back perfectly straight and his eyes calmly focused.

I did not as he explained that his retainer would be $30k. I wrote him a check from the professor's account and he explained that he would be in touch in five days. Not a week, but five days.

I felt assured that if anyone could do what was needed this was the man and I was able to put it out of my mind as we shook hands and I let myself out.

# MORE QUESTIONS AND A LITTLE SOUTHERN HOSPITALITY

Our business was still fairly slow so I called my new trucker buddy Jerry to take him up on his offer of getting together. We set it for two weekends down the road and when the day of the party came I picked up a good bottle of bourbon for him and a box of locally made pralines for his missus. As I made the 40-minute drive out to the country my mind drifted to events of the past while at the same time swirling with visions of the possible pasts of my new friends and associates. I always knew the professor was a private box of nefarious secrets and Mango and Marie were what you see is what you get kind of people with some mischief thrown in. L.C. Wrigley was the one who challenged me the most as I conjured up imaginary stories of his exploits that I assumed would never be either confirmed *or* denied. The only thing that worried me was a call I'd gotten from Kata several days ago. She informed me that she had been diagnosed with a very rare blood disease that was going to require a lot of time and money if she wanted to live. The clinic where she worked was cool about giving her the time off that she would need but the treatments for the disease could become very expensive and she wasn't sure if she could cover it. She wasn't asking me for help money wise, our relationship was not like that, but she was my best friend and as a single man my expenses were minimal so in my mind, I was ready to start cutting checks if I needed to.

I found the address I was looking for and as I drove up the long dirt driveway, I could smell something good and hear music as the large house with two pole barns came into view. There must have been 20 trucks and cars and twice that many people walking about, sitting in folding chairs drinking beer, or watching me as I parked. Jerry came over first and eagerly gave me a bear hug as his people started to gather around us. I met Mrs. Jerry first and gave her the candy I'd bought. Next was his four children of various ages, his two brothers and their families, and three cousins with their kin as it was called down here. I met several other folks, mainly friends and neighbors as Jerry asked what I was drinking and his wife asked if I was ready to eat. They had roasted a pig for the party and he shared that he figured as long as they were going to cook they might as well throw down so he had done several chickens, beef briskets, sausage and deep fried alligator tail to boot. His wife was a master in the kitchen and had made baked beans, potato salad, macaroni salad, turnip greens, sweet potatoes, dirty rice, and two different fruit cobblers for dessert. I was glad I wore my comfy pants as food started appearing before me and the liquor flowed. Jerry had to go over the whole scene where we met, slapping me on the back numerous times as he kept calling me the dude who saved his bacon. His brother thought it was funnier than hell that he'd lost his pants when I dragged him out of the truck and we all had a good laugh over the visual of him running down a dirt road in his underwear but Jerry laughed the hardest as he raised a glass to toast and said, "that fire got my pants, and that piece of crap rig, but it didn't cook my chubby butt and I'll drink to that!" We all raised our glasses and agreed heartily as the band started to play.

It was a wonderful, authentic night, where every person I met was as genuine as your first pair of Levi's and even if I hadn't saved the man's life I think they'd have treated me about the same. As our buzz began to grow the conversation opened up and at one point, Jerry pulled me aside and wrapping his big arm around my shoulders whispered drunkenly into my ear, "brother, all bullshit aside, you saved my life and I owe you. I got some interesting friends and family and trust me when I say if there is ever anything you need you just say the word and old Jerry's got your back." I looked at him sheepishly as the bourbon from his breath floated over and thanked him as I said, "Ok." Right then a woman with thick brown hair and particularly large breasts insisted on meeting *the hero* as she gave me a hug and a kiss that was more intimate than a simple greeting. Jerry winked and later shared that his cousin was recently divorced and wanted to play the field. Apparently, I was the ball for that night but she treated me very nice and when we woke up the next morning in Jerry's guest bedroom she insisted on another quick romp as I smelled coffee and pancakes. Yes sir, I was really beginning to enjoy southern hospitality.

When we came downstairs Jerry laughed and said, "damn son, you didn't damage my wall banging that headboard last night did you?" His wife laughed and punched him as his cousin just took a sip from the steaming coffee mug, smiled and thanked him for introducing us.

Over the next couple months things began to pick up and as expected one day I got asked to get back into the underground body parts business. Things had quieted down up north and no one here even knew about my past hassle. The market was growing and once again the people in charge needed a guy like me to help them meet demand. The system was very much the same as before with two of the same players involved. The pay was also the same and I'd never have to drive through snow so that was a plus. I'd questioned myself occasionally about the merits of this dark side of my profession and had also been questioned by the few people I let it on my little secret. The main point of both my conscience and other's sense of right and wrong was the money. It always amazed me how so many of us directly attach right and wrong to cash. Mother Theresa was a saint, but someone who didn't live in misery and enjoyed a decent salary for helping others was a bastard? You will never get me to agree with that. Our clients were dead and to be frank, were going to rot in their graves. Emotion had no part in that concept it was simple biology, and to me it always came back around to performing a service. You can label it justification on my part but the insurance companies were making millions off from it and they didn't give two shits about any further motive. I still gave a damn so good for me, right? Our clients were dead and my true opinion was that we might as well try and use their deaths to keep other people alive, dark money or not. We ran a lot out of New Orleans with its large homeless population, tourists, and drunken accidents. There was plenty for me to do. The harvest center was still our main facility but a large funeral home just across the Alabama state line started getting more and more of our business and at first, I didn't care. It was more hours and more money and I wanted to build my savings back up anyway, but I started noticing trouble with them soon after and what I came to find out would rock me right down to my core.

# MARGE AND THE CHOP SHOP

The first time I went to the facility I was surprised at the rural setting of it. It didn't look like what it was, more of a ranch with a bunch of buildings, and security was obvious right from the get-go. As I pulled up the asphalt drive there was a six-foot fence on both sides of the road with groups of large mixed breed dogs barking furiously at my intrusion. I liked dogs as a general rule but these looked more feral than house broken and I made sure they were still on the other side of the fence before I got out.

Ricky and his mom came out of the office to greet me and even though they both smiled and warmly welcomed me some-thing about the place gave me a very uneasy feeling. They showed me which building to pull my truck into and when I did their people unloaded the gurney and quickly disappeared into the facility. Marge, Rick's mom, told me it would only be a bit for them to take care of the client and she had lunch ready. I still felt odd about the place but figured maybe it was just me and, not wanting to be rude, let it go as I smiled and followed her into the main house. She had a table with breads, cold cuts, salads and sandwich fixings lain out. Two pitchers of sweet tea and lemonade with a fresh plate of snicker doodle cookies rounded it out as she introduced me to her other sons. With five of us at the table the conversation varied back and forth from me and my background to them and theirs. I asked how they had gotten into the funeral home business and how it ended up being in such a quiet, remote setting. The boys all gave me a hard look at my query but Marge gave me a matronly smile as she told me how her grandfather had been the first to begin way back when. He never even had a mortician's license, but the local law was amicable to his request, the cemetery was only a mile away, and her grandmother was a nurse which was apparently good enough. I wondered to myself how in the hell that was adequate, but things were done a little differently down south and it was what it was. Marge had since struck a deal with a man who had graduated mortuary school but was also an alcoholic and chose not to practice so legally they were right as rain. Being that the closest funeral parlor was over 50 miles away also helped as it was basic demand and supply but again things were done different down here and you just dealt with it. She told me how farming and cattle had been the main business back in the day because there were not enough local folks dying to support a full-time parlor. With the growing demand for transplants they had built two additional buildings over the years and were considering a third. The money they were bringing in was obvious with several expensive and fully decked out trucks and luxury cars parked just outside. I had noticed a bright red F-350 ford pickup when I pulled up, Red Neck Cadillac custom painted on the tailgate and in one of the barns you could see several off-road vehicles and other toys, not one of them over a year old. These folks were bringing in the dough and you could see they were enjoying it.

After lunch Marge walked me back out to my sprinter and my gurney was already loaded in the back. It was obvious they liked to control things and while they were professional and pleasant enough something about the whole thing just gave me pause but it wasn't my business and I wasn't looking to make it mine as I shook her hand firmly, thanked her for lunch, and went on my merry way. I began to make more frequent runs out here and as our familiarity grew they became more relaxed. I ate lunch with them several times and Marge always proved a cordial hostess. I knew she was all business but we got along, this wasn't the case with her youngest boy Quinn. He didn't like me and gave me shit at every opportunity, making me wait longer than was needed, bringing my gurney back with blood on it more than once, he was just a dick. It was Marge, Quinn and the two older brothers and I didn't dare say anything about the young dude's crap. We might have all gotten along but he was family and I was not. That was reality so I put up with it but after a while I found myself getting bored many times when I was waiting and started exploring around the place a little. They didn't have cameras that I could see and most times they were all busy either in the office, the harvest building, or the transport cooler. One particularly nice day I decided to go for a walk while they processed the client I'd brought and walking maybe a couple hundred yards up a dirt road that went into the woods behind the house I came upon two smaller buildings in old, run down condition, as well as what looked like a large, long chicken coop. I sure as heck didn't want to get accidently shot so I called out as I approached. One thing I knew was that these boys had plenty of guns and they made sure you knew it. This alone should have kept me from ever walking up the damn road in the first place but even though something inside me told me I might be in danger and to head back to my truck, and even though I knew curiosity killed the cat, I assumed I still had all of my nine lives and for some stupid reason I needed to know what was in these buildings.

When I opened the door my first thought was why wasn't it locked, my second was what the fuck is that nasty smell? They had large canna-filters, like the ones used in marijuana grow operations, attached to even larger exhaust fans. That was why I couldn't smell on the outside what I now clearly smelled on the inside and as I blindly moved towards one of the many lidded plastic 50-gallon drums along the walls I knew what I was about to discover. Popping the first lid I was overwhelmed with nausea as the flies swarmed out as thick as the stench of rotting human flesh. The first container was full to the top with severed hands and partial arms. Rob Zombie couldn't have thought up anything more horrible as I opened one container after another, all filled or partially filled with various human body parts. The last barrel held nothing but heads and the psychological impact of it finally made me puke as I staggered towards the door. I assumed the other building would be the same but the chicken coop pegged my curiosity again and kept me from running like a madman back to the safety of my truck. I was still alone and for the life of me couldn't figure out why they wouldn't have secured these buildings. In the end I found out it was one very simple fact, they didn't give a fuck. They also never planned on anyone making it past their house and office based on common sense alone, which apparently, I was lacking. When the hinges on the wooden door creaked open what I saw inside shook me to a level I didn't even know existed, as well over 100 embalmed or partially embalmed corpses were stacked in front of me like firewood in various stages of decomposition. My legs carried me into this storage crypt for the dead as my eyes couldn't convince my mind that what I was seeing was even real. It was every stage of life in what human forms had once been. Men, women, kids and even babies of different ethnic groups were stacked or piled all around me and the damn place was running out of room to put more. I vomited again and felt horrible about it as surely these people had already been disrespected enough but I continued to walk through the building operating now on auto pilot. I was standing at the far end when Marge appeared in the open door, "sorry you had to see the less pleasant part of what we do," was her only explanation.

I stood absolutely dumbstruck as I stared at her in a state of disbelief, no words could come out of my mouth.

"What do you say we leave these folks alone and get a cup of hot tea back at the house?" as she motioned for me to come out.

It was the easiest thing to do right about then and I complied as she closed the door behind us and calmly walked next to me down the dirt road back to sanity. Neither of us said anything and when we got to the house she started a kettle of water on the gas stove, making ready two cups and saucers with a sugar bowl next to them.

"You take milk in your tea?" she asked.

I just shook my head.

"Right about now I'm pretty sure the main thing going through your mind is what the fuck? Is that a good guess?" as she looked at me with a crooked smile.

I didn't answer her, wanting to keep whatever cards I might currently hold close to my chest, but inside I was thinking many things. What the fuck certainly topped the list. Who the fuck are you people and how the fuck can you do this to other people, let alone live on the property like some goddamn third-world slaughterhouse with expensive cars, big screen televisions, and hot tea as your blanket of acceptance for what you do? How have you gotten away with it, why haven't you been shut down and locked up long ago? Lastly, what on God's green earth happened in your life where you all could be okay with any of this?

I was glad she couldn't read my mind like my clients could, or at least I didn't think she could, as she set a cup of hot water and a Lipton tea bag in front of me. Marge sat down across the table and met my gaze with the confidence of a black jack dealer . She methodically dunked the tea bag in and out of her cup, looking down at the table and up towards the ceiling as she appeared to be trying to think of what to say. In my mind I knew without any doubt that this was just a tactic. This woman was a stone cold, calculating, all business piece of work and nothing in her life ever came out of those lips that she hadn't planned right down to the finest detail. As she spoke I knew this shit was chess, not checkers, and I was a damn good chess player. Because of this I always recognized a worthy opponent and I knew the only advantage I currently had was letting her speak, so I kept my mouth fucking shut.

"It isn't easy, or pleasant, this job we do, but it needs to be done," she began. "Those parts you saw in the first barn will be incinerated next week, the original owners were left indigent and we have no one to piece them back up and return them to so they get cremated."

I found out later this was complete bullshit, they fed the dogs with human meat which helped make them as vicious as they were and probably kept their dog food bills down as well. They had a crematorium on the property but not wanting to pay an excessive gas bill they rarely used it hence, the chicken coop of horrors. Cheap AND fucked up right?

Marge poured some rum in her tea cup and offered the bottle to me which she figured I needed right about then, and she was correct.

"Most of these folks you bring us got nobody back home that gives a tinker's damn and after we've harvested what needs to be taken we get left to clean up the mess. At first, we were able to keep up the proper procedures but after a while, things started stacking up and when you combine that with the states not paying for the indigents, I had to figure something out. I'm not sure what your life is like but out here we do what we got to do, it's always been that way and I don't imagine any-thing changing anytime soon."

Again, in my mind I call bullshit when I see it and like my grandpa used to say those shiny new vehicles out in the driveway didn't fall off a turnip truck. Santa Claus sure as shit didn't bring them either, but I drank my tea with rum and let her keep on.

"You must know what it's like to worry about money with that girlfriend of yours being sick and all?"

This stopped me in the middle of a sip and don't think Marge didn't notice. They knew about Kata and her illness! What the fuck?

"She has a nice little second floor apartment in the garden district, she works when she can right now at Our Lady of Sorrows free-clinic, and on Tuesday night she likes to have supper at Dominick's Italian Bistro three blocks from her place. Should I tell you what she had for dinner the last time she was there?"

Right now, I was the bird in the cage and she was the cat, and it seemed obvious. One thing I knew though was when you were in a situation where someone thought they held all the cards you need to show them you aren't even playing with the same deck as I forced myself to chuckle and lean back in my chair. I set the cup down and looking at her hard and straight said, "lady, just like the man said in that movie *Cool Hand Luke*, I believe we have us a failure to communicate.

First, don't think for a second I haven't done a little diggin' on you and your family too. Second, whoever is giving you your info owes you a refund. Kata isn't my girlfriend, hell we've never even kissed let alone fucked. I've helped her where I could, because I could, and that is that. You do have one thing right though, I am in this for the money and only the money. Saving the world or these dead folks ain't my business and I'm not looking to make it mine. So, at this point maybe you and me have more in common than you thought." The part about never even kissing Kata or sleeping together was the truth so it was easy to sell.

I took another sip, keeping a steady gaze on my opponent, and after maybe 15 seconds or so she burst out laughing as she slapped her own leg and said, "boy god damn, you northerners are quick on your feet but I like it! The question is now that you seen what you seen what's it gonna take to keep you quiet?"

Taking another sip at the bottom of my cup I turned it towards her in acknowledgement and said, "I think you're beginning to understand me. Let me think on that a minute. You're making money. You know it and so do I, but greed doesn't help anyone so how does $500 a run, cash, suit you?" I didn't know if I was high, low, or in the middle but I knew she'd tell me.

"Tell you what," she answered as she leaned forward, "I'll do you one better and I'll give you $600 per run, but I want more runs coming to us."

I felt a little better about our relationship, forcing myself to put what I had witnessed behind me for now, but I wasn't sure what she was talking about with bringing them more runs. Filling both of our cups half way up with liquor she began to explain. "I was only a girl the first time I saw Eldon. It was down at the ice cream parlor where me and my friends used to hang out on Saturday nights. He was a couple years older than me and walked with a swagger like he was Elvis or something. He slicked his hair back and wore too much cologne but it all appealed to me and it stirred the first sexual thoughts I can recall. I wouldn't actually meet him until four more years had passed and by the time I did I had filled out, my large breasts now attracting his gaze. One Saturday night he came over and introduced himself. Shaking my hand and smiling with his brilliant white teeth I was smitten at once and it wasn't long after that we began dating. My parents were never much on socializing and his were too busy with their own friends to watch over what their only son was doing. It was a wonderful summer and the weekend of our homecoming I lost my virginity to the man I knew would be my forever but like the change in the seasons it wasn't long after he got my cherry that his ambitions were set on other conquests. I was devastated, and looking back, naive as hell. He was a player and anyone not running on teenage girl hormones would have seen it ten miles away, but I didn't. I really thought he loved me as much as I did him and when reality set in it tattooed pain onto my wounded soul that would never heal. A year later we ran into each other at a Halloween party and the bastard played me like a pawn shop fiddle, telling me how much he had missed me and wondering how he could ever have left such a beautiful and special person. I didn't consider that the beer on his breath or the hard on in his jeans were the ones doing the talking but we ended up in the back seat of his car never the less. The next day I felt a little excited but nervous too, recognizing my own immaturity but hoping the last night was to him what it had been to me. The phone not ringing told me what my fears didn't want to admit and I sure wasn't going to tell anybody that I'd been duped again. Three weeks later mother nature made the decision for me when for no reason I started feeling funny and throwing up in the morning. August first of the next year I gave birth to my oldest boy Ricky, the only consolation being that I had graduated early that spring so only my family knew about my pregnancy.

I wanted to tell him he had a son, partly in hopes that it might make him love me, part out of common decency, but my father forbid it. We had plenty of work to do on the farm and with a new baby I chose to focus on the things I could control as little Ricky grew into a toddler and I began to plan our future. My sisters were basically worthless and left the farm as soon as they legally could but I was a hard worker and my parents were getting older so eventually I ran the parlor, as well. For whatever reason dead bodies never bothered me and I learned the trade from my grandfather before he died. I began to add things we could offer to the families of the deceased and our profits grew. I purchased the 40 acres next to ours and the one behind as our property expanded into the current 400 acres we now own. Three years after Ricky was born I met a man who could be what I needed in a husband and after a brief courtship we married. He worked at the saw mill and was nice enough at first, hard working as a mule but also hard on the inside. Eventually the bottle got to him and one night he laid his hands on me.

I took it at first, my daddy being an occasional wife beater himself, but one night when he knocked out a tooth I decided that if I didn't do something this fool was going to straight up beat me to death. John always had a healthy appetite and I always had supper ready the minute he walked through our door every night. I'd bring him a cold beer as he washed up and a second with his meal so it made sense that I began poisoning him either in his drink or food. I made sure I did it slowly, knowing he would never go to a doctor, and that winter he died in his sleep. My second cousin was the M.E. for the county and never liked my husband much so long story short, not saying my cousin knew I'd killed the man, the report listed the cause of death as heart failure which was easy to sell since nobody was going to care that much about one more drunk dying of a heart attack anyway. He had given me two more boys and I had a good amount of life insurance on him so when they were putting the last bucket of dirt on his grave, I lit up a smoke and lied while I assured my grieving boys that daddy was in a better place and everything would be alright. Everything was going to be much better, but that red neck asshole was shoveling coal in Lucifer's oven sure as shit and I still had my payback on Eldon to keep me warm at night.

As it turns out my former lover had married a gal whose family had a funeral parlor over in Haggard county. Not that long ago they caught wind of my success and sought a contract with the State to start competing against us. As of now they are getting one half of all the body business for a hundred miles around and probably a little more. That needs to stop."

The place they were talking about was familiar to me and had gotten a few bodies from us but they weren't getting even close to half of all the local business, which I would lie about and have it work in my favor. They were completely legit and had a spotless reputation. I think this pissed Marge off as well but as I came to know her more, I learned it was anyone's guess what might set her off. The whole damn family was touched in the head but as long as we kept it all business I could steer my ship just fine. Make my money and keep on rolling was my motto and I was sticking to it particularly with the given circumstances.

I was tight with a couple of the dispatchers and convinced them that Marge's place was easier to work with and did a better job with turnaround times which was a lie but translated to my truck being on the road more and our company making more profit so it was easy enough. The thing is Marge didn't know the numbers, neither did her competition. We handled three states and God knows how many counties in those states so at the end of the day only my company had that info and I could manipulate it in my favor. I would have assumed that a smart woman like her could easily surmise this but emotion and particularly revenge fueled anger makes people do crazy shit. Whatever was my attitude, as long as things kept in my favor and the bullshit was kept to a minimum I'd just do my job.

The other business did try to up their numbers, asking me how I thought they were doing, and asked me to do the same thing that Marge was doing. I smiled as I told them that dispatch handles all of that and I'm just a driver but if they kept up the good work our business with them would eventually increase. Our business continued to expand so just by default

I began upping my numbers, which Marge interpreted as me keeping up my end of our deal so we continued to get along.

One night I brought them two clients, one that required multiple removals and was then to be returned so I would have about four hours of down time while I waited. Marge apparently had her work caught up and seeing me just hanging out asked me if I wanted to grab a burger at the local tavern. I couldn't drink but I was hungry and I knew I wasn't on her bad side so off we went. When we got there she ordered up a tall gin and tonic, I had a coke. We made small talk, ordered our food, and she threw back her first drink as she ordered another. She was a smart and capable business woman but I had observed some erratic behaviors growing more common, I assumed due to an increased personal comfort level on her part but it was anyone's guess. As she finished drink number two she reached into her purse and grabbed a pill bottle of some sort, popping two into her mouth and washing it down with a fresh gin and tonic.

"I have some back problems," she shared. I didn't care one way or another but the combination of Vicodin and liquor was rapidly easing her inhibitions and this could quickly enter onto dangerous ground if we didn't wrap it up soon. She seemed to be flirting with me and although not an unattractive woman I did, and always would, associate her with the chop house that she owned and operated. The possibility of her sexually arousing me was about as likely as the Easter bunny walking through your living room but I ate my burger and let her talk.

"You know I ran into that pussy son of a bitch right in this bar once a few years back," she said it more of a statement than a question. I wasn't sure which pussy son of a bitch she was referring to and I kept eating, hoping she'd finish her food and we could leave but she had a story to tell and apparently I was the guy who was going to hear it.

"I know you think that me and my kin are a bunch of hillbillies, and we are, but I ain't ashamed of it. Nobody ever gave my family a damn thing, but we made our way just the same. We seen and lived through times that would kill most folks, drive them to the bread line or suicide, but not us. We do what we need to do to get by," as she took another drink and smiled at me across the table.

"You know my grand dad killed a man once when I was just a little girl. I still remember seeing it. He didn't know I was outside playing and I don't think he'd of done it if he did, but he shot that man dead as a Dixie just outside of our front porch. The man owed him, or he owed the man, nobody ever said, but I watched him fall and also watched my grand dad stand over him as he finished him off with two more shots from his pistol. I stood quiet as he went through the man's pockets, retrieving a sizable fold of green bills and then loading the dead body into his old pickup truck. He buried him somewhere out back and had his younger brother drive the man's car across the Florida state line. Nothing ever came of it after that but it set the tone in me of what my family was capable of and a few weeks later grand dad took me aside after supper and said he was sorry I had to see what I saw, but life ain't easy and we don't let nobody take from us. You won't survive if you do, he told me as he looked down at me with his kind but serious brown eyes

I loved Eldon, I truly did. I think part of it because his family was from the other side of the tracks and I wanted that. I wanted people to look at me and smile as I went by, not calling me white trash after I did or whispering amongst themselves. In my young mind I believed somewhere deep down that being with a man like him would give me that and it would forever change my life. In reality it was just a fucking fairy tale and my white-night wanted to get in my panties and not a damn thing more. You know the pain of him loving another woman wore off, but that night I seen him in this place I got up my courage and maybe blind hope along with it, but I told him about Ricky. That boy is a spitting image of his daddy and even though I could have demanded a DNA test and made him pay child support I never wanted his charity. I only wanted him to love me but after I told him he had a son do you know he laughed in my damn face? He was drunk for sure but when wasn't he. That didn't bother me but he went on, laughing at me and telling me I was just some crazy podunk hillbilly like my whole damn family and that no one would ever listen to my lies. He got loud and told anyone in earshot what I had told him. This whole place had a good laugh at it, and you might think I'd have cried but it was just the opposite. The crystal-clear revelation of who this man was burned me so far down inside you can't place it, but I swore that day that I would pay him back."

Tipping her glass up and emptying it she set it quietly back down as she seemed suddenly very sad and said, "You know the funniest part? What hurt me the most wasn't his distain or his disrespect, it was him not having the goddamn balls to at least consider what I was saying as the truth, and with it acknowledging my boy. Ricky deserved to know who his daddy was, every child does. I wasn't a whore and Eldon knew it. We had sex nine months prior to my baby being born, and he knew that too. I guess at the end of the day, in this world anyhow, there ain't no way in Hades that somebody like him is going to marry someone like me and he will take to his grave what he and I both knew as the truth and never miss a minutes sleep over it. She paid our bill, waiving me off as I brought out my wallet. We listened to the radio on the way back and when we got there my truck was parked out front with the engine on. I thanked her for dinner and as I walked away I could see one of the bigger dogs standing on the other side of the chain fence holding something in its mouth. We still had daylight and as I got closer to see what it was, simply out of curiosity, I almost lost my dinner. I thought he was chewing on a big short stick or maybe a dead squirrel but resting firmly between his large brown jaws was a human hand and partial forearm. It honestly didn't shock me as much as it should have and Marge came up behind me as she took a look at the beast.

"Damn dogs must have got into the burn pile again. A word to the wise don't ever go inside that fence. Heck I love dogs and I think these boys are partial to me, but no way in hell you will ever see my butt on the other side. It does keep the riff raff away though," as she turned and walked off.

# ON THE SIXTH DAY

True to his word L.C. Wrigley contacted me five days after our first meeting and we set a time to meet for lunch the next afternoon. We met at a small and little-known cafe on the out-skirts of the French Quarter and with the afternoon heat both ordered iced tea and salad for starters.

His inquiry had given him a road map to start off but he explained that travel to Great Britain would require an add-itional $10k. I had no idea what his work entailed and to be honest he could have stuck me for triple that and I would not have been able to question it. Not that I would have, the pro-fessor instructed me very clearly that money was not to be a limiting factor at any time.

Our salads finished, the detective ordered cold crab cocktail and an absinthe cocktail. A small filet steak sounded good to me but I was curious at his choice in libation and followed suit with one of my own. The cloudy drinks were served proper with a sugar cube on top and iced water dripped slowly over it into the liquor-filled martini glass beneath. It was bitter and tasted like licorice which might have thrown me off but for some odd reason it went perfectly with the story I was about to hear.

L.C. had been working in a small town in the south of France when he met the one and only love he would have in his life. The cocktail had lowered his guard or perhaps he felt I was trustworthy, he didn't say. What he shared was like something out of a romantic spy movie and I sat back and didn't interrupt as he painted a picture of a young CIA agent that passion turned into a schoolboy in the summer of '92.

"Carcassonne was a military stronghold many times in its history. The agency dropped me there due to its remote yet central location. My cover was that of a liaison to the French government for a recreational development but I never believed that the locals believed it. I looked the part and had studied architecture and the local history enough to sell it but those farmers had all survived treachery and manipulation longer than I'd been alive, so my interactions were always met with skepticism and the occasional eye rolling. At least they were polite and they had fantastic wine, bread and cheese so I could have had a far worse duty assignments. The Berlin wall had come down the year before and anyone who knew Europe could feel the impact. I guessed being here now was very much like the 70's were in the states with the people, both men and women, wanting to let their hair down and party. I had a limited degree of engagement myself, but I had a job to do and that always came first. Then I met Georgette.

I will never forget the first time I saw her as she strolled through the cobblestone streets with a basket of fresh picked flowers and a sparkling blue barrette in her jet-black hair. She was a vision and every man she walked past could hardly gather his words, their women frowning as if they could read the wicked thoughts going through their husbands at that very moment. Every afternoon it was the same but as curious as I might have been work was always my bride, until the day she walked up and asked to join me for tea.

It was a very bold move, local culture considered, but it stirred me and I motioned her to a chair. She had a firm grip, confident but not overbearing, and her perfume was as intoxicating. She was raised Armenian gypsy from her mother's side and wouldn't share how she ended up in this little town but at that moment all of my training flew off with the warm summer breeze and all I wanted was to listen to her songbird voice and look into those dangerous eyes."

I was enjoying the story and my drink when L.C. suddenly paused. Looking at me with what I can only say was a sheepish grin he said that he needed to apologize for misleading me in a few areas. Taking another drink of his cocktail he smiled as he confessed that he was never in the CIA but the majority of his other qualifications were legit. I sat back a bit confused and annoyed and yet sill intrigued as I asked him to clarify.

"I was stationed in Europe and I did perform intelligence and counter terrorism work," he explained, "but when my tour was up a man from Lyon, France approached me with an offer I simply could not turn down. I had one month of leave saved up so I had decided to use it exploring the various countries around me before I came back to the U.S. I traveled through Germany first, then France, Austria, Switzerland and the northern end of Italy and it was on my way back to Frankfurt that I was approached. I must have looked like a G.I. or at least that was what I presumed when the man offered to buy me a beer. Kristopher, or Kristoff as he preferred, approached the conversation softly but it wasn't long before he got to the point. His organization was expanding and they needed people that could not only come and go through U.S. borders but were also experienced in various high level security protocols. I never did much back and forth as they had plenty for me to do right there and as expected it began with small, testing assignments. I would do a pick up here, a drop off there, and eventually it grew into a more supervisory position. The job challenged me which was something I always enjoyed, and the money was good, but the real hook was the danger. I love living close to the edge, always have, and while I've grown less fond of it in my later years, at the time I'd have preferred doing what I did than being a CEO of the biggest company on earth."

I wasn't exactly sure what L.C.'s position had been but I had a pretty good idea even though it surprised me a bit, and there isn't much that does that. He didn't go into details and I felt no need to pry as the conversation, timed appropriately, drifted back to Georgette.

"I'd love to tell you that I held firm and was strong enough to defend against her temptations but to this day I don't believe any man could have. The mountain air is an intoxicant all on its own and when she invited me to picnic with her the next day I accepted, literally lying awake the entire night and counting the clicks on the wall clock until sunrise. I woke the next morning, shaving and splashing my face with an expensive cologne I had picked up in Rome as I dressed in my best wool trousers and brown wool vest. When I picked her up she kissed me softly on the cheek as she complimented me saying I was her dashing suitor. We drove one hour into the countryside and found an old estate with an orchard that was long since abandoned. I've always wondered if the location was pre-arranged but never got the chance to ask as our mutual passion took over. We lay in the afternoon sun, the smell of lavender I will never forget. After finishing the first bottle of wine our only appetite was for each other as we made love on the blanket she had packed in her basket until it was almost dark. The relationship lasted the summer and while, truth be told, I had inner thoughts of making her my wife I knew a wild stallion like her would never be happy under any confinement, so I kept it to myself. We enjoyed so many days and nights, spending hours discussing the arts, music and poetry, and I am more grateful for the time we had than I am remorseful over her leaving, which in the end inevitably she did. In retrospect, I have wondered if she was working me but being a woman of such incredible passion having taken me on as a mark would have been so far beneath her I soon banished the thought from my mind."

I asked if L.C. he had pursued other female interests after, assuming that he had. He smiled and shook his head from side to side as he looked directly at me and said, "my friend, once you have been with a woman like her anything else would only be a letdown. I had my work and it was always a close second to any romantic interludes I had enjoyed so I kept my focus where it needed to be and moved on with her memory and a smile."

I wondered to myself after our lunch why he had chosen to disclose information he didn't need to but perhaps he had achieved whatever level of comfort he needed to have, or again maybe it may have been the liquor. At the end of the day some people just need to have that one person to tell a secret to and perhaps with L.C. that day was today, and that person was me. I honestly don't know but it sure was an interesting tale.

# SEEING THE SKY AGAIN

Over the next few months two things started to happen, I started drinking more and my clients stopped talking to me. Neither thing bothered me that much. I drank at home and I'd heard plenty already from dead folks, but I was heading backward and if I couldn't admit it my friends' behavior did. The neighbors seemed to be busy more often than not when I asked them to get together, Kata was dealing with her health but still we had developed a block in our communication and our coffee shop conversations became nonexistent. The Prof was awaiting trial and with the lawyer he had he'd be dead before he'd ever face a jury. L.C. was doing what we paid him to but it was going to take a little while and I knew that from the get go. In the movies people get found with a computer search, a little street cash and a phone call but in real life people who don't want to get found don't or they make it damn hard for you to do it.

I was falling back into a place that I thought I'd left behind. I went to the gym less and less. The magnolia trees and the sweet smells of the French Quarter became lost on me and I was hardening again inside. I had plenty of time to think as I made my runs but the dreams and vigor I'd come to know so recently seemed to roll off into the distance as darkness once again became my flavor. I didn't want to look in a mirror and I couldn't tell anyone what was going on with Marge. I was racking up the cash but it didn't motivate me any longer and the whole ordeal took on the taste of salted dirt. It was hitting me hard in both body and soul as the energy I had tied myself to became a repellant to the same people I'd grown so fond of. I was spinning into a downward spiral but one afternoon I got the run that would put me back on track.

Miss Edna was a 63 year-old black woman who never had any children, worked two and often three jobs when she was alive, and was at the Trinity Baptist Church on Ursilines street every Sunday morning at 10 am sharp. She volunteered at the church and several other places, helping to cook and prep for a homeless shelter during the holidays and knitting scarves and socks to give away when she had time. I don't know if she'd have qualified for sainthood but she had to be in the thick of it with all of the good she'd done while amongst the living. As fate has it her ticker had a defect and one beautiful Sunday morning as she left the service, she grabbed to her chest just for a moment and as quick as a hummingbird's wings she was no longer among us. They performed CPR on her and technically she was still alive when she got to the ER but as she would share with me all of the effort that they put into her was a waste. It wasn't within anyone's control but the man upstairs and he had sent her a one-way ticket to the promise land.

We didn't have much small talk when she appeared in my cab and she didn't strike me as a woman of frivolous conversation as she quickly made it quite clear she had something to say to me. She lit into me with the passion of a preacher on the pulpit and in retrospect what she had to say was something I needed to hear.

"What you been doing ain't right, and you know it!" she lit in.

"The folks you letting get sawed up and tossed around like trash are people and you are disrespecting them in the foulest of ways by letting your friends do what they doing."

In my mind I thought they aren't my friends and Edna was

quick to scold me again.

"You just doing it for the money, plain and simple. You just as bad as them, maybe worse, for helping."

I couldn't disagree with her and maybe that was the main reason I'd taken to my old ways.

"You think?" she replied. "You don't seem like a stupid man but what in the Lord's creation got you to thinking anything about what you been doing with these people is okay? The other end of it is fine, and respectable, you are helping people you most certainly are, but this stuff here, its deplorable and it don't happen if you don't agree to be a part of it."

I had to disagree with her on that part, knowing damn well if I didn't they'd find ten guys to fill my position in a hot country minute.

"It don't make it right, nothing you are going to tell me will, and don't lie to yourself."

You know sometimes this whole read your mind thing could be a real pain in the ass but I let her keep on, inside knowing I deserved it.

She began to tell me about her life and as she did I began to feel cleansed in a way foreign to me for the better part of my life. This was a woman of pure spirit, the polar opposite of most people walking around and nothing close to Marge. She had been brought up in great poverty, much like my first talking client Tabor way back but she wasn't bitter or broken by it. "We are all blessed," she said, "it just comes to us in different ways. Some people have money but will never know love either of themselves or from others. Some folks are smart as a whip and the world will tell them so, but it may not always feed them in the places they hunger." as she kept on. "My father had five children and only one leg from the war but he was one of the happiest and kindest men you'd ever know.

He loved my mother and she loved him in return. Forty-three years they were married and even when my middle brother died they kept their faith. I had me plenty of bad examples I could have gravitated towards at one time or another, whiskey and wickedness never being far away in this town, but my parents were my rock and I learned early on that having peace in your life is something many people work hard to get but are never able to. I think part of it is simply because they working too hard to achieve something that's right in front of them if they'd just slow down a touch."

She didn't tell me I was a prime example, she didn't need to, but I was taking her words to heart and I was listening.

"You know I've never known much luxury in my life and I never missed it, but do you know I have money in my savings account that would make them folks over in the garden district shake their heads in disbelief. I lived simple, I worked hard and I saved my money. My church and the places I volunteer are gonna get themselves a big check once my affairs get settled and they won't ever know it came from me. I hired me a smart lawyer and a good tax man years back and by putting my little something -something away every pay day what I did in this life is going to help a bunch of folks now that I've gone on. That makes me really happy and to me my life meant something because of it. I worked down at the soup kitchen and over at the jail helping them young people learn to read and write and get their G.E.D so they can make something of themselves if they choose to. I've drank coffee with young men and women, murderers, drug dealers, many of them in gangs and you know the one common denominator I figured out in most, they never felt loved. These people not much older than children was raised in families that beat them or sometimes molested them and they took that fear, that hurt, and that anger and put it out on the street. I was raised dirt poor but like I told you I was loved and I knew it. Many of these kids I worked with, not all but many, were created by the hardness that life molded them into. That's how they learned to survive and fear kept them from learning anything else.

Do you know I have had some of the hardest, scariest looking people you'd ever meet break down in tears when I hugged them or told them I loved them? That was all they needed to heal. One person who genuinely cared and believed they weren't a bad person, so many times that was all it took and little old me with my worn yellow dress and bifocal glasses was blessed to be that person for them.

She went on a little while more but her point was taken. I had agreed to work with Marge and her boys out of fear and money, but I was no longer afraid and I would make out just fine without being a part of dead people getting handled like trash. The next week I told Marge I wasn't going to work with them anymore and she took it far easier than I had expected, or that was what she led me to think. I couldn't just cut them off and agreed to give them two weeks to coordinate my replacement. It had to be handled delicately but that wasn't my problem. She didn't really ask why and I honestly thought she just took it as a business decision and would leave it alone. Wrong again.

That weekend I was coming back from meeting with the investigator when I saw the smoke in the distance. As I rolled up my garage was fully engulfed in flames but surprisingly, not my house. It was clearly arson and the firemen asked if I had any enemies. It had to have been one of the boys but my business with them would be kept personal so I told the man no one that I know of.

# THE PAYBACK AND
# THE PROMISE

The next day I drove back over to the chop shop and when I pulled up Marge was grilling steaks out front, a bright blue flowered apron saying Welcome All wrapping around her like one of those fake ass Christian billboards saying *Jesus saves* but the church needs to get paid.

"You here on business or just dropping by sweetie?" smiling at me like an alligator that had just ate your pet dog.

I told her she knew god damn well why I was here but all she did is offer me a glass of lemonade which I wasn't going to touch. I told her I knew it was her or her family that torched my garage and she just smiled as she flipped a steak and shook her head.

"Sorry, I truly am, but I have no idea who would do such a thing. You don't want to work with us anymore and that's your decision. I just hoped you were stopping by to tell me you'd reconsidered and we could get back to making money. If not there is no problem between us and we can all move on as she set a plate of steak, beans, garlic bread and corn on the cob in front of me.

"Really? You burn my fucking garage down and you think I'm going to sit here and eat like nothing happened?" That was what was in my head but I knew not to say it and as Ricky sat down next to me I suddenly got a different idea.

216

Marge wandered off into the house leaving me and her oldest alone to eat. I wondered if he was going to pull out a gun and shoot me but he just ate his food and told me about the deer blind he had built in the back forty. Ricky was always the nicest and also the slowest of the boys and he just kept on talking about hunting while I played with my food. He was a strapping lad of 32 and I believed very loyal to his family. That was why I knew my plan was a gamble, but it just might work. As he kept on I thought back to the many times I'd seen either Marge or Quinn talk to him like a third cousin, giving him the shit work and even making fun of him from time to time. The middle brother never said much, just working and not taking sides but I saw no reason for them to treat the man like an idiot. They did it just the same and although I'd never seen him sass back or call them on it, I knew it had to bother him. I let him go on for a while and being after five o'clock I pulled two beers out of the ice chest they always had on the porch, cracking one and handing it to Ricky. He must have kept a thirst that day and in no short order he put back three more like they were water. Marge had interrupted us a few times but she had work to do and this was an unexpected visit on my part so I was not a priority and she went about her business. As I cracked him his fifth cold one, I started telling him about me being adopted. It was a lie but it had the intended affect as he nodded his head to my fabricated sorrow of never knowing my parents.

"At least you know your mom is your mom," I told him.

He smiled as he said that momma always said he was lucky to have not been old enough to remember his daddy, telling him at the appropriate age about the alcohol and his physical abuse on her.

"But you know that isn't your real father," I said as he set the empty brown bottle down soft on the table.

"What the hell you talking about? He sure was and he's buried just up the hill in the family cemetery," he said with both hostility and distress. He started fiddling with his hands and feet and his face was changing color a tad as I made my move.

"Brother, I thought your mom had told you, she told me months ago and I just assumed you knew. Marge had you from that man that owns the funeral parlor over in Haggard county. They had a fling when she was younger and I guess maybe she is still embarrassed about it. I'm sorry to be the one to tell you," as I took a very satisfying swig off my beer.

Ricky was now clearly angry. I'd never seen him show any emotion and I knew I'd struck a nerve-hard. It was just me and him and he asked more questions, some I could answer and others I just made up to fuel the fire. By the time I got back in my car and left, Ricky had thrown back ten beers and had cracked a fifth of his momma's whiskey. Marge was walking up the road from the mailbox and waved as I drove past. I just smiled as I thought to myself try putting the pin back in that hand-grenade you psychotic bitch.

I still kept making my runs to Marge's competitor and as we had discussed they began getting more business. I had no idea what Ricky might have said to her or how many arguments they had had since my conversation with him but the whole thing gave me satisfaction, particularly when I had to pay the $1,000 deductible for my garage fire. The family had not been there this time when I dropped my client at Eldon's parlor and the on-duty tech would only tell me that the wife was tending to an emergency of some sort. Kind of weird but not my business so I waited for them to do their thing and then headed back to New Orleans. As I headed to the highway, I had to drive through the county that Marge lived in and when I heard the siren directly behind me my stomach began churning. I wasn't speeding and my truck was serviced weekly so I didn't think I had any lights out as the sheriff came up on the side of my parked vehicle and asked for my license and registration. Going through the motions he finally got to what he really wanted as he asked to look in the back of my sprinter. I told him that wasn't possible, or necessary, but the hand on his pistol was telling me otherwise and there was no one but me and him on this deserted stretch dirt road. As I complied with his next request to get out of my vehicle I opened the back, offering to help, but he told me to stay back as he disappeared inside. Not two minutes later he re-appeared holding two plastic pouches, one cheaply made nine millimeter pistol, and a smirk as he told me to spread my legs and put my hands on my head. I complied and minutes later another police car pulled up. How convenient I thought, no witnesses to him planting dope and a gun and the local judge sure as shit wasn't taking my side over the sheriffs, but I knew something that the sheriff didn't and I just needed to comply and not give him a reason to smoke my ass out here in BFE.

They impounded my rig and brought me to the local jail. Possession of a controlled substance with intent to distribute and possession of a stolen firearm were my gift tag when they walked me in front of the constable, but I had called the professor and a very expensive attorney stood beside me as I pled not guilty. The prosecutor pushed for keeping me locked up, me being a career criminal and all, but even the crooked judge couldn't comply with his request and I posted the $50k needed to breathe free air again. I thanked the lawyer and the Prof and headed back to my place to get a quick shower before I sorted things out with my employer.

The dope was heroin and I explained in no uncertain terms that fuck no, I wasn't an H-dealer, and I also never even owned a gun in my life but that was going to change. They sent another employee to get my truck released and thinking they had a slam dunk case the local law had never even searched the vehicle any further than what the sheriff had done during his stop. When it came back I asked to get my things out and as I grabbed my jacket and thermos I reached under the driver's seat, opened the concealed black box set back by the fire wall, and took out the tiny thumb drive that was my ticket out of this mess. I got home and popped it into my computer and watched the screen as first my buddy Quinn stuffed the two bags of low grade smack into the drawer where we kept our disposable gloves , the sheriff showing up later and going directly to it, and to put icing on the cake, pulling the gun that was supposedly mine out of his own jacket pocket. Quinn had made a key at some point and when I stopped at the local diner for lunch that day he had slipped into the back and planted the drugs.

The thing that saved me was my paranoia. A month back I had purchased one of those tiny motion activated cameras off Amazon. Taking my vehicle to a local car stereo shack I had it professionally wired up, with audio capability in the back and a hidden recorder that had stored it all. The cherry on top was the sheriff's ego and his big mouth as just five feet from the hidden microphone he said to himself, "we gonna pin a murder on your Yankee ass just for good measure," never having a clue it was all on tape. As it turned out my decision to quit had expedited Marge's original agenda and having the sheriff on her payroll, she had him shoot her former lover just the previous night. The ballistics on the pistol now in evidence would be an exact match and if I hadn't covered my butt they'd have sent me down to the county farm for longer than anyone would want to be there.

Even the crooked judge couldn't protect them and when my lawyer met up with him, the state's attorney, and what I'd recorded, they locked Quinn up in the same jail where they had planned to put me away for life. They would have put the sheriff away too but somebody dusted his steering wheel a couple days before with pure Fentanyl and he OD'd, foaming at the mouth like the rabid dog he was. I hoped he'd also shit his pants but dead and disgraced was good enough for me. I knew it was Marge but they could never prove it and anyone with common sense realized she was just cleaning up and he wasn't going to be making any deals with anyone, but that still left me.

When they went to serve the warrant and search the property Marge was in her kitchen making soup, her arrogance not allowing her to consider I knew a few things and might want to pay her back. As it turned out what I knew was only the tip of the iceberg. I have to hand it to them, they were ambitious and fairly creative. Quinn had given his family another avenue to make money and it was directly tied to the body parts gig. He had always dabbled in peddling pills, H, and bulk commercial weed; he wasn't picky. Being a young dude, he had plenty of friends, and they had friends, and their friends...you get the picture. He and his family weren't just shipping parts for legitimate or even the black-market needs, they were putting drugs inside of parts that were never intended for transplant. They literally UPS'd the shit anywhere in the states, knowing that even if someone opened the Styrofoam container with the cold packs, no fuckin way they would be looking inside a kidney, lung, or a heart, never wanting to even pick the things up in the first place.

The packages had all the legal paperwork inside with a big red EXPEDITEDED DELIVERY-BIOLOGICAL CONTENTS and a HUMAN TISUUE-HANDLE WITH EXTREME CARE tag emblazoned on the top. Most people handled them like a customs agent with someone's diarrhea-soaked underwear and didn't want to touch them or even be in the same fucking room so they had a fairly fool proof gig going.

It's kind of funny when you think of it, if they would have left me alone they could have stayed in business but I guess they never heard the old saying *best to let sleeping dogs lay* and here I always thought it was a southern thing. When the agents raided the property they found a room I'd never known about with large gallon zip lock bags stacked on the shelves. I was told later it was stocked better than a pain clinic and they were all going down for a very long time. I would have thought they'd cut a deal but either out of fear or hillbilly pride they weren't giving anybody up. Too bad, it would have been nice to read about them in the paper getting shanked in prison.

The other great thing to happen was Ricky had emptied his mom's safe and left town two days before the raid. The cops said when they knocked on the door she was cool as a cucumber even with her oldest boy now gone. Cold was more like it and the day after the judge sentenced her, Quinn, and the middle boy to 15-year sentences I got a typed letter in the mail with no return address.

Enjoy what time you have left sweetie. I promise it won't be long.

# THE STAKES GO UP

Not long after the whole Marge fiasco I was asked to meet with one of my bosses for lunch. I assumed incorrectly it was to tidy up anything left over in his mind with the dope and gun charges but he never even mentioned it as we ordered our lunch of shrimp po boys, coleslaw and french fries. I was still thinking about the death threat from Marge but for right now I couldn't do shit about it and worrying or wrecking my lunch wasn't going to change anything as I took a bite of the warm French roll stuffed full of fresh fried local seafood, lettuce, and a spicy mayonnaise.

"How'd you like to make some real money? Serious, six figure cash?" he said as he took a swig off his Coca-Cola.

I was still chewing and as always, with a proposition of this nature, I needed to only listen.

"First you need to sign an agreement not to talk," as he slid an envelope across the table.

Wiping my hands and mouth with a napkin I cautiously opened it, not having any clue what I was about to be told if I did in fact sign it. The form was basically a simple NDA or non-disclosure agreement; the attorney's name on the letterhead a well-known partner in a very large Texas law firm. What the hell I thought right before signing it,. How much further down the old rabbit hole can it possibly be than the crazy stuff I had already been knee deep in? Taking the signed document back Tony leaned in as he started filling me in on "The Client."

"We have an opportunity to help someone, and it will require both the decorum and professionalism we have come to expect from you. Mister Vizzini, or Carlo as you will come to call him, is in need of a heart. With his uncommon blood type and health issues he will require a very specific transplant. Even with the drugs to prevent his body rejecting it he's looking at a fifty-fifty chance of survival and he knows it. He is only in his mid-fifties and other than the issue with his ticker is a man of decent physical health-doesn't smoke, rarely drinks, no drugs or other bad social habits that he has disclosed. He and his family have substantial financial resources but with our country's medical system he is too far down the list of recipients to confidently expect to live unless we get involved."

I asked myself *why*, with his financial means, he hadn't gone to Europe or south America, both being areas of the world where money can buy your new life and bureaucracy would not get in the way.

"The Vizzini family is old school Houston money with their roots in shipping but they have expanded over the years into other areas including substantial real-estate holdings in the area. Long story short they can write whatever check needs to be written to get Carlo a heart, but the clock is ticking. We have a donor already lined up and your end, for your services, is a cool hundred grand. Again, you can never disclose anything about it to anyone, not even your priest."

This information caused me to pause. I didn't have a priest or even go to church so that wasn't an issue, but the "we have a donor lined up" thing raised some questions for me. *Who and how* but again I kept my mouth shut for now. Tony said they had a 45- day window at the outside and most of the other requirements where already in place or close. They had weighed using me against two other operators and unknown to me, up until now they had found out about the problem up north which actually sealed the deal.

"We know you can operate in the dark and you aren't a rat so you are our guy if you want the gig."

For whatever reason the client wanted to meet me so that weekend I drove to a large estate just west of Houston and was introduced to him, his brother, an uncle who was visiting the states and his quiet but watchful father Carlo Sr.

He was a stylish dresser and a cordial host. We enjoyed a bottle of red wine from his uncle's vineyard back in Sicily as plates of antipasto and warm tapas began to appear in front of us. I washed down a thin slice of braesola with warm bread as I listened to him share a little about his family.

"We come from humble beginnings," he began. "My grandfather arriving in this country in 1939. He came in through New York like most Italians but being from the hills of Palermo he sought out a more open area to make his home. He was familiar with ships and when he got to Houston he hired on as a long shore man down on the docks, with his short and stocky build the work was easy but the other workers held anyone new in contempt and only viewed them as someone taking money from their pockets. My grandfather got the hell beaten out of him one night after work by three men but having the wisdom he possessed he didn't retaliate, he made them friends and eventually business partners. He knew that their knowledge of the docks and the people who ran them was invaluable for what he needed to do and a few broken ribs was a small price to pay for the future he would certainly build. One of the men held the manifest of every ship that came in and no one would complain about or even notice a few Persian rugs missing, a pallet of coffee that disappeared, or ten cases of fine Irish whiskey that never arrived. They were smart and not greedy as they only took a little at a time, but it was all profit. Eventually the need for kick-backs increased but with 400 shipping containers coming through every day so did the amount of things they could steal. My grandfather married a local woman who had come from northern Italy and worked at the local country club. She had to slow down as their family grew but she still worked there enough to pick up on local goings on and business dealings that nobody talked about outside the club. Every night after supper my grandfather asked her about what she had heard at the club and one evening she told him about a man discussing a new industrial area that the Army Corp of Engineers was intending to re-locate their new headquarters to. It was only one mile from the docks and in an undesirable area of town so it had its share of vacant and run down warehouses. My grandfather intended to make his first real-estate venture a substantial one as he began to speak with the owners of the buildings he thought could be purchased for the least amount. He spent many nights in local watering holes and underground gambling joints as he put together a list of men who were either alcoholics and frivolous with their expenses or degenerate gamblers who were upside down to the local loan sharks. Houston wasn't any different than Sicily and weak men could be easily manipulated if you knew where to look. He got to know their bookies and found out where their mistresses lived. After having enough money wired from back home he went around and through quiet persuasion with a very real threat behind it, convinced 22 of the property owners to sell their warehouses to him with very little or no money down. He locked up most of the area where he thought the new facility would be built and not being a man who relied on luck he also made friends with the agent who would ultimately recommend one area or another for development.

It would be a government contract and with it a license to steal so my grandfather knew he had to proceed subtly. Over the next few months he groomed a friendship with the man by having him and his wife over for dinner and golfing on the weekends. When he thought he had laid enough seed he brought up the topic of where the new facility was to be built and the man shared that it was now down to just two areas. The several blocks where my grandfather owned significant business interest, and another less desirable area much further away. Still treading carefully he continued his inquiry when to his complete surprise the man sat his scotch down and asked my grandfather which area he owned property in and how much he was prepared to pay to swing the vote. The old man always laughed when he talked about it in later years saying that America is not that much different than Sicily.

The man was not greedy and neither was his new business partner. My grandpa told him that he could pay him $20k for his guarantee, or three times that once the properties had been purchased by the government. I'm told it was an easy decision and as luck would have it two months before the sale a hurricane leveled, or damaged beyond repair, all but one of the buildings. My grandfather had also made friends with his insurance agent and with it had previously obtained appraisals on all of his properties for 20% more than they were actually worth. First, he collected on the insurance and then he sold the lots to the U.S. government. He never even had to pay for the demolition or the excavation of the fallen down buildings and at the end of the day he paid back every cent that he'd borrowed from back home, paid off his new partners stateside, and with enough money to now completely stand on his own, killed all three of the men who had beaten him when he'd first arrived in Houston. He had used them for what he needed, but he never forgot what they had done."

This was all very interesting, but I was more curious about Carlo Jr. and exactly how close we were to his clock shutting off, anyone outside the room who knew about our arrangement, and if he had people paid to do the transplant or if it was being handled on our end. His heart was a complete crap shoot for now and even with the preventative meds he was taking it was at best a guess as to when he might take his last breath. The only people on the inside were him, his father, and anyone with a need to know in my group. I was satisfied as much as I could be that things would run smoothly and thought to inquire about the donor but something inside told me to avoid the topic. Right before I left Carlo thanked me and shaking my hand handed me a large and thick parcel envelope that I knew was filled with cash. I wasn't sure if I could or should accept it but this was all being done under the table so again I kept my mouth closed and thanked him.

"You just make sure that new heart gets to me and I assure you I will show you my appreciation tenfold."

When I got home and counted the contents, I had $50k in hundred-dollar bills staring up at me from my kitchen table and I was nervous as hell. Smart, very smart! The man knew to take care of the gate-keeper because at the end of the day he could grease our people, the cops if need be, even the doctor putting the new beats in him, but if I, for whatever reason, could not or would not deliver on my end he was a dead man walking. Now I had Marge to consider along with not fucking up a deal for a man that I assumed could have me killed if I did. Marge was locked up tight but I knew she could reach out when she wanted to so after much consideration I applied to purchase a pistol. I had plenty of people who could get me one on the streets but no way in hell I was going to run the risk of getting popped in Louisiana with an unlicensed or possibly stolen firearm. The law down here had no sense of humor when it came to guns or violence and I would respect it right down to the letter, other than transporting black market body parts that is.

# NO TURNING
# BACK NOW

Something that I found odd began happening as more and more of our clients began to come from the streets. Homeless aren't really a great source for what we do, with drug abuse and the ailments that usually frequent living on the street taking their toll on human organs, tissue, etc. Some recipients were desperate enough to take their chances and some of our clients went for research or teaching which could I suppose be a benefit for learning. A medical student seeing the real-life effects of drug abuse could certainly have its value but the devil's advocate in me, combined with what I knew people were capable of when money got involved, always questioned how many of these folks died in relative peace and how many just got clipped. The only solace I could find was knowing they wouldn't end up at a place like Marge's and I guess for now that needed to be good enough. I was heading out to Jerry's again the coming weekend and looking forward to decompressing with some good people. When I got there, it wasn't quite the shin-dig he had set up before but it was still a nice party with plenty of food and drink. He and I shot the shit for a while about life and the odd things in it. I told him about Marge and he smiled as he said, "she or her kin come around you just give me a call and we will set her straight." I thanked him but I knew if anyone from her camp did track me down it would not be much of a conversation, but I didn't expect to be hearing from any of them in the near future, so I just drank my beer and hoped Jerry had some other friendly ladies to meet.

Mid way through the evening he introduced me to a cousin of his and the point of the intro soon became evident. The cousin had a son who was 24 and who needed a heart. Like Carlo he would require a very specific candidate as the donor and while not able to guarantee anything I asked him to email me the son's specific requirements and I could reach out to a few people on my side of the fence. Without needing to be asked the man explained that he knew it would be expensive, but they would find a way to come up with the money when the time came. Jerry interrupted us and told the man that he and his family would help but we should see what I found before we started planning either a celebration or a funeral. I agreed with him. There was no sense in putting the cart before the horse and the night was young. As luck would have it Jerry had a friend, who had a friend, who had a daughter that worked at our dispatch. Small world isn't it?

I got the text alerting me to Carlos' donor three weeks later and even though it came in at one a.m. I was still awake. It came from an unknown caller just like I was told it would and I quick hit the Keurig as I got ready to go to work. Being ADD as hell and with everything I had swirling around in both my life and my brain sleep was a rare commodity as of late and I was dressed and out the door in 15 minutes flat.

I picked up Ernie, a young man who had been shot in an apparent robbery earlier that evening, without much fanfare. The morgue had me I.D. him and sign him out electronically, which I knew could and probably *would* be erased after I left. No further texts ever came from the dump phone and I'd already been told I wouldn't be bothered with any of our legitimate runs once this situation was in play. This was being swept under the rug from the get-go and all I needed to do was get him where he needed to go and I would wake up tomorrow a fairly wealthy man. Easy right?

As I was transporting Ernie to the underground medical facility, he came up to visit and of all the runs I had made, and all of the bizarre stories shared, this would top the charts and put me in a moral dilemma I never saw coming. Ernie was pretty much an average Joe. He lived his brief life as a bartender and then a manager in a local strip joint. He didn't really impress me as your usual greasy pimp wanna be that most of those cats resembled and I asked how this became his chosen profession.

"I like the ladies, always have, and most of my girls where real sweet hearts that were willing to give me some lovin' if I treated them right. I gave them decent shifts so they could make the rent, turned my back when they did their little something-something on the side and we all just got along. Hell, I had five of them at my place for Christmas and it turned out like a big old family dinner, the main difference being a ton of fucking after the gifts were opened. It was a great gig while it lasted but dope was too easy to get in that world and when I broke my arm last spring, I got hooked on the pain killers and eventually the junk. Man, my whole fucking life turned completely upside down in just under two years If you can believe it. Never saw it coming, and I'm a street smart man or at least I thought I was, but that devil grabs you by the balls brother and he does not want to let go."

I'd seen enough addiction in my life so I didn't doubt what Ernie was saying as I let him keep on telling me about the latter part of his life without interuption.

"I kept it under control, or again I thought I did but pretty soon I needed extra money to scratch my itch and what began as a $50 out of the register now and then turned into a $200-a-week habit. The owner was cool, even when he had to let me go. He could have, and in my mind should have given me a beat down but he didn't. He just wished me luck as he took my keys. I had no savings and my rent was all up my arm so it wasn't but a week and I was out on the curb. I sold what I could, pan-handled a little and even stole. I eventually got locked up and

I thought this was what I needed to clean up. Wrong again, I just made friends inside that could help my habit, for a price. When I got out I ran dope, getting mine for free and enough to rent a shitty room by the week. It was no life but it was my life and I accepted it until I met Brett from the free clinic. He was my savior and helped begin the long and arduous process of getting cleaned up. He got me a bed in a men's recovery house and although I fell off the wagon a couple of times, he always took me back and kept on straightening me out. I went through counseling for addiction, got a job in a place that didn't serve booze. Heck I even started going to church. I had turned my life around. You know I read the bible a lot but I must have ignored the part about man's wicked ways and the dude who I thought really wanted to help was actually the motherfucker fattening me up like a thanksgiving turkey to get plucked.

I met with Brett at the clinic on a regular basis. I was getting my health back along with the rest of my life and he kept cheering me on as he kept the progress in my chart. I'd been clean from smack going on four months and being a Friday night Brett asked if I wanted to go out for dinner to celebrate my short-term success. I wondered if he might be gay and if it came up I was prepared to politely decline any offer. One thing I know about this life is ain't nothing free and in the back of my mind a part of me kept on asking when would it be my time to pay up? I got the answer right after dinner as I walked the short distance back to my room.

I remember the man passing by and smiling in some sort of acknowledgement unknown to me. A minute after I felt a gun to the back of my neck and thought fuck, I don't even have any cash on me. Walking around in front he didn't say anything, just kept the gun pointed at my chest and I kept my hands up. Maybe he was just some freak or perhaps it was a beef with somebody else and he had realized I wasn't the dude, but I was the dude, I just didn't know it. The only thing he said to me was, "sorry brother," and then he shot me twice, once in the upper inner left thigh, and once in my lower right side which punctured my liver. As I sank to the ground It wasn't like I thought it would be from all the shit you hear on television. It was a cool night, but I was hot. My life didn't flash before me really at all. I just felt the warm blood flowing out and I looked at the man above me and asked him who he was, and why the fuck he shot me?

Then the thing that almost stung more than the bullets came into view as Brett walked in, crouched down by my side, and said, "brother, you are going to a better place and you are going to give life with your life, so you will not have lived in vain."

"Lived in vain? Seriously, this arrogant son of a bitch was saying that to me? My life may have been far from perfect but it mattered. I had not given up and I was determined to turn my addiction around and I would have if he hadn't MURDERED me! I mattered to my mom, I mattered to my sister, and even though they had needed to protect themselves from my violation of their trust, they always made it clear that they all still loved me. Even the friends I made on the street had a certain code among us and we looked out for one another to the degree our addictions would allow. Here's the worst part of it all though, I earned the street life, I did, and I don't lay that on anyone but myself, but I have a four-year-old son. What is going to happen to him?"

Fuck...fuck, fuck, FUCK! were the only words that came to mind as I pondered what I'd just been told. I knew the pain of this kind of situation but as you know mine was in the reverse of what Ernie was going through and I didn't have a clue right at the moment how to help him *or* his boy. Danny was born to a former addict girlfriend and after a brief court battle my man Ernie had stepped up when the boy was just a toddler and took full custody of him. It wasn't long after when he acquired his own vice and the kid was currently under the care of his grandmother. It was not an ideal situation by any means but I figured if I put my mind on it, after this current dilemma was wrapped up, I or someone I knew could offer a little help.

"So whose great life had I become the sacrificial lamb for anyway?" and then his spirit mind connected with mine and he looked over at me as he yelled, "son of a bitch! Please tell me this is all a dream or a bad movie or something!"

Son of a bitch was pretty much what I was feeling too, and I tried to explain to him that I didn't know anything about him getting killed. Nothing. Notta. For once the mind reading thing worked in my favor as he could tell I wasn't lying but it was still a great big what the fuck situation for both of us. The question was what were we going to do about it?

I had considered bumping up my price when the time came anyway so making my first phone call was not difficult, but before I did, I needed to think this thing through or my ass wouldn't even make it to the next sunrise and I knew it. The thought that they might kill me as soon as I dropped off the donor had already been in my mind and I had done a little pre-planning because of it. As I pulled my truck into the rural airport parking lot I drove back to a lesser occupied part where I had parked a slightly beaten up but mechanically solid grey-dodge-minivan a couple weeks prior. Inside I had removed the rear seats and installed a custom-built roller track system under a raised platform of plywood and two by four construction. Stacked on the platform were various boxes of window wash, paper towels, squeegees, and anything else that might be needed to sell the picture to anyone who happened to look inside. On top of the van was a ladder rack with two cheap and beat up extension ladders and on the side the words Rick's Window Cleaning-Licensed and Insured was tastefully done in the colors of the New Orleans Saints football team but hidden under a sheet of taped on white plastic that I would remove once I'd left the area, along with switching the plates. I pulled up alongside the van and after waiting five minutes to make sure I wouldn't be getting company, I rolled the gurney right out the back, lowering the deck to the level of my minivan, and then slid Ernie into his temporary home in the rear of my new, untraceable transport vehicle. Tearing open two cases of instant icepacks I began smashing them to activate the freezing agent as I placed them in a layer on top of the thick vinyl pouch. Not to be gross but if the meat spoils it's of no use to anyone and I planned on getting paid. Smiling to myself with a degree of quiet satisfaction I shut the plywood door on the back of my secret body stash, and off I went. My first big question got answered within ten minutes as my other cell phone received a text:

Is everything okay???

Smiling to myself again I texted back:

Everything is beautiful

I got no response for five minutes and I knew that whoever was on the other end was blowing up someone else's phone right about now.

After another five minutes, I assumed after they had activated and dispatched whoever would be looking for me, I received another text:

What is your location and ETA?

Now it was my time to play a little cat and mouse as I didn't answer. They waited another five minutes and repeated the last text.

Not very good poker players I thought but it was time to let them know the game required a re-negotiation so I responded:

I'm not at the airport, and we need to talk about the last part.

If panic could transmit through a text my phone would be screaming right about now as I knew that somewhere in New Orleans a few folks were shitting their pants.

What are your demands?

My demands? Hey, I wasn't robbing a bank or threatening to blow up a plane for Christ sake but I got their point and took a degree of confidence knowing that at least we weren't going to dick around.

I need to talk to whoever handles the money, was my reply.

Another pause of a few minutes passed and then:

Your terms have already been set. The client won't negotiate.

Fuck! I thought we weren't going to play games I thought to myself but such is human nature and I let them wait another 20 minutes until I was ready to move forward.

I hit the remote control opening the garage door of the small warehouse I had rented a few weeks back and into relative anonymity I pulled my vehicle in. After shutting it down I unloaded the client from the back, lowered him into a human sized plastic tub and covered him in ice from the small chest freezer in the corner. After hopefully throwing them into further panic I sent another text from a burner phone:

Okay, I guess I'll just throw this body in the river.

Realizing this would take a minute I took a quick peek at the vacant street out front and confident I was unnoticed for the moment texted a different number to let them know I had arrived.

I had pulled the battery out of the old phone ten miles back but just to make sure I could not be tracked I pulled the S.I.M. card out, smashed it and placed in inside the small lead lined box I had waiting. After a quick squirt of lighter fluid, I torched the contents just to be sure.

Please send all further correspondence to this new number. The old phone is no longer functioning I sent as the follow up text.

They had put a GPS on my Sprinter and I assumed they could also track the phone they had given me but now they were walking in the dark and they knew it.

You disappoint me. I thought you were man of honor!" came in on the new burner.

I wasn't sure who was doing the texting. Could be Carlos, could be his father, and it could be someone from my end but none of that mattered to me. Holding my anger I punched in my response:

People in glass houses shouldn't talk shit.

I had also sent a text to both my friends Jerry and his friends, friends, daughter who worked at our dispatch but had given me her personal cell phone when we had all met the same week I'd rented the warehouse. I nervously waited for their response as I sat with my own thoughts on the potential shit storm sitting right outside. The building I was in was set up completely to perform a heart transplant. I took part of the cash Carlo had given me and after speaking with Kata and a colleague of hers was able to purchase or steal everything required. Don't ask me how but Jerry once again knew someone, who knew someone. Get the picture? Anyway, with a promise to pay $100k cash after a successful surgery we had lined up a very qualified heart specialist who also enjoyed playing the ponies and apparently, wasn't very good at it, who would be willing to help. We had the facility, the equipment, the doctor and even a small staff just a text away. We even had the donor but here is the funny part, all of this had been set up without ever considering a Carlos situation. Jerry's cousin's son needed a heart and I felt confident that I could help them sooner rather than later so we had gotten our plan together in anticipation of today, but today wasn't supposed to go down this way and a young man's life was now holding in the balance.

How much do you want? came in first from Carlo's people.

Up and running came in next from the three from my side of the fence.

The first one I needed to calculate but the others I just replied with a thumbs up emoji knowing the cavalry was awake and ready to ride.

Three million is a nice round number I answered.

The sun was coming up and it was time to go fishing.

# IT GETS INTERESTING

By now I figured they had people tossing my house for clues, hoping they wouldn't need to do too much damage before they found the alternate receipts I'd left for the other warehouse and the used vehicle I'd gotten as decoys. They would eventually be able to track me down but by the time they got here the operation would be done and we would all be in the wind. Still I didn't want to get arrogant and I said a little Irish prayer for things to go well as Jerry, his cousin, two very serious looking and well-armed friends, and the doctor and his staff all arrived in quiet succession. The doctor and his people got to work quickly, checking and testing every piece of equipment in front of them. He was complimentary of my work in completing the list as it was by no means an ordinary shopping list. I had to spread a little bribe money around, five grand going to the guard at my company's storage facility over in the industrial district, but when the guard let me in to the large building where they kept back up or older medical equipment it was like going to Wal-Mart for the stuff you'd need to transplant a heart. They had everything I needed, and it was just the right price. They got Ernie out and began prepping him for surgery as I told him in my head that I would look out for his son. He didn't answer.

Jerry's cousin was now fully sedated and prepped as well as the doc closed off the room to everyone but those he needed to do his job. I walked over and sat down as I could now see three new texts had come in.

We won't do three million.

The client has authorized one million four hundred thousand to be paid anywhere you choose.

We need a response.

It had been half an hour since our last correspondence and the doctor told me at the earliest, without complications, we had a four hour wait for him to finish. Four hours might seem fast but I'd seen it done in less and wasn't concerned at all about his end of the deal as I answered the texts.

"So apparently your client values the inheritance to those he is leaving behind more than his own life?"

A minute later I got their hostile response.

You do know who you are dealing with correct?

Patience is definitely a virtue and I walked over, waited for the brand new Keurig to pour me a delicious hot cup of dark roast, topped it with a splash of Bailey's Irish Cream and thoroughly enjoyed the warm and satisfying beverage as I punched in my answer.

Yes, but apparently you don't.

For now I was just buying a little time and really, letting them negotiate all by themselves right into the deal I'd hoped for all along.

He will go two million. Please be reasonable.

Reasonable? That's a joke but I wanted to wrap this up in preparation of the next part.

Two-point-five or we are done talking and I let the client go the alligators. It's time to get serious and I have my retirement to think of.

I knew this was the money shot, or damn close to it, as I sat back and waited. Knowing that the cost for doing it legally, with no special requirements, was currently running around $1.4 million. I knew we were very close to moving forward.

We have a deal, but you don't seriously anticipate enjoying a long future do you.

I knew they were very serious but with two and a half I could do what I needed to do and still disappear.

Just for that it's two point six, or you can read about them finding this donor floating in Lake Ponchatrain.

I knew they wouldn't let it go for a hundred K and it was kind of fun fucking with the arrogant bastards.

Wire it to account #332-56-88923 at the Federal Bank and Trust of Grand Cayman. When I've confirmed it is done, I will deliver the gift to wherever you like.

I finished my cup of Joe. After only a minute their final response came in, just as anticipated.

Agreed. Will contact you when transfer is complete.

It was now just after eleven in the morning and by my figures it would take 45 minutes for them to confirm as we waited on things to wrap up on our end. The surgery was a success and just then a man who only Jerry knew knocked on the door. He owned an ambulance company and was well prepared to transport the man with the new heart to a pre-arranged recovery facility I knew nothing about, which was exactly how I wanted it. Jerry was full of surprises and connections, and I for one was grateful for them both.

I watched the ambulance drive off, thanked Jerry and agreed to get the money to the doctor in the next 24 hours as planned as I waited for everyone to leave and loaded Ernie, minus the heart), back into the rear of my vehicle. My phone alerted me to an incoming text and after I quickly called the bank to confirm I smiled to myself as two million six hundred thousand dollars was now waiting for me and my new life, but you knew it couldn't possibly be as simple as that right?

I had never planned on screwing Carlo on the deal but when I found out they had murdered someone to get him his heart I just couldn't do it. Maybe he knew, maybe he didn't? I could never be certain, but I knew one thing for sure, the only reason he was going to live was that he or someone in his organization had enough money to ensure that somebody like Ernie didn't. I couldn't live with that.

I delivered the body to the closest hospital, wheeling him in through the rear entry to the morgue where I knew I wouldn't be challenged and leaving a note taped to the outside of the bag with instructions and a certified check made out to Ernie's mom to cover the funeral. Knowing that Carlo's people could never have possibly known about my conversation with Ernie and would be left to their own assumptions my next move was to drop a dime on Brett. The N.O.L.A police found what was left of him a few weeks later but not before I sent him a card at the free clinic that read, "brother, you are going to a better place and you are going to give life with your life, so you will not have lived in vain."

I wasn't sure about someone like him going to a better place and the only life he was going to give with his life was to feed maggots, but I am sure it freaked his ass out with whatever time he had left and it was the least I could do for Ernie.

# HIDING OUT AND TELLING GHOST STORIES

Whoever tossed my house must have been told to show some enthusiasm and they tore the hell out of it. I'm not sure when they found the fake clues I'd left but they must have taken the long way getting to them and my place was trashed. I had already warned my neighbors to expect visitors again but not to get involved. I wasn't sure what might happen with the whole Carlo deal but a little precaution can keep people from getting hurt. I'd upped my home insurance coverage's recently and whatever damage done would get chalked up as the cost of doing business. I'd already pulled any personnel belongings that held meaning to me, used a burner phone going forward, quit my job before they fired me, and took Mango and Marie up on an offer to crash at their place while I kept my head down.

I helped with prep cooking at their bar where I would never be noticed and after things quieted down. Occasionally one of them, Mango or Marie, would whip up something fabulous for us to eat. Sitting down to an amazing plate of seafood thermidor one night the topic of family came up. I had avoided the subject up until now but we were getting closer as friends and I knew I could trust them both as I shared a reader's digest version of my past, and they part of their own. They had both seen and lived through their share of strife, like most of us much from making the wrong choice and plenty from just life being life but we shared something in common in that we all had made the decision to keep going forward. Marie had been in a bad marriage with a physically and mentally abusive first husband. The man coming to her family's bar one night which turned out to be the wrong night, wrong place, and most certainly the wrong time with the wrong dude on the far end of the ass whipping stick. To make it short he was a bully on top of his other sins, and he ran in to my friend Mango fresh back from the fighting. Mango told me he never dated married women and that was the only thing that had kept him from asking Marie out, but when her husband came in that fateful night and slapped her in front of him as Mango laughed he said that the parking lot was only a Texas two-step away and he was in the mood to put his boots on a wife-beater anyway.

He cleaned up the ground with the dude, went back inside to finish his beer, and as Marie thanked him she passed him her phone number on a beer coaster. She was divorced by March and they had a May wedding as they joined forces to make a new life. They asked me why I hadn't settled down my own self and I could only tell them I hadn't met the right lady, but I hoped to some day. We talked a little about my daughter and I could see the pain of my loss darken Marie's face as she said, "I can't imagine what that was like."

I told her that I couldn't either as I had drank myself through most of it and then I decided to take a gamble and I shared with her what one of my clients had told me about my daughter having cancer unknown to anyone and that she was happy I hadn't had to watch her go through it.

"Brother," Mango said, "I smoke some really good ganja, but come again. Are you saying you can talk to the dead?"

I thought by opening my mouth I had just lost a friend but it was quite the opposite. They were both incredibly curious, startled, but curious, as they prodded me with questions about it for the next two hours. In that two hours neither one of them hardly asked a question as they sat back in amazement at some of the folks I'd carried and what they had told me about their own lives. I wasn't sure they believed me at first but they confessed that they had always been very curious about the subject and living in New Orleans had plenty of Gris-Gris and voodoo talk around them so I guessed it was like people in Milwaukee talking about beer, or those in Chicago comparing the best pizza. Everyone may have had their own preference but the topic itself was as accepted as the rising sun.

They both got a kick out of Jesse but like me felt that he had been cut short far too soon and would have liked to know him as a friend. Funny part is that as I shared some of the different stories we found a common root in that love, the pursuit of love, or the loss of it impacted so very much of who we all were as people. Mango had lost many friends in combat but it made him more kind. Marie had suffered loss of love and the violation of the trust that was supposed to come with it, but it had not broken and with a man in her life that she knew would love her and never hurt her she had grown into a far stronger woman then she ever dreamed possible.

Me? Well I still wasn't out of the woods yet. Chloe's death was easier to live with but it was still often a part of my day and I had to accept that it was probably never going to change. The one thing I was happy inside about was that I was evolving. Truth be told before my divorce I was a cold fish. My wife and I had come to have sex on special events, watched the news and let it put us to bed every night with a sense of dread and forbearance as we bitched between us about what other people were doing. I was embarrassed to acknowledge this in retrospect. How much of my life had been wasted on negative bullshit? How much of my time with my daughter had been taken by my complacence and sitting on the couch? I still wasn't sure exactly where I was headed or how it would all end up but I knew one thing, it wasn't going to be like it was before and it was damn sure going to be interesting and full of good people and great memories.

The cat was out of the bag so I told them about the Ernie situation and how I was trying to find someone to adopt his boy if I could. Ernie's mom was not in good health and I wasn't sure what other family might be an option but I would try and work something out if they'd let me. Right then I caught Marie looking over at Mango somewhat coyly and I asked "what?"

He looked at me and said that they had been talking about family for a little while now but he was sterile and neither of them wanted to go through the process of artificial insemination. Call it archaic but they just thought it was weird and would rather try and give someone else's baby a good home. They asked about the possibility of Danny and although I knew they would be great parents it was a situation very much out of my control, but you just never know how life will turn out and I was going to see what I could do to help.

# THE FATHER-DAUGHTER DANCE

My cell phone rang a few days later and on the other end was J.C. telling me he had found the professor's daughter. I was glad to hear this as I didn't know how much longer the old man had and I was eager to meet up and find out the details. We were able to meet the next afternoon and when we did, he presented me with a packet documenting his inquiry, the results, and the expenses. He had used the entire retainer plus some, but the Prof had already told me that if she was found within three months to give a bonus of $10k on top of the original amount and I wrote a check to settle it right there. As I leafed through the report I followed along as J.C. had searched and traveled through Great Britain, Louisiana, Florida, and for a brief and interesting but inconclusive three days, to Peru before winding up right back in the Big Easy.

Willow, the lady we had been looking for had at one point or another lived in all of the places mentioned but love and loss dropped her permanently in New Orleans. The Bean and the Berry was a funky little coffee shop slash art studio she had opened ten years prior and was now a thriving joint that the locals tried in vain to keep to themselves. I read the entire report while J.C. replied to emails and when I was finished he asked if I had any questions. I didn't but I expressed both the prof's gratitude and my own as we shook hands and he handed me his card saying that if he could ever be of further assistance don't hesitate to call him. I hoped to never need his kind of services again but you just never know what life is going to throw you and I tucked the brown linen business card securely in my wallet.

I knew full well the next step would require kid gloves as this woman hadn't remained absent from her father life without her own reasons. I figured the easiest way to address it was probably also the most basic. The next morning, I walked into her coffee shop, ordered a latte and a fresh baked fruit danish as I asked her if she had a moment to hear news about her father. The look she gave me was somewhere between distain and disbelief but she shook my hand and with a wispy wave of her hand ushered us to a more private area of the shop. I thanked her and apologized for what I'm sure was an unexpected and unwelcome intrusion into her life, the circumstances of which having forced me to act. I shared with her the minimum details of my personal affiliation, quickly getting to the main point that her father was terminally ill and had asked to see her one more time before he passed. A server brought her a glass of iced earl grey tea and another latte for me and as she took a long drink I could tell she was processing the revelation I had just laid on her.

"How much is he paying you to do this?" she asked with a calculating gaze. I told her I wasn't making anything off from it, it was only a favor for a dying friend.

"How good of friends are you?" her gaze unwavering.

I knew to lie and I did as I gave her the minimums and painted the story of being a former art student who was doing what I was more out of service than dedication. I honestly couldn't tell how much of it she bought into but I noticed her relax her posture a little which assured me of some progress in my endeavor. Normally I would have continued on with some small talk but this was one practiced and prudent bird and I knew inside to let her lead as she eventually opened up about the topic.

"You know I had not heard from Papa for years. When my mother died, I was in my early 20s and after the funeral I never heard another word from him until now. They had been divorced but he was still my dad and I guess inside I always hoped for a relationship he was either unable or unwilling to deliver. I remember the day he left the UK when I was just a young girl and he gave me a pretty gift-wrapped box. I still see the beautiful pink rose wrapping paper and the letter he had written on his personal stationary inside.

> *My dearest Willow,*
>
> *It is with great remorse that I leave you and your mother. I cannot offer an explanation other than to tell you both that there are things about me that I've never disclosed and your lives without me will be for the better.*
>
> *I love you and I loved your mum but life sometimes returns its history and I can only offer you my deepest love and nothing more.*
>
> *I know you won't understand and I sincerely hope that someday I can explain. Please look out for your mother, she is a good and honest woman.*
>
> *Love always,*
>
> *Papa*

Inside was a jade and silver heart pendant with the words Papa engraved on the back," and as she continued about life in Britain she reached up and pulled it out from hiding in the neck of the light lavender sweater she wore. The Prof had somewhere along the way gotten word to her mother that he was living in New Orleans but had sworn her to a secrecy and she finally broke it to her daughter the week before she died. With no certain ties to London she sought out to find her father but when she did, anger and uncertainty had kept her at bay. She did however find the same infectious soul of the city that her father had, and even though she refused to reach out to him it gave her some sort of odd comfort knowing they at least lived in the same place. She told me how she kept quiet ties on him, having watched him teach his students in the park on several warm and sunny afternoons in the past. I asked her why she didn't just confront him but she said part of her figured fuck him, he was the one who left not me and my mom. Another part though had to respect the validity of his note to her and in the balance of them both she found a numb but comfortable acceptance that had worked up until now.

"You know my mum told me some bits about him," as she fiddled with the paper napkin in front of her. "She said that he wasn't necessarily a bad man, he just wasn't a good one. He had done work that helped our Country but it was at the cost of many lives and she didn't know how the man she loved could also be the man who had done such awful things. He hadn't given her many details, or apparently ones she felt confident in sharing with me, but before he left she started seeing strange men in our neighborhood and at night she would find him up or roaming about the flat always lying and telling her that everything was fine, he just couldn't sleep.

She believed him at first, but it was odd, whenever he could not sleep in the past he always got up with a hot cup of milk tea and either vanilla biscuits or rosemary scones as he sat in his tall leather chair in our tiny living room by the fireplace. Near the end however, she never heard the whistle of the tea pot, she never found the crumbs on the counter from the biscuits or scones, and the fireplace was ice cold and then one morning he was simply gone."

"You know I never believed what she told me," Willow began. "Maybe I was protecting the inner version of what I needed my dad to be but I also did some research. He was in the war and he moved around plenty on assignments but the men he had soldiered with described him as a quiet and intelligent man who loved his family, his country, and an excellent single malt on occasion. Nothing about murder or other atrocities but in retrospect they wouldn't have, would they?"

We both sat there and nodded our agreement as I asked her what she would prefer to do now.

"I want to see my papa," was her response, and we set a date.

Our conversation had set in place a few questions for me but I would be asking them in private after my job was done and I phoned the old man.

# THE CONFESSION

I could feel the emotional release on the other end when I phoned my friend to tell him I'd found his daughter. He asked some basic questions and was very surprised to hear she had lived near him the entire time. She had matured in her appearance from the old pic's I'd seen and I'm not sure if he would have recognized her if they ran into each other nose to nose on a city street. None of that mattered now and I coordinated a dinner with the two of them at the Commander's Palace the coming Friday. Initially they balked at my request but when I explained who it was for the books opened up like Noah parting the Red Sea. This man was one interesting fellow and he had connections.

I got there before them and made sure they had a secluded, private room for the duration of their dinner. The small dining area had been tastefully and simply decorated with vases of seasonal flowers, one table, two comfortable chairs, and a small framed photo of the professor, his wife and his daughter when she was very young. The old man showed up dressed as dapper as a nobleman and as he assessed the room he placed a small wrapped gift on the table. We made small talk as we waited and although normally a very confident man he was now as giddy as a school boy pondering his first date. When Willow arrived it was all anyone had expected. She offered her hand and he took it. He ushered her to her seat and they ordered cocktails as the icy silence of a 500 pound gorilla hung in the room. He asked a few questions, she answered with one syllable answers at first but eventually the liquor loosened her tongue and the dialogue grew more heated.

Of course she wanted to know why he had left, why he had abandoned her and her mum. She went on a 15-minute tirade about how much they had worried about him, hated him, and loved him again at the same time. A few tears flowed down her cheek but time had numbed her emotions and she was the type to keep it in check. After he let her get it all out and he asked if he could please speak? They ordered lunch first and two Caesar salads on chilled plates appeared in front of them as he began.

"First, and I hope you can believe me, I am sorry. Your mother was the love of my life and I never dated another woman after I left, but that was not even close to the hardest part. The evening that I departed I went to look in on you one last time while you were sleeping and it was the hardest thing I've ever done. I have killed men and women, had them killed and in effect ended several family names, but having to leave and not see you again, not see you grow up, go to your first dance, go out on your first date, those were things that could not be replaced and yet I knew full well I had to leave just the same."

A steaming plate of oysters Bienville appeared in front of them but the professor had only fiddled with his salad and his daughter had not done much more with hers as he continued.

"There is no easy way to say this, your mum did not die, she was murdered." At this his daughter got red in the face and challenged him saying that her mother had cancer and she herself had sat by her bedside as the disease had eaten her mind and her body. Leaning back he looked at her from across the table and shook his head.

"In a way I wish that was true, perhaps it would be easier for us both to accept, but it simply is not. I never told your mother everything I was tasked to do during the war but you are intelligent enough to know it could not have been pleasant. With my position I was responsible with performing deeds that would never be forgotten, and they weren't. The war eventually ended but the wounds from it never healed for so many both on our side and the other. It wasn't just the Germans either. In the course of our duty we assassinated Turks, Italians, even people from the Middle East and many of them of substantial means. When the war ended many of the families made it their mission in life to avenge the deaths and we were not the only people with resources and intelligence. Money can buy almost anything in this world and information is far easier to obtain than you might believe. I was warned that my identity had been revealed and for several years I was able to protect us and keep our whereabouts secret but it was a brief reprieve and I always knew it. One day a man from the agency called on me to share that reliable sources had verified a contract on my life. I never doubted it and in the next few weeks I made the decision to leave, the main reason in removing you and your mum from being used as a pawn. My heart was what gave me away and also caused your mother's death. I never forgave myself for that weakness.

You see I just could not go on in life without speaking with her and knowing you both were taken care of. I had set up an endowment to provide for your needs but it was no substitute for the sound of your mother's voice and in a few moments of weakness I phoned her. There was someone on the other end listening and while they knew they couldn't get to me, they could hurt me much deeper if they killed her. Children are seen by many to be off limits in matters like this, so I always considered you safe to a reasonable degree but when my enemy realized I was not a cad who had abandoned his family and run off they set their sights on her. Her illness was sudden and not particularly prolonged was it?"

Willow nodded her head and agreed as her father continued.

"Even when I was in service we had certain poisons that could mimic a variety of illnesses and I'm sure they've advanced over the years. All you need is a cooperating doctor or medical examiner and no one is ever the wiser. They didn't perform any kind of autopsy did they?"

Willow shook her head as she whispered through her tears. "No."

The professor had visibly aged in the course of the discussion and sat back into his chair wearily, a look of great sadness and defeat on his face. The rest of the afternoon was spent filling in some blanks with Willow gradually opening up and sharing some of her experiences and more so, her feelings. They both agreed that It wasn't a complete fix but it was a start and when they parted ways late in the day it was with a hug and a promise to rebuild what had been lost with what time was still left. That night I went to visit him at his flat to wrap things up but this labyrinth of curios turns was not quite finished. When I arrived he shook my hand with a warmth and gratitude, handed me a wooden box with a bottle of 2003 Lafitte Rothschild Bordeaux to share with my neighbor ladies and nestled beside it a bottle of Hine Triumph Cognac which I knew I'd enjoy for years to come but would never have bought for myself. As we sat down he also handed me a substantial check which I looked at and tried to hand back, telling him I did what I did for a friend and he smiled as he said he realized this, but that I should please accept it just the same.

"I have plenty of money, what I don't have and never really did are true friends, so please take it. Finding my daughter will give me a certain degree of peace in whatever the next life holds and for that I don't believe you could calculate a value."

He had hired a man servant to help in his last days and two snifters of warm Benedictine were offered to each of us, the warm golden liquor pausing my senses and giving a slight reprieve to the surreal events of past months.

"There is one more thing that I must ask your help with. It is fairly simple and I insist an additional fee be paid to you for it."

I was curious I admit, but I had come to learn that nothing with my friend was ever simple as I tilted my glass in acceptance and then outward towards his passing man servant for a refill.

"You heard me tell Willow that I never dated another woman after her mother and I didn't. I did however consummate an act of service for a colleague of mine who could not bare child and had asked for my involvement. That act produced a child, a young man named Nathaniel who lives with his Mum in the Garden District, attends Isidore Newman private academy and excels at both academics and lacrosse. Out of prior agreement and decorum I have never met the lad but I have attended a few of his games and he bears a striking resemblance that I hope never betrays him. I have been in contact with his mother, a single woman who never married, and she has agreed to allow a financial contribution for his future. She has been apprised of my situation and has agreed to accept you as an executor to disperse funds for the boy's scholastic needs. I could have simply written her a check but for her own reasons she preferred it be handled this way and I did not think you would refuse."

I did not.

The professor passed into the next world three days later and per his request I organized a small, private service with only a handful of his friends in attendance. We had a small lunch catered in with wines, cheeses, and rich desserts that I'm sure he would have enjoyed if he were still alive. When lunch ended his daughter thanked me for what I had done and offered her help if I ever needed it. I handed her an envelope with a handwritten note from her father inside. While the contents were unknown to me, I assumed it offered a final apology as well as substantial financial support for her future and that was that? Wrong again.

# TOO CLOSE FOR COMFORT

I went back to work eventually for another company that was getting into the market and didn't care about the stuff with my former employer. They had contracts but very few drivers which is the biggest problem in this business, so while I couldn't run down the streets naked chasing chickens I pretty much had job security.

I got the email for Frank in the late afternoon on a Wednesday and it was as basic as basic could get with no cut off time and a straight hop from New Orleans General to the college harvest center one hour and thirty minutes away. As always I did my toe tag I.D. and cross referenced my paperwork against what the morgue had. As I zipped him up I noticed he was a very run of the mill looking type with average looks and seemed to be in decent shape for a 50 year old man. He'd suffered an aneurism and other than the bruises and marks from the E.R.'s lifesaving efforts he was just an ordinary Moe who could have been a bank manager or an insurance salesman.

I rolled him up into my truck, locked the gurney down and turned on the a/c for both the back and the front. It was going to be a hot one and while this may sound weird to you, I absolutely hate to sweat. Probably shouldn't have moved to a friggin' swamp right? Well they had some damn fine cooking and some good people so I'd just needed to invest in extra deodorant and keep my mouth shut. You know I had done hundreds of runs over my years of doing what I did and truth be told most of them were ordinary people. I've only told you about the ones whose story really stuck out but honestly most of the time it was a fairly boring job. You had to maintain your timelines or people could die but between the loading and unloading all I did was drive, think, and listen to the radio. The other thing that stood out is that the energy I had gotten from most of my clients, even the suicides, was of a fairly peaceful and calm place. That all changed when I got on the road with Frank.

He started talking me up just outside the city limits and his first words to me were actually with a bit of a chuckle as he said, "Man, that was close."

I had no idea of what he was talking about and I asked him what he meant. As he said my name, obviously reading it from my badge or paperwork I guessed, he said, "you know, two more days and you'd have been the one on ice and I'd have been eating a steak dinner over at Dickie Brennens."

I still didn't understand and he went on, explaining to me that he was a hired killer and I had a contract out on me that he had planned on fulfilling the coming Friday.

"Yes sir, thirty grand and I had it all set up. Been watching you for over a week now and the only thing I hadn't exactly figured out was how to make it big and loud without getting seen doing you."

"Holy shit, are you serious?" I thought.

"Serious as a heart attack my friend, no pun intended." He further elaborated saying, "you know I already had my mind set on surf and turf for my dinner. I called earlier this week and they told me they had some fresh Maine lobsters just flown in so I was going to do it up nice. It's not often that I get a solid pay day like this. By the way, who the fuck did you piss off to get that big a bounty hung around your neck? An ex-wife, some girlfriend or boyfriend you dumped? You do this for a living so I assume it wasn't somebody you screwed in a business deal."

By now I was getting a little pissed at his cavalier approach to the thought of taking my life and I said to him, "you're the pro, why don't you tell me. It's not like you can get arrested or killed over it."

"That's pretty funny but I don't know. We usually don't know or meet the client. It's all done through an agent to keep things in the dark. I really never wanted to know anyway. To me it was just my job and that's the only way I'd ever looked at it ever since I did my first hit during college.

I think back to that first guy I shot, me and two other guys, all clean cut and preppy looking got recruited by a local biker club to do some work. It's funny you know, those bikers may look rough but those are some smart people and all business. The reason they recruited guys like me was because we looked nothing like them and could come and go from a town without anyone every looking at us twice. Shit, I don't even have one tattoo and my hair has never grown past my collar."

"How in the hell did someone like you get into that line of work?" I asked. "Are you a sociopath or something, where you abused as a child and kept looking for payback your entire life, what?"

"No" he laughed, "can't say any of that was the case with me. I just never cared much about anything or anyone. I can't recall ever having much emotions one way or the other except with my mom. I liked her a lot, never loved her, I never loved anyone but she was special to me maybe simply for giving me life. I know it sounds odd but that is the god's honest truth and it has served me well. I never went through all the emotional bullshit other people do when someone dies, or leaves, or does something to hurt me. I just never cared, never.

My first test was when they, my parents, were killed during a robbery. Everyone around me was messed up, my aunts and uncles beyond words and I give my one aunt credit for stepping up and taking me in. What I didn't know, what I couldn't have known, was that she had a thing for me and one Sunday afternoon when her husband had gone golfing after lunch she pulled a naughty Nancy on me. I wasn't sure yet if I liked girls or boys, as it turns out both, but when she came onto me I never thought to resist. My only thought, ever, was on self-preservation and I laid her down hard as I gave her a fucking I knew she never got from the old man."

We agreed to keep it quiet and I started working her for nicer clothes and eventually my first ride-a '68 Camaro. They had the money and I think she enjoyed the game so it lasted into my college years but by then she was looking worn out and I had other plans. It should have bothered me that I was balling my mother's sister, and it should have bothered her if she had any kind of conscience. It didn't and I guess maybe the whole lack of emotion is a family trait that skips around a bit. I graduated with dual degrees in biology and English literature and while I could have lived off a teacher's salary I didn't want to plus, my other work gave me a little travel and I always found the hunt very stimulating."

"Wait a second, you're telling me you were a school teacher?"

"Yes sir, always enjoyed teaching but some of those parents came far closer to a free *house call* than they will ever know. Fucking 'my Johnny is a good boy, or how can you fail little Sally? Shit. Tell you what I never put it on the kids, they are after all kids, but those fucking whiny-ass parents I could have lined up ten deep, put a bullet through the lot of them and never lost an ounce of sleep over it. Not that I ever did any way, just sharing my opinion on their ridiculous lack of accountability.

261

I worked doing hits for the bikers through college and after they told me I was getting too old to suit their profile which I understood but I asked if they could make a call on my behalf and after a while I hooked up with my current handler Jeff. I had only worked for him about five years when we finally acted on mutual attraction one night. It only lasted a few months and being practical men we knew it wasn't smart to mix business with friendship, especially this kind of business, but our working relationship was mutually beneficial so we agreed to never act on our desires again and I've been doing contracts through him for over 20 years now.

I only work out of town, it never being wise to allow even the possibility that someone local witnesses a hit and recognizes you. I learned that little piece first thing working for the club, that's why they brought us in from outside. No one to recognize us and we were gone before the first composite drawing could ever be put up. Hell, before they even notified the families of the target I was a hundred miles away wearing brand new kakis and a turtle neck sweater, driving a rental car and using my own perfectly legitimate identification. The one time I got pulled over for a random stop I was just a clean-cut sophomore coming back from seeing his girlfriend for the weekend. I still remember the twinkle in the trooper's eye as he joked and told me to practice safe sex as he handed back my license and registration. I'm sure in his mind right then he was visualizing me banging some young, hotty that could have been his daughter but he let me go and that's all I wanted as I smiled back and said yes sir!

I worked a lot in Texas and Florida, with a little work out west when the need arose. The main thing until now was never in my own backyard but I've got retirement to consider and the payday on you made me bend the rules this once. Not that it matters now anyway."

I was curious and asked what the bulk of his work was, I assumed drug dealers, people who talked to the cops, you know the typical stuff you hear in the movies? Laughing again he verified my assumption were pretty much false as he told me that I had watched too many movies.

"No most of it is just business. Someone has a partner who is ripping them off or maybe they just get greedy and want them gone. I've done a bit of club work here and there, clipping legitimate business people who crossed the line somewhere along the way. The funny thing is I've probably done as much or more work for people just wanting their spouses gone. Insurance money, inheritance, other lovers but the best one was a dude who was molesting his step daughter. I have to say I enjoyed that work and I could barely tell you any details of all the hits I did over the years accept the very first one.

He was an accountant who was stealing from the bikers and one Friday night they drove me to the county fair, pointed him out, and put a short barrel 38 with a crude silencer on it in my hand. I didn't have any kind of formal training, never even a fight in school, but for some reason both they and I knew I wouldn't have a problem with it. Mack, the guy who brought me in had an eye for talent and I think back to that first time he approached me on campus at an after- game kegger. He pretended like he was a dad or uncle of a student but in reality he was there looking for prospects. After a few beers he shared a little about the work and it got me curious. My first question was how much it paid and he smiled as he said we would get to that later, I needed to meet a few more people first. I must have passed whatever sniff test they had and three weeks later I was at the Lee County fair holding a pistol and getting ready to do my first job. They had me do a little shooting prior and I found the entire situation just a matter of mechanics. You point the gun where it needs to be pointed, you pull the trigger, and the work is done.

DANIEL LEE SILVERTHORNE

I think back to the ridiculous red bow tie the accountant was wearing and with my preppy college look I fit right in to his crowd. I noticed him with a lady who was obviously not his wife and what appeared to be a male co-worker and they were all walking around as they laughed and watched the rides and the carnival around them. I think back and the smells and noise are what stand out as much as anything else. Grease in the air from the frying elephant ears, onions and peppers from the sausage sandwich wagon, and a mix of chaotic but pleasant noise. I still recall the joyful screams of the people on the rides, the bad music piped in from behind the carnie games and how it all kind of blended together. It was very surreal. The only advice Mack gave me was try and hit him alone so I wouldn't face the possibility of shooting someone else and hopefully wouldn't be recognized. I noticed the men were passing a brown bag between them and from the flat look of it I was pretty sure it was liquor and not beer or wine. After a while the mark started walking towards the porta-potties and I could tell that his buddy was using the opportunity to put his moves on the woman as he stayed behind. As luck would have it all the urinals were three people deep and my slightly intoxicated target opted to piss in the woods behind them. I followed him and let him begin to do his business as I drew out the pistol. The funny thing is I was told to shoot him twice in the back of the head, you always put two in them, but I wanted to see his face so I stepped around in front of him almost close enough to get pissed on. In the moonlight he could see me I'm sure but he didn't know what to make of it as he zipped up his fly and just stared at me for a quick second. I pulled the piece and shot him straight up through just under his chin as he grabbed at his throat and stumbled back. I stood over him and was going to shoot him again but it was the oddest thing, with the moonlight shining down the blood began to soak his white shirt and with that ugly red bow tie the dark crimson began to fan out like tassels hanging beneath it. He had this vaudevillian artificial smirk plastered on his lips like something out of a bad Joker movie and when his eyes got big for just a second he looked more like a cartoon than a man. It was like art to me and I didn't want to mess up my work by shooting him again and disturbing the picture, so I just left. Besides the bullet had shot straight up through his brain and he was gone before he even landed in the grass.

I got back to the car, Mack asking for the gun and I lied as I told him I had wrapped it up in a popcorn bag and dumped it in a trash barrel. He was kind of pissed but I was a first timer and I knew I could get away with it. Besides, there was no fucking way I was going to give a murder weapon with my prints on it back to someone I had just met. They could never trace the gun to the hit. I saw the bullet come out the top of the accountants head, but still I knew then to always cover your ass and that kind of thinking combined with a little luck is what kept me out of prison and alive until now."

I hate to admit it but listening to Frank go into the details I found myself engaged. As he continued on describing his resume I found myself living vicariously through his story telling. Come on, admit it, we have all at one time or another experienced someone who we wished we could kill. I know for a fact I have, and more than once. If you say otherwise you are either up for sainthood and good for you, or you are the only one I've ever known but this isn't confession and I'm not here to judge. I'm just telling you it gave me a rush listening to someone take people out. Maybe I'm a little messed up but I've been straight with you up until now, no sense in starting to lie. I asked him if he had various ways of taking care of people and although he had been forced on occasion to use alternate methods he always preferred a gun.

"Pistols, revolvers to be specific, are my tool of choice. They are easy to find at gun show parking lots, you can pick them up for two to three hundred bucks, and I always make my own silencers. I use steel wool, aluminum tubing and black athletic tape and all you need to do is notch the one end of the tube, drill a bunch of small holes crosswise through it, wrap the tube in steel wool and finish it off with the tape. I tape it right to the gun so I don't need to mess around attaching it or un-attaching it. I use a bullet that fragments so even with one or two shots the interior damage is significant enough where they will bleed out way before they get to any hospital or ambulance, if that even happens. I wear a basic disguise when I make the gun buys just in case, and if the serial numbers aren't already gone I've got a little hand held grinder to remove them. I always ditch the gun right after I use it but just before I toss it I run a drill bit down the barrel with the same grinder and if the bullet ever does come back, and the gun is ever recovered, the ballistics won't match. That's how thorough I am and for me only an idiot would do the work without it."

I had heard and seen my share of depraved human behavior and Frank's cold indifference to what he had done for a living sent a chill down my spine, but I had to ask him how he became a donor. I mean it was quite obvious by now that helping other people wasn't exactly a high point on his resume but I also know the hardest of people can have their reasons, and their unknown soft spots.

"Really, like most of the other things in my life, it was mechanics without emotion," he replied. He went on to describe the situation in terms of burnt toast which completely perplexed me but he was really good at describing and explaining, I assumed from his years as a teacher.

"You see I, as a human being, am very much like when you sit down to breakfast and you see the bread has been over toasted, burnt if you will. You have your coffee, delicious, hot and stimulating. You have your eggs, scrambled, perhaps over easy, but tasty just the same. Usually you have your hash browns or home fries, I like mine with onions but the meal is never the same without potatoes. Most people have meat, bacon, ham, sausage, or down here sometimes fried chicken, but most pick a side of meat to go with the breakfast. I don't.

Coming from a family with heart issues and high blood pressure I've always watched my saturated fats. Kind of a joke now seeing the way I went out. If I'd have known that I was going to die from an aneurism of all things I'd have eaten bacon, sausage, and steak for every fucking meal, but such is life. Anyway, most people also typically include a bread option of some kind.

"Being in the south obviously biscuits are a standard, I never cared for them due to texture but I know a lot of folks love them. I usually choose toast, rye to be exact, and there is nothing worse than having your meal come, hot and fresh, and they burned the god-damned toast. You can scrape it 'til its thin as a cracker but somehow it still tastes burnt. You can cover it in butter or honey, but that nasty burnt taste will not go away.

You can send it back for sure but now you're stuck waiting to eat because you cannot eat a proper ratio of bites without some sort of bread to balance it all out. It just doesn't work.

Now with me, realize that I look good physically, I certainly look very good on paper and at cursory inspection I pass any test that your basic human has for the whole good or bad thing. After all I teach kids for a living, but no one knew of my side gig. If they did all the awards and successful students in the world wouldn't change shit. I'd still be burnt toast with no honest remedy but to throw it out and wait for un-burnt toast to show up.

That's just life and I was always fine with it but I figured on the way out maybe I could help someone who wasn't like me to live a little longer," as I heard him sigh.

After listening to his explanation I wasn't sure what to think.

It sounded fairly plausible but at the end of the day my current riding partner had killed a bunch of people for money and I knew one thing for sure, he had just completely ruined break-fast for me for as long as it was going to take to get the whole *burnt toast* analogy out of my mind. Thanks dude.

# TAKE ME OUT OF THE GAME

I had opted for part-time for a number of reasons including trying to get Danny adopted, meeting with Nathaniel's mom occasionally, and trying to finally get my house back in order but even at 20 hours a week they kept me on the road. I ran only straight business with no extra jobs and I made it clear right off the bat but as luck would have it my time with this career was about to come to a close anyway and as with many things in this life I had no control over it.

I got the call at 3 am as the only real fear I ever had about this job came across on the text:

Sarah

Female

weight 67 lbs

D/O/B ******

Children's Hospital

New Orleans

What is your ETA?

Damn it! This girl was only ten years old and I had never had a child client. I had talked about it before with a few of the other operators and the consensus was that if you have one you either get through it and it doesn't affect you or consider yourself done. To me you'd need to have just a tiny bit of socio-pathic tendencies for it *not* to bother you but maybe that's being judgmental. Either way I was about to get tested and I took a breath as I texted back my ETA and started my truck.

When I got there security had me park out front which was very unusual. Anytime you moved a client from one point to another decorum and a tad of security was basic protocol so it was always somewhat covert. We parked by the loading docks out back, sometimes by a remote out building where the morgue was, but never through the front entrance. Parking our front? WTF, do they want me to shoot off fireworks too?

They escorted me with my gurney up to the fourth floor and on the way I asked why this wasn't being done in the morgue where it always is done? The stocky guard kind of shrugged and said, "the little girl just died an hour ago bro and they haven't wanted to move her I guess," as the elevator doors opened. I wheeled out with my clipboard resting on the gurney and I could see that the skeleton shift of three nurses all sobbing behind the nurse's counter.

Great, this is going to fucking suck, I thought, little did I know at that time just how much. I gave my introduction to the supervisor, showed my ID and the clearance for transportation and through tears she pointed to a room across the hall, low lights on and four people visible through the thin curtains.

"The family is still here?" I blurted out in measured exasperation. Normally I can keep it all cool but this was like walking into a weed whacker with boxer shorts on, I knew I'd survive but it was going to hurt like a motherfucker before I did. I paused as I both got my shit together and came up with a plan to handle talking with a family that I was about to take their daughter, sister, or aunt away from while she was still closer to being alive than she was dead. It's odd the stuff that flies through your head under times of great stress but in a nano-second I thought to myself that right now if someone had offered me walking into this room, or walking into a bar full of outlaw bikers with the promise of getting pounded with a bat, I'd have chosen the bat. As I taped gently on the glass a quiet voice told me to come in. Rolling my gurney in ahead of me I figured out the pecking order and reached my hand out to shake the father's as I offered my sincere condolences. Mom had already been taken home by a family member and an uncle and two neighbors were standing watch over the fallen angel as I nodded my head at the three of them. They didn't nod back but I couldn't blame them. If I was in their shoes I would have had a very hard time not telling me to get the fuck out of the room even though we all knew this young girl's death would mean that several other kids might live. It just was what it was, and it fucking sucked, but I had a job to do as I wheeled my gurney up along the tiny girls hospital bed and lowered the deck to the proper level. As I put on my latex gloves I gently moved her tiny body over onto my cart and after asking everyone in the room if it was okay to proceed, zipped her up in the grey plastic that would wrap her and keep her safe on her last physical journey. I shook everyone's hand, had the father sign off where he needed to, and into the night I went with my precious cargo.

I hadn't gotten to the first stop sign when I heard a giggle beside me as a beautiful pink vapor began to form into the shape of a blond-haired little girl.

"What's your name? I'm Sarah," were the beginning words of the last conversation I would ever have with the other side. I told her my name and asked her if she was okay, which in retrospect was such an amateur response from someone who had done this as many times as I had.

"I'm fine, it's a beautiful day and I am so happy. I haven't figured out something though, why can I see everyone in my life and why are they all crying?"

I swear to God I almost lost control of the truck over the emotion this sent up in me as inside I frantically tried to consider how I was going to talk to this girl and how was I going to explain it to her. Fortunately, I didn't have to as she answered her own question. I assumed that their spiritual being evolved at a pace unimaginable by those of us still alive and right then I was grateful for it.

"Now I'm not happy," she whispered. "I know this had to happen, it's just nature's plan except I can feel the pain of everyone that loved me and its growing, and it hurts me to see them sad."

We allowed a silence to take hold as the insecurity of both of our spirits sorted itself out. After a few minutes I told her that I had a little girl that I lost and it still hurts, but that if she was going to be in pain I wouldn't have wanted her to suffer here on earth.

"Her name was Chloe and I think about her every day."

"I know," Sara quietly said, "she said to tell you she thinks of you too."

One of the small gifts I got from my spiritual friends I thought, and brother did I appreciate it as I asked her to continue.

"I've got two sisters, one brother, a barn cat, and a mom who's a great cook and reads to me every night. My dad drives a cement truck and works a lot but he's super funny and always gets us kids laughing. My mom isn't always so sure about his humor but I can tell she really loves him and her favorite place to be is in our house, but not now. I can see our house and all the animals. We have cows, chickens, pigs and an old grey dog who doesn't listen to anyone but my mom. I think it's because she feeds him. She doesn't know I know it but she feeds him extra scraps and treats even though she thinks my dad will get irritated and say she going to make the dog fat. There's the fort that my brother and my dad built last year. I remember how proud my brother was that day and at night when mom served supper my dad's chest stuck out like a Christmas turkey. Now I see my brother sitting out in the fort and he's crying. I see my dad driving his cement truck but the radio is off and he is just looking off into the horizon with a blank stare. I see my mom sitting in the living room brushing one of my sister's hair while the other one is curled up on the couch in that old purple throw my grandmother made. Her face is very pale, her face is never pale. I'm not sure if we have emotions up here but seeing them hurt I feel very guilty. I don't want them to hurt. Is it my fault?"

Now, finally my time as a dad might become of some use again as I asked if, with what I had seen and learned in my life, I could answer her.

"Yes, please," she said.

"First off it is absolutely not your fault," I told her. "We are all going to have our time here on earth to do what we are intended to do but then the time is over and we have to go. I've carried many, many different people and everyone had a different purpose for being here. It sounds like you and your family gave each other a lot of love and one thing I know for sure is that we all need it to get through our lives but so many people don't have enough of it and sometimes it turns into something else not so good, but that's another story and you are too innocent to hear it.

As a human my mind tells me that you are far too young to have had to leave already but the universe has its own plan and we can only try to do the best with what time we have. I don't know why you had to go so young but it sounds like while you were here you gave those around you a love as bright as a summer sun and that will help them to get through the clouds that

273

they find themselves in now, but again, it is in no way your fault and I know that for me and your parents they would not want you to feel that it was.

Sometimes bad things happen to really good people and I've learned that the only thing we can do is to try and make sure that the love we got from those who we loved gets passed on to the rest of the world sill here on earth."

I asked Sara if it made sense and she said that it did. She told me more about her life and much of what she shared reminded me of my own childhood and it brought me back to a level of innocence I had not known in a long time. We both laughed as we talked about her aunt that talks too much, acknowledging between us that every family has one, family suppers and all the home cooked food and the smells that went with it. She said her mom made the best pies in the county and baked 20 or more every year to give to the local 4-H so they could raise money.

I said, "I'll bet there the best damn pies anyone's ever tasted," apologizing after for having cussed.

"It's okay, my dad swears sometimes, but he works a lot and I know he gets tired and frustrated. I think me being gone is going to hurt him the most. My mom loved us for sure but me and my dad had a different connection than the rest of them. I kind of knew it while I was alive but here now I see it more clearly. We had an emotional energy and a vision of life that was different than everyone around us and now I am gone. How is he going to fix himself?"

I told her more about how I had dealt with my daughter passing, trying to minimize the drinking part but not wanting to lie either, summing it up to the end fact that every one of us handles it differently.

"Your dad has your mother and your sisters and brother to

keep him propped up. That's the biggest thing most of us need when death happens. That is what makes the difference for most I think."

"What about you?" she asked.

I was a little ashamed at the inquiry but the truth was that I, and I alone, had made the choice to deal with my situation in the past the way I had. I could have reached out to get help but maybe I was just too stubborn or stoic, and I had lain my table the way I did. I told her about Jesse and how he helped me to get back in the saddle.

"It sounds like he had more pain than a boy that young should have had," Sara said and I agreed but also reiterated that it was somehow the universes plan and that even in death my friend Jesse was appreciative of what he had enjoyed on earth.

"He was a better friend to me in the few hours we had than most people I'd ever known and he was raised rough but he didn't let it break him and he didn't let it make him bitter or keep him from caring about others. I guess that's also part of the lesson. I think you would have liked him, I know he would have liked you."

I hadn't read Sara's paperwork but from what I'd had seen when I first walked in to the hospital room I knew she had endured some type of trauma that someone her age should not have had to. I figured it was cancer or a disease that required continual invasive and disruptive treatment, and if I was her family I would have asked to let her go so she could find peace but it was not my girl and not my call. When we got to the harvest center she thanked me for talking to her and told me she hoped I could be happy in my life.

"You're a nice person and you deserve it" she said.

I quieted my own thoughts as inside I admitted that this wasn't always the case but I was trying to get back to being the man she thought I was.

"You just took a detour. Even at my age I know sometimes people do that, but what matters isn't so much of where you were, but where you are now. Does that make sense?"

I chuckled a little at this as I pondered Sarah's wisdom and said, "the student becomes the teacher," as I watched the big garage door to the harvest center raise up.

I went home that day with a sense of peace I had not had in too long. Still a little sad over seeing a child so young pass away but happy, if you can call it that, that she was no longer in suffering from whatever disease the universe had put on her. That night as I sat down to eat dinner I turned on the local news and after a few minutes the story was about the little girl that had been taken off life support earlier that day. The news anchor explained how she had been in a really bad auto accident several months ago and her family had been forced to finally stop the machines from keeping her alive. I sat there by myself, numb for at least 20 minutes, as my silver cloud of peace and acceptance regarding her death shattered into a million pieces. It's hard to explain but I had formed my own emotional insurance to the situation, painting it in a picture that would make it be okay, but now it just wasn't. Sure, we had a great, positive conversation but she was still dead, and she was still too fucking young to be dead. In my head I had conjured my own letter of acceptance about the situation that I felt I could live with but now I had lost my illusions and I knew I could never transport another client ever again.

# WHAT ROAD TO TAKE NOW

After Sara my mind wasn't right for several weeks. I gave no notice to my new employer, I just quit with no explanation as I turned in my badge, security card and uniforms. I found the ghosts of the past dancing in my head again and not in a kind way. I questioned everything, waking up several times each night with the thoughts of this poor decision or that. For about two months it seems like every single thing I'd ever fucked up in my life or even some shit that I borrowed as my own came calling in the dark hours of the night. I found myself diving way back into my days as a kid, questioning the way I'd treated ex-girlfriends, challenging all of the major decisions I ever made about the future, even going so far as to ponder my influence and impact on other people lives when in reality there was no way I had made any difference one way or the other but that was something a *sane* person would quickly acknowledge. I just wasn't sane right now.

Kata knew something was amiss and I reluctantly agreed to spend some time with her if nothing more than to placate her and limit her phone calls. I felt like a dick, knowing that the things she had endured made what I had seen look like fucking Disneyland but as I've said before our troubles are our own and when you are neck deep in shit you don't look over the edge of the shit pool to look for sunshine. Still I appreciated what she was trying to do and she agreed with me that seeing a child dead was never an easy thing to process but she was at peace and that was something I could build on, if I chose to. It took a while but eventually I was able to settle my head and look to move forward in life again. I had financial security from saving the majority of my salary and what the professor intended for me, even with my plans to disperse most of the money from Carlo to a few people in need I had plenty of options on what to do next.

Now that my thoughts were clear I dreamed about what I might do if I could do anything I wanted. Move to Key West and buy a bar or start a fishing charter, move out west and open a small cafe or coffee shop in one of the fancy ski resort towns, the only thing that wasn't a consideration was moving anywhere back in the Midwest or the east coast. I had changed my way of looking at life and had begun to thoroughly embrace the easy living of the warmer weather or maybe the live and let live flow of Colorado, Montana or Oregon. I loved New Orleans, I truly did and at some point I'd love to come back but for now I needed to spread my wings and make some new memories someplace else, doing something else. I was meeting Kata at a little barbeque shack about a mile east of the Quarter and with the sun now down I was enjoying the solitude and the warm breeze coming down the way as I walked along without a care in the world. I don't recall what I was thinking about as I got within 50 feet of the restaurant's front door but just as I did a car parked on the street in front of me turned on their headlights and I heard two gunshots behind me. As I turned around I didn't realize I was the target and watched curiously as a non-descript figure in a dark coat and hat walked briskly away in the other direction and then I felt the blood begin to flow down my back.

I'd been shot twice, one bullet entering my right lung, the other missing my heart by merely an inch but the people inside, including my friend, had heard the shots and came out to see what was going on. I remember an off-duty cop standing over me, waving his pistol around as he surveyed the area for the shooter. I remember Kata telling me to stay awake and that help was on the way, and then I don't remember anything as I drifted off.

I wasn't sure if I had died or not. I had heard plenty of expert testimony over the years on the subject but still I was inconclusive. I felt no pain so maybe I *was* dead as I had a show of emotions, visions, and past loved ones swirling about in what was now my reality. It reminded me a little of a Grateful Dead show but the main stage was in the middle of a circus with people and machines flying overhead and music, beautiful, exotic music that I couldn't recognize played from every direction. I don't know maybe I died and came back, but I did see my daughter and while it seemed like only a minute it also seemed like it would never stop as our spirits connected without an audible word having ever been spoken. I knew, finally, that she was alright and with that I was ready to go on to the next world but it was not to be and after a few days I woke up in the intensive care ward with only the hum and beep of the machines to welcome me back.

Finally, a nurse came in and cleared a few things up for me as she asked if I was thirsty. Man was I but all they could give me for now were ice-chips. I'd have given my left leg for a glass of iced tea or a margarita but that would have to wait as things started coming back to me and my pain announced itself with a bang. When I was ready the police wanted to talk to me which was fine but between the warm embrace of the morphine and self-preservation I wasn't going to be a very reliable source. I knew it had to have been either one of Carlo's people or Marge's and just as soon as I could leave I was getting the hell out of dodge and I wasn't about to complicate it with the possibility of becoming a witness in some drawn out trial. Either way I knew they could both get to me again and I wasn't sticking around any longer than I had to and give them another shot. I was on day seven of my hospital stay when I got an unexpected visitor. Carlo walked in, dressed in a thousand-dollar pair of wool slacks and a cardigan sweater. Even with the temperature being in the 80s his heart problem kept him cold all of the time but he wore it well I'll give him that. I didn't figure him to pull out a gun and finish me off in a well-lit, public place, but you just never know as he asked to sit.

Leaning back into the vinyl cushioned chair he looked as casual as a man getting ready to watch a movie, not an ounce of caution or malice on his face and for a minute or so he said nothing as I assumed he was preparing the speech.

"I want you to know that I don't hold any anger towards you. My family and my people do, but I don't. You have my word on that."

That wasn't the words I expected but this wasn't a tea party and I knew I still had a button on my back so I wasn't going to let my guard down as I asked him directly, "why are you here?"

He paused and I assumed it was just the way he had been molded as a person in his position that needed to ponder everything said to him and always calculate the impact of the conversation but, crossing one leg over the other, he continued.

"I did not know they were going to kill a young man to get me a heart. You may believe me, you may not, but the one thing I keep in this world is my honor and with it, my word. I have no issue with life being taken, it is often simply a part of our business, but we have certain codes that we live by and I did not give the order, nor would I if I had known about it. Again, you can believe me or perhaps not, we both know my days are limited so I won't waste the time for deception or false pretense."

I still didn't know why he was there and as he stood he said, "I just wanted to shake your hand," as he walked up to my bedside and offered me his manicured palm.

"You had to have known the danger you placed yourself in and for some odd reason, I'm guessing your own set of rules, you did what you did. My people want to give you a horrible death for your thievery, I however, respect courage and cunning even when it comes in the oddest of forms." He shook my hand firmly, a look of acceptance in his green eyes as he turned away.

Glancing in my direction one more time before leaving he wished me well and informed me that given the circumstances I wouldn't be receiving the bonus. He pursed his lips firmly into a grin and walked out.

# LET ME TELL YOU ABOUT THE SPECIAL

They kept me in the hospital another week but I'm told I healed rather quickly and was released. Marie insisted I stay with them and even though my place was back to being in livable conditions I must admit the company was something that I couldn't refuse. I'd never had anyone try to kill me, let alone been in many fights so the protection of being among friends as I tried to sort this out felt good. They didn't expect me to do any work but I got restless and could do some easy stuff like bussing tables and seating people so the following Monday I began working with them again. It was a slow day and I sat down in one of the back booths to eat a little. I had a cup of chicory coffee, some biscuits and strawberry jam in front of me when I got a surprise visitor.

"May I sit?" came the voice of Willow.

Smiling I said sure as I motioned her across from me in the worn but colorful booth. Marie approached and brought her a coffee and water, setting a menu in front of her. Smiling but shaking her head Willow moved the menu to the side and said, "I won't be staying long."

Marie smiled back and said that she would just leave the menu in case Willow changed her mind and she left us to our conversation. I wasn't sure why Willow had visited. I wasn't really sure how she even knew how to find me in the first place but that question was quickly and uncomfortably answered as she kept one hand under the table and began to speak.

"You're an easy man to find unfortunately, not so easy to kill. I had hoped to be in Houston already getting ready to pay my respects to my lover, the man you took from me with your greed, but that can wait for now."

I was dumbfounded, WTF my main thought as even with the pain killers flowing through my blood it all came to me quite clearly.

"You and Carlo?" I said with what must have been a deer in the headlights look in my eyes.

"Yes, we met ten years ago," she answered. "He was on a business trip to Peru and we met at a little cafe one afternoon. I had begun my real work of importing stolen artifacts and he was an unexpected but very valuable partner to my success. We tried to keep it business but that quickly fell away as the wine, the high mountain air and our mutual interest in ancient things had us become lovers rather quickly. He was a gentleman in bed but firm with his desires and not only did it turn me on I also had the same penchant for pain and dominance that he enjoyed. He was a king among men and unique in so many ways. He made it clear straight away that it could never become anything more and I accepted it for what it was. He was a brilliant business man and our clientele grew quickly. Supply was never an issue and with his family's shipping business transportation wasn't much of a challenge either. At first, he came up every month, delivering the goods in person and always following up with a three-day sexual excursion at one of the city's finest hotels. We ordered room service and spilled the finest wine as we were like two debaucherous children in a sensual Disneyland without boundaries. After a while it calmed considerable as I knew it had to but two or three times each year he visited and while our trysts became more sedate our mutual affection grew. It wasn't love by any realistic measure, but it was the closest thing to it I'd ever seen and I was happy.

Then a year ago, during his last visit, I noticed his enthusiasm had dwindled. I thought that perhaps he was losing interest or had met someone else but he assured me neither was the case. As we lay in bed he held my hand and told me about his failing heart. I was devastated but he assured me he had the money and means to address it and that he didn't want me to worry. I was still worried but I trusted him, I always trusted him, and we spent the rest of that weekend just enjoying each other's company. We talked about art and life, I shared with him for the very first time about my father and he listened. He never offered advice unless I asked and he knew that I was just looking for someone to understand. He did. We took a car to the zoo and gardens and as we walked we were as little children might be, only soaking in the beauty around us and not considering anything past the moment. Like I said it was the closest thing to love I had known in my life. He told me when you came to visit. He described you as a competent and honest man. He trusted you with his life. I never would have. He resisted giving me your name out of obvious discretion but when you double crossed him he knew his time was getting more precarious and I was able to get it out of him. He told me that for some odd reason he didn't hold it against you but he never explained why. He died yesterday. I'm sure you didn't know it and I'm just as sure that you didn't care, but I do and I am here to do what he wouldn't," as she pulled the arm she had kept under the table into view, a 38 semi -automatic pistol pointed directly at my stomach.

She had balls I'll give her that, but we were in the back and being the only customers no one was going be coming to my rescue or at least that's what I thought as I watched her eyes shift to someone walking up behind me and tucking the gun back under the table I heard Marie's cheery voice say, "did you happen to change your mind?"

I sensed someone else come up and as I tilted my head to the right I saw Mango standing right next to the booth as he said, "why the hell didn't you introduce your friend?" reaching his hand out to shake Willow's hand.

She glared over the table at me and glanced downward as she wanted to acknowledge the weapon still trained on my abdomen but then she looked up at the wiry one-armed man and smiled as she said, "we aren't actually friends, just acquaintances," offering nothing more cordial than that.

Quicker than I could have imagined Marie said, "well at least let me tell you about our specials," as Mango grabbed me hard by my shirt and pulled me straight sideways out of the booth, a nano second later Marie leveling the hidden revolver she had on her waitress tray straight at Willow and without any further talk putting a .38 bullet right between her eyes. Willow managed to get one round off but it hit the red vinyl covered cushion of the back rest and with no other customers to hear the commotion my friends quickly went into action. Marie wrapped a large dish towel around the dead woman's head to contain the blood and Mango rushed around to lock all of the doors and put the closed sign out.

I told them what had been explained to me but neither of them seemed too enlightened by it. Unbeknownst to me the little bar-restaurant had several points throughout it for covert observation of its clients and they had both seen and heard what had transpired at our little booth without ever tipping their hand. They would explain later that during the civil war many of the local pubs had a similar set-up to allow random spying. I was never much of a history buff but I was damn glad for it this time and after downing a couple shots to calm my nerves we began to discuss the what next part. All that mattered was that a friend of theirs was in dire harm and they did what they had to for my safety. No frills, no questions asked, but now we had a body to deal with. Mango offered to make her disappear and I was confident in his ability but I was never much on disrespecting the dead and I couldn't really fault her for wanting to kill me. This, combined with the fact that her father had been a very good friend of mine-had gotten my butt out of that legal jam and I was now the executor of his estate lead me to an easy choice.

We wrapped her up securely in a large drop cloth they had in back. When the coast was clear Mango backed his white ford van into the alley next to us and after double checking once more we loaded Willows remains into the back. New Orleans has its share of less than desirable places to frequent and that night after the sun had gone down he dropped her behind a vacant warehouse that he knew had local drug traffic, pulled the cash and credit cards out of her purse, and from a local pay phone, made an anonymous call to the local precinct about a possible dead person laying in an alley. I waited a few days and then under the guise of stopping by for a chat, dropped in to her coffee shop. The woman there had seen me come in before so it didn't set off any alarms as they informed me of her unfortunate demise. Making the appropriate gestures and comments of sympathy I explained that I was the executor of her father's estate and if no prior arrangements or executors were already in place, I would be happy to handle the burial, including expenses. I knew none were in place and the man-ager readily accepted my offer as I'm sure she didn't want to do it herself no matter how close they might have been. It was a bit surreal having to view the body and plan a service for a per-son who had wanted to trade places with me but sometimes that's life. By now you all know I've seen some strange shit and all I can say is that truth is many times stranger than fiction. With that, I wrote the check to have her buried right next to her father and coordinated with a friend of hers to dress her in a lavender and sun flower dress that had apparently been her favorite. I drove over to Cafe Du Monde and ordered a cafe au lait-no donuts, as I watched the crowds stroll by and pondered if, when I died, it would play out that I too was buried beside my own daughter. Life is uncertain, and at the same time if it mattered to me that much I could easily pre-arrange it, but I had not and I did not. I missed her still every day but I wasn't ready for the dirt nap just yet. Funny how getting shot will make you reevaluate things like that.

I didn't attend the funeral nor the burial. I may be a hustler from time to time but I am not a hypocrite and a week later after the dust had settled I drove out with a spring bouquet and a fifth of cognac. It was only a $50 bottle and even with money no option I knew that the Prof would have rolled over if I poured anything more costly on to his grave. I placed the flowers by his daughter's headstone, said a few words that didn't mean shit, and walked back to my car. I missed my friend but people die and as I still remembered from Jesse I was among the living and I needed to respect that.

# A LITTLE FAITH
# COMES BACK

The following week I got a call from Ernie's mom. She was in her 70's and dealing with health issues so raising a small child had her both concerned and worried. I stopped over the next afternoon and when she asked about my bandages and my arm in a sling I lied and told her it was a work injury. After pouring coffee out of one of those old G.E. electric percolators she began catching me up on the Danny situation. Watching the small boy play in the living room I could only hope his dad was watching and could see that he was happy and safe but I knew the old woman was spot on with her concerns. I asked about other family and I knew there was an aunt but it turned out she was a crack head with plenty on her plate already just keeping her shit together. They had some family up north but as is the case with many families they had fallen distant over the years and it wasn't like you could just make a long distance phone call and ask hey, can you take in a kid? The relations they had in the area were either incapable for one reason or another or still held a grudge over Ernie's drug problem and wouldn't even take the call let alone consider any request. I thought that was kind of fucked up. I mean it wasn't Danny's fault, but another thing I knew full well was that people, especially those closest to you, could be real dick-heads when you needed them the most and this little boy didn't have the luxury of us making a bad choice and fucking up his future just to find a solution convenient to us. My thoughts went back to Mango and Marie.

I was smacking myself at first, having taken so long to think of it, but that stuff they gave me for pain was still making me fuzzy as a Teletubby and as I watched Danny roll a little choo-choo train across the carpet I broached the subject with his grandma. I told her a little about them, Mango a war vet, Marie from a large southern family but unable to have kids of her own. As she sipped her coffee I could see her nodding in agreement as I laid out my plan. They were financially stable and I would be adding to it from the cash I'd taken in the Carlo deal but the biggest thing, the most important thing, was that I knew they would always love that boy as their own. I asked if they could come out to meet her and her grandson and she could size them up for herself and not be forced to just take my word on any of it. She agreed and we set it up for that coming Friday. When Friday came Mango and Marie showed up five minutes early and with her flowered dress and stuffed teddy bear she looked like a hallmark mom if I ever saw one. I knew Danny's grandma felt it too as she visibly relaxed within minutes of meeting them both. Grandma, Mango and me sat in the kitchen drinking iced tea and eating Johnny cakes with fresh blackberry jam that Marie had made as the jubilant mom to be played with Danny on the carpet in the other room.

It didn't take much, I knew it wouldn't, and with a handshake and then a hug, the arrangement was made an hour later. I told grandma that I would handle and pay for all of the legal expenses and when Mango protested I just put up my hand and told him, "I got this, and it is absolutely my pleasure."

I'd have done it even if they hadn't saved my ass but with that in consideration and plenty of cash in my account I wasn't taking no for an answer. I also told one more little lie as I told Grandma that they had caught the guy who killed her son and there would be a settlement coming soon to help her in her golden years. I started cutting her a check the next month from the fake trust I had set up and while I didn't know how many years the old girl still had in her I knew she would live them in comfort without having to worry about surviving off social security.

I spent quite a bit of time with the new parents over the next few months as they both doted on the boy, an obvious void having been filed in their hearts and truth be told, mine too. Mango was a heck of a fisherman and he had a nice little flat-boat that he took his son and me out on many mornings before heading into the bar. I was still recovering from my wounds but getting stronger and I always cleaned the fish that we brought back so Mango could have time with Danny.

One day after supper, when I thought it would be received the right way, I shared with them both my current bank account and what I intended to do with it. I told them only what they needed to know about how I got the cash, not wanting to put anyone else in possible jeopardy from knowing things they shouldn't have. Like me, no one had ever given them anything in this life and I wanted to change a few things in their future as I showed them the other trust I had set up for them and their young son. With what I had managed to save, what the Prof had insisted I accept as payment for my continued services along with the Carlo cash I was able to quite comfortably set up trusts for them, Danny's grandma, Kata's medical bills, and a college fund for both my nephew and my niece and never need to haul another body ever again.

# THE GIFT

For the first time in my life I wasn't worrying about the future. I caught up on my painting, visited a bunch of local art galleries and small mom and pop pubs as I made a few new friends along the way. I slept in an hour later than usual each day as I was still recovering from the gun shots but inside, I felt better, more at peace if you will, than I could ever recall. With it came a clarity also new to me. I pondered my past in the afternoons as I either sat for coffee or enjoyed a leisurely southern lunch, smiling to myself at the amazing and curious people I now considered friends. My life currently reflected almost nothing of my life before and that was okay. Change is a constant whether we want it or not and for me it was more forced than I'd have ever accepted with the old me, but I was grateful for it now. I wasn't sure what the rest of my life would look like but I knew I would be the one writing the script. Sure, the money would help but to say I never had options before it would have been a cop-out on my part. Even going back to my developing years, I had always been a kind of meal in the box type. I knew I got that from my folks and with no disrespect to them the wisdom and experience of my later years clearly shown it. How many times do we find ourselves in the supposedly *safe* places in life where we wake up every day telling ourselves we are in a good spot, life is good, and this is where we wanted to be-maybe just because it's what every other dead soul around us had chosen to do. More often than not our choices turn out to be mundane and crippling to the spirit and they damn sure aren't safe, but I get it. I did it too.

I lived a boring, impassionate life partly out of security but also from insecurity on my part. I wanted, no, I needed to appear a certain way to the people around me. Thinking back, I woke up every day just wanting to look in that mirror and be okay with what I saw even if the fake ass smile, the polyester shirt and the white picket fence out front never had fit who I really was. Jesse brought part of it out but inside, hidden from popular opinion, I was always a rocker and a bit of a deviant but not in a harmful way. I thought back to an Aunt Christy I had growing up and while she may have been an alcoholic she was an honest one. She had her demons for sure but she owned them and I'm convinced that every morning when she woke up, whiskey still on her breath and a new man snoring next to her, she knew exactly who she was. She was the black sheep for sure but she kept her wool shiny, dancing when she felt it, saying the shit everyone around her was thinking but didn't have the nerve to let out. Inside of me she had always been one of my heroes and until now I had never known why. Just then my phone rang and on the other end was my buddy Jerry inviting me out for another little get together. I had plans with a local gal friend but he told me to bring her along because they had a little surprise for me and I would not want to miss it. I thought to myself that the old version of me might have found an excuse not to go but the new me was like a teenager with thoughts of great food and beer swirling about as I chuckled at his persistence but agreed to go just the same. I picked up flowers for Mrs. Jerry and hoped my date wouldn't be too shocked by their southern charm but if she was she'd need to figure it out. These people had come to be like family to me and besides I could always find a new cuddle buddy.

We rolled up to pretty much the scene I'd expected and other than a big dual-axel Ford pickup with Georgia plates it was going to be just another Jerry Q as he liked to call them. I shook hands with a few people I had met before, got a big old bear hug from my friend and gave the flowers to his misses who demanded to meet my guest and quickly ushered her off to meet the others as Jerry grabbed an un-cracked fifth of bourbon and motioned me to follow him. He had several outbuildings on his farm and the furthest back was an old chicken shack he had renovated into the poker room/man cave. As we walked in I saw two tanned and leathered men, both over 200 pounds and serious looking, sitting at the bar well on their way to getting a bona fide whiskey drunk. I knew I was safe here but they still made the hair on my back go up a tad as they were introduced as Jerry's cousins from the east coast. I shook their hands and they both had the grip of someone who lived a life of hard work without a cushion for mistakes. Eldon and Cleo were Jerry's cousins on his momma side and they had driven down from Georgia last night for what they were told was a very special occasion. I didn't gather these fellows to be the black tie and cuff links crew and I had no idea what the occasion was but Eldon began to tell me a little story as he poured tumblers of that good whiskey for all of us.

"I'm a fisherman, just like our daddy, me and Cleo here been running nets off the Georgia coast as far back as my memory serves me. We were both raised with the good book and a hard hand and we live right, but sometimes this life lays out some things for you that don't quite seem fair," nodding over to Jerry who took a sip and nodded back.

"My cousin told me that's something you can relate to," as I glanced over at my friend, took a cautious sip, and agreed.

"Well a few years back my little brother here and his family were on their way home from one of them drive-in movie theatres. His wife June and their two boys had just lit up with excitement when papa told them they were all gonna have themselves a night out. They got a letter in the mail that day that their oldest boy had gotten accepted to the biggest college in the state and Cleo was beside himself knowing that one of his was going to get a college education. His wife packed a cooler with ham sandwiches, potato salad, cokes, beer, and a tray of fresh baked chocolate chip cookies and they loaded up for a night of family fun. They could have afforded the stuff they sold at the concession but we weren't raised as fool's with our money and besides the stuff June made was way better than that junk that came in a greasy cardboard container. They had themselves a time that night *yes sir*, but on the way home, just a mile from their house, a damn drunk rolled through the red light at over 60 miles an hour and almost cut their mini-van in half.

Cleo and June both had some damage but thank the lord above their youngest boy walked away without a scratch. It wasn't the same for their son Carter. The fire department came and had to cut him out with them jaws of life. According to the sheriff and the doctors the boy should have died. The only thing that saved him was the grit in his guts and his guardian angels above but the boy who had just received a scholarship to play linebacker at Georgia state the next fall would never again be playing football, let alone walk. They had that driver dead to rights but wouldn't you know it he got the judge to throw out the blood test on some chain of custody garbage and the charges were dropped down to reckless driving-causing a fatality. That old boy got himself a $2,500 fine, 100 hours of community service that he paid someone else to do and six months probation. He didn't even lose his license or get a alcohol breathalyzer put in his car if you can believe that.

The family filed a lawsuit and were quickly approached by some hot-shot attorney from Atlanta who offered to pay all medical expenses, now and in the future, and write them a check that had more zeroes in it than a flight of Japanese fighter pilots. He told them in a very politically correct way that they'd be fools to refuse as his firm had been ordered to make the offer but also ordered to make their lives hell if they refused. As it turns out he was a local fella who had knew my family when he was just a boy and even though he now got his paychecks signed by the devil he tried to give them the real world end of it as nice as he could. He wasn't telling them anything they didn't already know. Poor uneducated people have always gotten rolled over by the rich and they always would, but with the money they could at least take care of their family a little better and Carter could still go to college.

They took the pay-off but it always bothered my brother, as it should. Well wouldn't you know it that drunk driver had a place down here where he and his crooked family came for vacation once the snow was flying up north. He's been coming here since he was a teenager and he had a rap sheet to go right along with it, but his family's money always got him out of trouble. That old boy loved to party and chase the girls but the only thing he loved more was chasing fish and wouldn't you know it just last year he phoned me up to rent my boat for a charter. You'd have figured he'd recognize the last same of the people that had sued him but I don't truly believe he'd ever gave a damn enough to even ask. He rented us out several times that first year and we hit the fish hard, the day always ending with him wanting a bunch of pictures of his catch and handing us each a couple hundred bucks in tip. My brother had just returned to work the last run and I swear he was going to throw that fella right off the boat when we got a few miles out to sea but we were raised by the good book and as much as we truly wanted to, we just couldn't kill him.

This year he came back down and wanted to rent us out again, catching a trophy tuna on the first charter and getting his name and a picture with the fish hung proudly in the waterfront fishing store. My cousin Jerry here just happened to come up the next week and once he saw that dude's name he told us about how something similar had happened to your family, and very possibly by the same man. Got to give Jerry credit, he ain't afraid of killing a man, but he does his research and once he confirmed the facts the rest just needed to happen."

I thought back to a few months prior and Jerry had asked me what the man's name was who killed my daughter in that accident. I didn't think much about it at the time, I had no reason to, but now I realized why he asked. We were having fun drinking and such and no disrespect to my daughter, but I had been forced to put the past in the past and that is exactly where I intended it to remain. I had no idea what Jerry now knew and in a way I'm glad I didn't. What would I have done? Gone over and killed the man? I'm not sure I have it in me. I'd have wanted to confront him that's for sure but what would I have said that he'd have given two shits about anyway. It was obvious that nothing inside him had changed and he was still drinking and driving and hurting people, just like he always had. I wasn't sure exactly what I was being told by the man speaking and a part of me was terrified to hear anymore but right about then Jerry started talking.

"You know bubba, me and you are friends now and I told you that day you saved my life that I always pay my debts. Then you go and get that heart for my cousin's boy so now I owe you twice. I know you told me that I didn't owe you anything for either but that just isn't the way we do thing where I come from and once I'd confirmed that the son of a bitch who crippled my cousin's son was the same trash that killed your daughter, mister I just couldn't sit on my hands anymore.

He isn't the first man I'd ever put down, and I truly hope he is the last, but I got a code that I live by and it does not allow for situations like this to go on without being rectified. I'm not sure what your thoughts are about it but it doesn't much matter now," as he tossed a driver's license on the bar, the name John Kruger lll and a smear of dried blood telling the rest of the tale.

"I went up to catch some fish with my cousins but just like Eldon said once I put two and two together I couldn't let it rest. I told them to call me when Kruger wanted to go fishing again and I didn't have to wait long. Eldon rung me up two weeks ago and told me he had been hired again by that old boy that killed your baby. They introduced me as just another helper and once I broke out a bottle of Gentlemen Jack wouldn't you know it that Yankee took to me like we'd been running together for 20 years. I sat back listening to him spout off about all his accomplishments, all the women, all the big parties and money, but I just smiled and sipped my whiskey until I couldn't see the land or another boat anymore. I helped him rig his pole and once we got him settled in the chair we got hold of his arms and zipped tied his ass to it. He didn't have any idea what to make of it all and wouldn't you know it that fool thought we were trying to rob him. At first, he went off about his daddy's lawyers and what his men would do to us all if we didn't bring him back to shore directly but once he saw the dead grey in my eyes he got the picture. He tried to protest a bit more, still not knowing who we were or what we planned. Brother, I don't usually get any pleasure out of having to handle business like this but seeing that fella about ready to shit himself gave me a rise. We let him jabber on a while longer and then first we told him about Cleo's boy. He remembered it but tried to say it wasn't his fault. With people like him nothing ever is, and then I asked him about your daughter. He didn't say a word and I could tell by the look in his eyes that he knew he was done with. He pleaded a while longer, promising money or whatever he thought might save his butt and he was still talking when I stuck that fishing knife into his right thigh.

Dude had no tolerance for pain I'll tell you that but this day had been coming for a while and I took the time I needed. Had to tie him off twice so he didn't bleed out and I have to say the look of utter terror on his once cocky face was almost as much payment as knowing he was about to become shark shit. We chummed the water with some chopped raw fish to draw in the eaters and once we untied him he could barely stand but do you know I made him stare over the side at that churning water and I grabbed him by his face as I had him look at me."

"You remember that little girl you killed, you remember that boy who can't ever walk again because of your worthless, white trash ass? Well today my friend you pay the piper," as I threw him over the side.

"I spotted a big black tip shark and some smaller ones tear right into him, he screamed but they took him under quick and all he left was a blood slick on the top of the water and that there driver's license. My kids keep telling me we're supposed to keep plastic out of the ocean so I wanted to do my part," as he grinned at the group of us.

My mind was fucking spinning now, I'd just been told in graphic detail about a murder and even if it was one that I'd wished for many times it was still a murder. Jerry could see I was shook, hell even his younger cousin was a bit off about the whole thing and his son was in a wheelchair, but at the end of the day John Kruger lll had gotten what he deserved. Jerry and his relation had become family and as they taught me in the south, family looks out for family.

Jerry cracked another bottle and we were damned sure going to need it as I heard the woman yelling about dinner being served and we all piled out of that chicken coop without another word ever being said about it.

# ONWARD AND UPWARD

I was still a bit shook for several weeks after but I had the future to focus on as I worked on getting my life more in order and thought about going back to college. I only had my associate degree and had thought about becoming a teacher for a while now. The professor was part of it but I also just wanted to help young people. I knew I didn't want to teach high school or below, no offense but Frank the hit man had sold me on leaving that alone. The thought of working with young adults that wanted to make something of themselves really appealed to me but I knew I'd need at minimum a masters and in reality a PHD to get into anywhere good. I had the advantage of not needing the paycheck but even at full time I had five or six years of hitting the books ahead of me if in fact this was the route I chose. I went to bed feeling good about the future and right before the sun came up the next morning I heard a dog bark and the trash man yelling at someone out front of my place. I threw on my robe and slippers and walked out the front door to see what all the commotion was about as the garbage dude was holding a tire iron, looking off in the distance at somebody running up the road about a hundred yards north of my place. I couldn't tell if it was a man or a woman but whoever it was they were headed anywhere but here and they were doing it as fast as their legs would carry them.

I walked over to Sam and he told me he was just pulling up to grab my trash cans when he saw somebody messing around by my car. He figured it was kids trying to steal something or just fooling around, either way he yelled at the person and they lit out without giving an introduction. I must not be as street smart as all of my recent trouble should have taught me to be but I was just going to write it off to teenager shenanigans as I thanked Sam and started walking back to the house. Thank God he was the curious type and just before I walked in he said, "hey buddy, you may want to see this."

As I turned and walked back I watched him kneeling on the driver's side and when he stood up he was holding a fairly well made pipe bomb, a spool of wire and some extra strength gorilla tape. Looking at the bomb he glanced at me and said, "whose wife are you screwing?"

That was certainly not the first thing that came to my mind, first off I wasn't screwing anyone's wife that I knew about, and second I had a couple people in mind that wanted me dead. I still had a button on my back apparently and I guessed that with the first hitter dead the job had gotten passed along to whoever was next in line. I had no idea if it was Marge or Carlo's people, hell there were a couple other possibilities on top of it but the one thing I decided right then was that my college career was going to have to wait. I needed to get gone and I needed to do it quick.

I couldn't tell anyone about it but just as soon as I got the coffee brewing I made sure my gun was loaded and I sat down to think. I had options and plenty of them, but my first reality was staying alive as I chewed on the whole situation and began to form a plan. I reached out to Jerry first. I knew I could trust him and he had a street experienced way of seeing things that I did not. We talked briefly and both agree it was better to meet in person and keep the chatter off the phone lines just in case anyone was listening in. Luckily, he was off the road for a few days and I drove straight out to his house. Once I got there he questioned me at length, taking notes as he did. New

Orleans has its share of people that could have gotten the call to take me out and he knew a few of them. Unfortunately for me Jerry didn't have anyone he could reach out to that he figured would provide useful information about my situation. I told him what Frank had shared and while he was still wrapping his head around me talking to spirits he didn't question it. The only thing he said as he shook his head was, that $30k is a heavy hit for a nobody like you with no offense intended.

"None taken," I replied.

We talked about it for a while and after weeding a few ideas out we drew up what we both considered a solid short-term exit strategy. Like any plan you want to work it would require some in-flight touching up but the basic premise gave me the first comfort I'd had since daylight. As I headed back home I called Kata and without telling her what happened explained that I had decided to relocate and wanted to meet her for dinner soon to say our goodbyes. She was sad over the phone but we both had seen enough in this world that we knew change was always inevitable and it's what you do with it that makes your life either suck or evolve. Mine had sucked long enough in the past and even with it now in question my focus was on what to do with whatever I had left of it. I got back home, packed a shaving bag and called a realtor as I poured myself a cold beer and sat at my kitchen table for what was going to be one of the last times. I drove my car to a 24-hour parking lot just outside the Quarter and after looking underneath it was fairly confident I had no tracking device but I still wasn't taking chances and switched the license plate with one that Jerry had given me. I had already pulled the battery and the S.I.M. card out of my cell and stopped at the first convenience store I happened upon as I paid cash for a cheap burner phone.

Out of precaution and on Jerry's advice I had left my watch and clothes at home, now only wearing a running suit, an old pair of running shoes and cheap sunglasses. I needed a place to stay for a few days and while I could have gone anywhere, I needed something nice but not too nice. I considered a B&B but most of them were family owned going back several generations and even the slightest chance that I could be recognized and dimed out wasn't an option. After circling the block twice, I settled on an upper mid-level hotel that had been recently purchase by a Japanese corporation and significantly upgraded. Two things I knew about the Japanese, one they were very security minded by nature and I was confident they wouldn't want anyone messing with a guest. Second, if they had just put the $30 million into renovations that the local newspaper had said they would have cameras everywhere so no one was going to try and hit me on their property. I gave the clerk my fake driver's license and credit card and giving the concierge a $50 gratuity hailed a private car for a little shopping.

First place I stopped was an outdoor store, much like Cabella's but smaller. I found a suitable hard travel case and filled it with three walking shirts, two pairs of comfortable travel slacks, two pairs of comfortable walking shoes, a G.I. style kaki boony hat, socks and boxers, two pairs of rugged sunglasses, a spool of fishing line, a marine aerosol horn, a small can of pepper spray and a small but razor sharp skinning knife with leather case. I added a few odds and ends but that was the bulk of it as once again I paid cash, leaving my old shoes and running suit in the trash can outside the dressing room. In my new attire I hailed a cab and headed to a men's hair salon he recommended. My hair was always just over shoulder length but today that was about to change as I had the girl crop it tight and bleach it three shades lighter than it had ever been. Getting back to my hotel I shaved my beard up leaving only a short narrow mustache and once I was satisfied with my new look I arranged to meet Kata for dinner at a local crab shack.

I was already there when she arrived, and she looked good. Not in a sexual way, again it was never like that with her, but she looked healthy and as a friend that made me happy. I knew I could trust her and I shared my little pipe bomb experience. No stranger to violence or the people who create it she wasn't stirred but she was concerned for me and she confided, for herself as well, that she was worried. As of late she had noticed strangers sticking around too long and while she was not a hundred percent sure she was being watched she was fairly confident of the possibility. We ate and drank very light, both now absorbing the change in our situations as we discussed what we could do to protect her. For me the first thing was to remove the target. If whoever was following her didn't know where she was she would be much harder to hit. She had a new boss at the clinic and the woman was an absolute bitch, only looking at her position of director as another step in climbing the corporate ladder. She treated her employees with disrespect and their clients with obvious distain. Kata did not enjoy the job as she once had and I was glad to hear it as she continued.

As of late she had been in contact with a cousin back in Croatia and I could see in her eyes the longing for home as she caught me up on things back in her country. The war had taken its toll and there was a great need for medical care in the underserved areas which included more of the country than not. My friend was now a certified P.A. and while not quite a doctor she could do almost everything a doctor could. It was obvious where her heart was and I knew she cared about people. As she went on a plan began to grow in my head. After she finished, I asked her what she would do if I could arrange for her to open her own clinic back in Croatia. She was startled and not sure how I could do this but I told her to let me worry about that. It only mattered if she was up for it and I was not one to tell anyone how to live their life or what to do with it. As we paused for a moment and I let the thought sink in she got this look on her face that was part day dreaming and part long sought serenity.

We discussed my idea and as we did it was like a time lapse video of a flower growing in the sun as I watched peace and simultaneously a new hope arise in my dear friend's eyes.

"I could go home, and help my people," she said, nervously tapping her finger on the yellow tablecloth.

"You could, and although I would miss you greatly, I think you should."

Her smile, her awesome and pure smile sealed it for me right there but again it had to be her call which, after one more glass of wine she agreed to. We ordered chateaubriand for two as we needed to celebrate and we both now looked towards the future. I convinced her that until we left she needed to lay low and also quit the clinic. Anyone following her would by now know where she lived and worked and we couldn't chance it if she wanted to get out of here alive. After dinner I convinced her to allow me to walk her home and being such a nice evening neither one of us minded the exercise as we strolled through the garden district en route to her small flat. I always loved the smells of her neighborhood with its abundant foliage growing all over and among the old Victorian homes. This part of the city had a sultry romance about it that was lost on most people as we walked past the grand estates of famous authors and artists along the way and I listened to Kata go on about her plans for her new life. I was happier than I had been in some time and once again the future was calling me down a road that I didn't know but was excited to travel. The wine had given us both a comfort that in retrospect we couldn't afford but once again my guardian angel was looking out for me and thank God for that. I was consumed with the evening and the splendor around us and didn't really consider anything when Kata suggested a shortcut down an alley that came up behind her place. We walked along with the rhythm of our shoes making a soft clicking noise on the old brick but just 20 feet from the back gate my ears and my instincts sensed a danger that had been lost in my own complacence as an attacker sought to strike.

With the man only steps away I turned and at the same time Kata yelled but it would have been too late if not for the rapid spit of two silenced gunshots coming from of the darkness behind him. Whoever was trying to kill me, or us, collapsed to the ground with a semi-auto pistol still in his right hand. Before either of us could think or react our protector rushed up, shot the man on the ground once more in the heart and looked around for anyone who might have witnessed it besides us. Convinced that we were now only a party of three he briefly introduced himself, explaining that Jerry had enlisted the help of he and two others to watch over us until we were out of town safely. The timeline would now become expedited with the obvious threat and he instructed us to get inside Kata's place, gather only the essentials, and phone Jerry when we were ready to move. He would get rid of the body and give my friend an update as we made ready upstairs. We had 30 minutes and no time for further explanations or courtesy as the seriousness of our situation was abundantly clear. I called Jerry and he told me what kind of vehicle to be ready for as I watched out the window for our escape and any other potential threats. Ten minutes later a black suburban pulled in fast as the driver remained outside with the vehicle running and two very capable looking men got out and rushed up to the front door. Kata had two bags and I grabbed one as the bodyguards, both carrying Heckler and Koch 9mm submachine guns, scanned the street front and the tops of the buildings around us as we rushed back out to the waiting vehicle. I directed them to my hotel and the driver pulled into an underground attached garage that I was not even familiar with as he backed the large vehicle into a handicapped spot right next to the service elevator. Keeping the ride running once again the two other guards escorted me up to my room where in rapid fashion I packed up all of my earlier purchases and was back in the waiting suburban in under ten minutes. I called Jerry back and we both agreed that for the moment his place would be the safest as we roared out of New Orleans into the safety of the countryside.

When we got there we went through a type of debriefing, sharing with him the events of the entire day including the phone calls leading up to our dinner. He took both of our phones and said he had a buddy in the D.E.A that might be able to track anyone who had intercepted or listened in on our conversations but it was a long shot. For the first time coming out here was not a party and the serious, methodical side of my friend took over as he got us situated in spare bedrooms, told us to make ourselves at home and disappeared down the driveway-leaving the three trusted bodyguards to watch over us. I didn't sleep much that night and woke up several times looking out the window in apprehension of what might be coming. Our security was more than adequate but this was now the third time in as many weeks that someone intended to end my life, Kata's life, or both and sleep wasn't going to come easy. When Jerry finally got back we set about building the exit plan as I gave him power of attorney to sell my house and temporarily manage the trusts I had set up. All total I put him in charge of well over $3 million but I knew I could trust him. I'd have bet my life on it and with the stroke of a pen that's just what I did as we finalized plans for the next morning's departure. Mrs. Jerry made us a fine meal and we all drank beer with it but no one was looking to put on a buzz as a very real threat was still out there and it affected every person in that house. We joked little about how Jerry and I had met, told a few stories about the shenanigans of his Jerry Q's, but I was going to miss him and I knew the same was true for him as we toasted our friendship with a solemn clink of our bottles.

The next morning two suburbans were parked outside as Jerry, Kata and I piled into one and his security team the other. Jerry was driving and leading the way as our little convoy headed south to a private airstrip outside of Baton Rouge. En route we stopped at three separate branches of my bank, withdrawing enough cash to get us where we needed to go but not set off any alarms for anyone who might be monitoring my activity. I had thought back to my client that kept a stash of gold and after brief discussion Jerry agreed it was a solid idea and also knew someone who could make it happen fast. We stopped at another bank and withdrew what we needed to purchase the gold and with only one more stop to make life in the big easy was all but over for me. When we arrived Kata and I thanked Jerry and his team, hugging him tight as I now knew I would never see him again. The plane flew us down to another private airport in Miami where a private car and guard were waiting and drove us the short distance to the international airport. Just before checking in with our fake passports the guard disappeared without saying a word and for a couple minutes I felt a panic come over me as it was now just me and Kata with no one to save us but I was confident in Jerry's planning and after downing a short glass of Maker's Mark at the airport bar my nerves settled a tad. I found myself constantly scanning the crowd until I heard woman's voice come over the intercom, "Flight 4325 to Frankfort-Germany now boarding." When I heard it the events of the previous week must have come calling and I almost fell back into my chair at the thought of release. Kata wrapped her warm hand around my wrist and as she looked into my eyes it was a realization of what we had and what we must also now put behind as she kissed me softly on the cheek and got up to board her plane.

# A NEW BEGINNING

Jerry had me set up to make multiple flights, changing my I.D. three times along the way as I flew first to New York-then London, and finally the British Virgin Islands. Even with flying business class, catching some sleep and a massage in one of the V.I.P. lounges I was exhausted when we touched down on the lush tropical island. I found a middle of the road hotel and after a couple hour nap and a hot shower walked down to a beach front bar, ordering a plate of grilled shrimp and rice but no libation for now.

I stayed at my hotel for two weeks and as I walked around the village during the afternoons the warm hospitality of the culture came back to embrace me like a friend from long ago. Eventually I rented a tiny but adequate place on one of the smaller islands and after a short boat ride was now walking up to the brightly painted pink stucco shack that would be my new home. I thought to buy a car or motor scooter but for now hiring a taxi was the right move as I spent my days getting to know the people and the place. It was only thirteen miles long and three miles wide but on the leeward side was a little cove called Smuggler's Bay that was very popular with the wealthy vacationers that wanted to hang out but not be bothered. It wasn't a celebrity nest so accidently getting caught in a photo was not a worry, although I still considered it. I had to.

During one of my visits in weeks that followed I had lunch in a little waterfront cafe and after striking up a conversation with the elderly owner her thoughts for a new tenant came up. I had no restaurant experience but she assured me that in just a few weeks she could teach me everything I needed to know, if I was serious. I was and although her current menu was focused on seafood she agreed that so was everybody else up and down the beach. Being a Jimmy Buffett fan from way back I had an idea and I shared it with her. Truth be told I never saw myself as owning and running a beach-front burger joint but Lola, the current owner thought I could avoid competition and besides everyone likes a good cheeseburger. I needed to chew on the whole thing for a bit, security and exposure being an obvious consideration, but I had been here now well over two months and hadn't seen or felt any warning signs. There was no disputing the contract or contracts on my old identity, but it wasn't like I had ratted on the mafia or stolen hundreds of millions and I had to realistically consider how far anyone would travel to kill me for only $30k. Along with my new identity and haircut I had been walking every morning and with it had lost 25 pounds that I would probably gain back owning a burger joint, but for now I looked nothing like the guy who used to drive around with dead bodies in the back of his truck. After careful consideration I decided that I could only walk around and hang out on the beach so many times. There was no sense in me worrying about an assassination if in the end boredom would be my killer and the following Monday I met up with Lola and signed the deal. I had Jerry wire the money and didn't ask questions as the next day she handed me the keys and a personalized apron she had sewn for me saying with a smile, "if your flipping burgers you're going to need it"

Jerry had been very clear about how I would survive and with his instruction and a little common sense I should remain safe. I bought a dog which was his idea but I'd always wanted one and Jake became my confident and protector as I settled in to island life and my new career. Jake came to work with me every day, serving as both security and greeter to my growing clientele as he walked freely around the cafe catching an occasional nap in the shade under one of the many palm trees.

Lola helped me whip up a menu and stayed on twenty hours a week, partly out of my need for her help and partly out of not wanting to sit on the couch every day. The one thing we both agreed on was to keep the burgers solid and simple-no fucking guacamole or brie, only the proper toppings and hand cut French fries that we triple cooked to make them come out crispy every time. We only opened the last four days of the week leaving Monday, Tuesday and Wednesday for reading, swimming, or scuba diving which I had always wanted to learn. Sometimes the customers bitched that we weren't open more but we both agreed that customers were always going to bitch about something and not being too available was a prudent decision on my part. Lola never knew that part of my choice was also to limit my being out in the public eye, another of Jerry's suggestions.

Business hours were 11 a.m. until 9 p.m. and we poured way more rum than we sold burgers but that my friends is island life as a constant mix of reggae, Buffett, and Caribbean salsa played over the outdoor speakers from open to close and many nights afterwards if we had forgot to turn off the stereo at closing. No one ever bitched about that.

Occasionally Lola would serve up some fresh spiny lobsters or fish that I had speared during my dive and I could always count on her to surprise the customers with an amazing Caribbean rice dish or salad to go with. Even with her being only ten years my senior she became like a grandmother to me, telling me about growing up out in California most of her life. She was a friendly but private lady and it took a year until she shared how she had come to live in the islands. Like the Warren Zevon song it involved lawyers, guns, and money but out of respect and consideration to our friendship I'll leave that for another time. She was a sweetheart, a great person and a friend and I had landed on my feet once again. One afternoon when the lunch rush had settled down I came out to the bar to have a beer and catch up on the restaurants paperwork. As I sat there, friendly but not trying to interrupt anyone, a man sat down next to me and asked if this was my place. I shook his hand and told him that it was.

"You got a pretty good gig here, you interested in selling it?" he asked.

Glancing up I took a quick once over of him and taking a drink out of the cold sweating bottle I leaned back to think. I had lived through some things that I knew I never should have. I had seen some truly crazy shit but I didn't let it bury me. I had learned to appreciate the simple things in life, like true friends, and I was blessed to never again need to have money steer the direction of my ship. I was living the dream, or at least my dream, and as I finished pondering his request, I thanked him but declined.

Looking down at the name on my apron he said, "well Jesse, if you ever change your mind here is my card. Say, your last name isn't James is it? Like Jesse James the outlaw? That would be a hoot!"

Smiling I said, "yes sir it is. Jesse James, but no relation," as I thanked him again and whistled for Jake to come up from the beach...

* * * * *

Thanks for taking the time to read my work. All the best to you and yours.

D L Silverthorne

Made in the USA
Monee, IL
27 June 2020